Dear Ann

ALSO BY BOBBIE ANN MASON

Fiction

Patchwork: A Reader

The Girl in the Blue Beret

In Country

Shiloh and Other Stories

An Atomic Romance

Zigzagging Down a Wild Trail

Nancy Culpepper

Midnight Magic

Feather Crowns

Love Life

Spence + Lila

Nonfiction

Clear Springs

Elvis Presley

The Girl Sleuth

Nabokov's Garden

Dear Ann

A Novel

Bobbie Ann Mason

HARPER LARGE PRINT

An Imprint of HarperCollinsPublishers

HarperCollins books may be purchased for educational, business, or sales promotional use. For information, please e-mail the Special Markets Department at SPsales@harpercollins.com.

FIRST HARPER LARGE PRINT EDITION

ISBN: 978-0-06-302970-5

Library of Congress Cataloging-in-Publication Data is available upon request.

20 21 22 23 24 LSC 10 9 8 7 6 5 4 3 2 1

DEDICATED TO
Gurney, Ed, Wendell, and Jim
And to the memory of our writing teacher,
Robert Hazel

But oh! that deep romantic chasm which slanted
Down the green hill athwart a cedarn cover!
A savage place! as holy and enchanted
As e'er beneath a waning moon was haunted
By woman wailing for her demon-lover!

—FROM "KUBLA KHAN,"
SAMUEL TAYLOR COLERIDGE

AT SEA

2017

Those old letters from so long ago burned in her memory now, as she stared at the relentless azure sea.

Berea, Kentucky
October 11, 1965

Dear Ann,

When you graduate, please go straight to California. I know you can get a Stanford fellowship. I will put in a word for you. It will be liberating for you out there. When I traveled from Kentucky to California, I began to understand America through our fellow pioneer, Daniel Boone. I remember standing on a cliff at Santa Cruz, at the edge of the Pa-

cific, and watching all the seabirds soar out to sea, and I thought about Daniel Boone atop Cumberland Mountain, surveying the unbounded promise of the wilderness. And I was stupefied to be there. Of course I was stoned, and for a while I felt I was Daniel Boone. Ann, what is your opinion of Daniel Boone these days?

Your erstwhile professor,
Albert

P.S. Please do what I say.

Berea, Kentucky
November 15, 1965

Dear Ann,

When I was at Stanford on the Stegner with Kesey and McMurtry and that bunch—before they were big!—I knew I was at the center of the universe. Mr. O'Connor regaled us with his hilarious Irish tales. I loved to hear his thick brogue. And Mr. Cowley gabbed about his pals Hem and Dos. Imagine, knowing those writers! At first I thought he meant Dostoevsky, but of course he meant Dos Passos. He and Dos Passos were thick. And as for Hemingway, we just quivered in admiration.

But you are wise, Ann, to go the academic route. It suits you.

Your servant and literary pal,
Albert

Berea, Kentucky
January 9, 1966

Dear Ann,

I won't listen to your self-deprecations. Or your oddball notion of striking out for New York. New York! Maybe Scott Fitzgerald went to New York, but Daniel Boone went west, where everything was new. What is happening in California these days is radical. And I was there at the beginning of this transformative time. This is cosmic.

I know some fine folks out there who will take care of you. You will bloom, Ann. People are so free and willing to explore. California is just what you need to drag you out of your shell.

We loved to go to San Gregorio Beach at sunset. A bunch of us would drop acid and have a square dance on the beach. We'd mire up in the sand and fall down crazy with laughter and desire. We were just barefooted freaks wild by the ocean.

Your pal,
Albert

What a featherhead she was. She should have followed Albert's advice. Even though Albert had never understood her, he claimed to know just what she needed to do—get stoned and practice "free love," etc. Perversely, she had blazed her own trail. With her unsophisticated rural background, she believed graduate school at Stanford University was obviously out of her league. Harpur College, where she had gone instead for her graduate degree, was in upstate New York, in the snow belt. There was no real springtime, just a June burst of summer after a long, dismal, chilly season. There, she spent each spring in a blue funk, romanticizing the sweet balminess of April in Kentucky. She should have gone to California.

Now, fifty years later, shut in the lofty stateroom of a colossal, farcical cruise ship, Ann wondered what would have happened if she had gone to Stanford instead of Harpur College. Her life would have been different. The dread she faced now made her feel like a weatherbeaten mariner, under a bird's curse.

If she had gone to California she would never have met Jimmy.

Jimmy. She could still hardly bear to think about him.

But she felt a whir of excitement, an unexpected pleasure in imagining her youth following an alternate path. People always said, *Oh, to be young again, knowing what I know now.*

Being young again, in the sixties. What a blast it

would be to start over—in California. Wasn't California something of a dream by definition? She could reimagine her life. And Jimmy wouldn't be in it. Or it could have turned out differently with Jimmy. She wouldn't be in this nightmarish mirage on an alien sea.

PALO ALTO, CALIFORNIA

1966

"**D**on't be afraid" was the last thing Albert had said to Ann before she left Kentucky.

If she had gone to California, she would have driven cross-country alone, following the southern route he recommended. Her two-door antique 1952 Chevrolet, black with a tidy rump, was like an elderly lady in sensible shoes. But the car was a mismatch. Ann sallied out with an innocent boldness, despite a shyness that sometimes made her tiptoe and hide. She kept the windows rolled down until she reached the Sierras. The car had no radio, but the friendly chug of the engine, with the wind whistling and whooshing against the little push-out corner window, made a soundtrack for her journey. Across the vast deserts, she felt she was in suspension, the past receding, the future nowhere yet. Daniel Boone never entered her mind.

In her mind, California would be a kaleidoscope of sunny skies, convertibles, bright blonds, unusual trees. Albert was right, she thought. Out there, she would open up like a flower. But Palo Alto, when she arrived, was cloudy, and the farm fields were dry and dusty, spreading a haze over the coastal hills. It appeared to be a quiet little city, hardly larger than Paducah. Something sweet-smelling drifted through the air, and flowers bloomed luxuriantly everywhere.

She had arranged to rent an apartment from a woman in a white wood-frame house with a dark Victorian interior. From the landlady's hallway, Ann glimpsed fringed lamps and velvet drapes, with incongruous arrangements of artificial flowers crowding the front room. A stale odor of cigarette ashes and bacon, with an overlay of Evening in Paris perfume, assaulted her. The landlady, in exaggerated lipstick and a lace shawl, was sullen and curt.

Ann rented an upstairs studio unit in a nondescript stucco building behind the house. The rooms were plainly furnished, but painted screaming pink throughout. The carpet was voluptuous mauve cabbage roses, and the bathroom was a deep burgundy color. The sink, the shower tile, the commode—all a somber burgundy. She stared in the mirror, aghast. The lighting made her skin sallow.

The university was at the end of a long avenue lined with lofty palm trees. Ann drove slowly, the car creeping along as if it too was nervous about the ultimate destination of the cross-country journey. Halfway down the avenue, she pulled over. Stanford displayed itself lavishly in front of her, both tantalizing and threatening. The amount of wealth it held in its history was beyond Ann's imagination. The palm trees on either side of her made a path to Xanadu. It took her breath.

She was three weeks early, and the campus was nearly deserted. At first glance, Stanford was a pleasant park, all manicured greenery and earth tones, but as she wandered past the imposing Hoover Tower and along the arcades of the sandstone buildings around the Main Quad, she felt as though she had stumbled upon a hidden ancient kingdom. The tall palm trees, with their bushy tops, seemed to have blown in from the tropics. She didn't know the names of the flowers spread at their feet.

The harsh sun glared off the walkways, making her feel exposed and uncertain. But she almost laughed when she noticed a group of palm trees, their moptop heads peering curiously over a red-tile roof. She walked on, map in hand, wandering bug-eyed past majestic buildings and landscaped oases. Ahead of her was a bold fountain, a sculpture made of green slashes of metal. It erupted like a sea creature rising.

She had not expected the campus to be so large and quiet and leafy. The giant oak trees splayed their limbs like lazy gymnasts. She saw trees that might have been redwoods—tall and gaunt, pinpointing the sky. She ambled through a grove of what she thought—from their fragrance—were eucalyptus trees. Their peeling bark lay shredded at their feet, like ragged gowns.

It was a grand and lonesome place. But she wasn't afraid of being alone. She was afraid of Yvor Winters, the prominent literary critic who would be her adviser. She had heard he was a curmudgeon and rationalist. What would he expect of her? She had made little progress on the reading list—seventy-five recommended books. There would be a test—but not until next summer. She knew some of the obvious books— *The Great Gatsby, Moby-Dick*—within the list of unknowns. But *Humphry Clinker? Erewhon?* She was sure that a more backwards bumpkin had never crossed the threshold of almighty Stanford University.

Hopewell, Ky.
September 4, 1966

Dear Ann,

   Glad to get your phone call and to know you are getting settled. I know you must be excited about all your new classes and your new apartment. That woman you rent from sounds like a character!

   That neighbor of ours who always keeps squirrel on the table brought us some squirrels she shot, and I had a time cleaning out the buckshot. Back in the summer, she kept wanting to get some Indian peaches off of us and I told her, I'm sorry, but you come to a goat's house to get wool. We ain't had any Indian peaches in ten years. Oh, what I'd give for an Indian peach right now. The only peaches I could get this year were wormy. . . .

Love,
Mama

Ann had brought everything she owned, even her notebooks from college and her stamp collection from childhood. On a whim, while shopping at Macy's for a skillet and a bath mat, she bought a new stamp album and a grab bag packet of stamps (a thousand for fifty cents).

She spread the stamps on her desk—a long table fashioned from a door. All afternoon, she played with them, engrossed, as if she were back in sixth grade. The countries were still mysterious, and the African countries had changed. Wars had obliterated some, brought others into being. There was something fragile and tentative about the very existence of borders and identities, she thought.

At the time, she would not have seen herself as young and naive, but years later she saw herself as even more innocent than she probably was. She blundered into anything promising, but when faced with a hard-banging hurdle—hitting a stump, her mother called it—she had a habit of escaping into mind-numbing pastimes. She hadn't changed. She was always thinking of somewhere else.

On a cruise ship, there is nowhere to go but overboard. Her mind, though, can rewrite history. Or learn Ger-

man. There are Zumba classes on the third deck. Those embarrassing moments of innocent youth can be obliterated. She shudders, a chill rippling across her shoulders.

She didn't want to meet new people yet. Who needed them? As she sorted the stamps and placed them carefully into the new album, she lost track of time. She imagined traveling to Newfoundland, New Caledonia, New Zealand. Folding the delicate cellophane hinges and taking care not to glue the stamp to its rectangular berth, she felt like an entomologist, cruelly but patiently pinning a colorful assortment of butterflies. All day, the radio played. She heard "Sunny Afternoon," "Sunshine Superman," "Just Like a Woman," and "You Can't Hurry Love" over and over. On the weekend, she listened to Monitor Radio. Every evening at about six, an aroma of spices drifted into her kitchen. A man from India lived on the floor below.

Albert's friends lived in a commune out in a redwood forest. There was time enough to look them up. Albert had told her about A. C. Skolnick ("Speedo"), who talked a mile a minute without repeating himself; about Spinning Jenny, who performed fluid dances in flowing, see-through nylon dresses; about Hungry Robert, who would eat anything and who had once imbibed a double dose of peyote and had to be talked down from a tree. Albert mentioned Freaky Pete, who you thought would shatter at a "Boo!" but who, with two tokes, became as relaxed as a sloth. And Albert seemed enamored of a girl who had thrown her clothes out a car window, leaped from the car at a stoplight, and paraded naked across Sand Hill Road to the Stanford Shopping Center. Albert also told her about Ned and Frieda, who outfitted a special tripping room in their house with large bright pillows inside multicolored silk panels hooked to the ceiling light and the door facings. The undulating colors breathed. California was the edge of the world, Albert had said.

Back home, a PhD was an unknown, as far-fetched as travel to the moon. It could have stood for Pursuit of Hound Dogs, she mused. As she sorted stamps, she felt courage simmering, like a chuck roast in her mother's pressure cooker.

She met the man from India at the bottom of the exterior metal stairway. His name was Sanjay, a PhD student in chemistry. He wore a yellow Henley shirt appliquéd with a small alligator. They were standing outside his door. He made chitchat in good English.

"I have stamps from India in my stamp collection," she said.

"You collect stamps?"

"It's a regression to childhood while I'm waiting for school to start. Never mind." She was embarrassed. "Your cooking always smells good."

"I'm making biryani."

"What's that?"

"A vegetable dish. Won't you join me?"

"Oh, no, that's all right. Thank you. I have something already started." A potato. A ragged iceberg.

"O.K., I'd love to," she relented when he urged her.

Sanjay was sautéing cauliflower florets in a strong-smelling spice that turned the vegetable orange. A chemistry experiment? It was astounding to learn about his hometown, a city of over two million people, a city she had never heard of. She realized she had never met anyone from India.

The layout of his apartment was the reverse of hers, and his bathroom was lime green, the same degree of shrieking intensity as her burgundy bordello decor. His walls were apple green. His books were all on esoteric science topics. His shoes matched his belt, and his argyle socks had yellow diamonds to echo his alligator shirt. He served no meat. He offered her sparkling water and hot tea. He sprinkled cashews on the food. On the side, he served a dish of sliced cucumbers and yogurt with a pinch of something. Cumin, he called it.

She was surprised by how talkative she was with

Sanjay. He seemed so nice, so cultivated—suave, even. He was orderly and confident. She thought of him as an adult, even though he was probably not much older than she. It came as a mild shock that a visiting foreigner from a poor country would be more educated and cultured than most people in her small town in Kentucky. She wondered if she felt even more out of place at Stanford than he did. She wondered what it would be like to kiss him.

The Pepto-Bismol walls were shouting at her. With a gallon of iceberg white and a roller, she painted the walls. She left the pink margins at the top, not bothering with the expense of a paintbrush to fill in the gaps. If she pinched pennies, she wouldn't have to get a roommate.

She went to see these movies:

Georgy Girl
Blow-Up
Who's Afraid of Virginia Woolf?
Morgan!

Often, late at night, the couple next door began jiggling their bed frame, knocking it against the thin wall, grunting and sighing with it. She listened, won-

dering how married couples could sit and read before bed. How could they wait? The sounds made her
grumpy. Ann had never really had a boyfriend—a
relationship, that is, the term in vogue. Although she
wasn't without sexual dalliances, nobody she had ever
cared about had said "I love you" or given her a gift.
She had been lovelorn throughout college over a certain Thomas from her sophomore art history class
and had not gone steady with anyone since. In the
mornings, when she heard the couple next door, their
shower was like the sound of time whizzing by.

Wanted: Natural, attractive women to model for professional photos in specialty magazines. $10 an hour. No experience necessary.

It was in the neighborhood, on Stanford Avenue, a short drive. Ann was not beautiful, but she thought she was pretty, and she was slim with fairly good legs. Ten dollars—an outlandish amount—would buy some curtain material, she thought.

She entered a rental room in a plain white house set back from the street. A camera on a tripod faced a rolled-out screen. The man, who was short and thin, showed her several display folders of his work. His photos were not lewd. The models were ordinary people. In bathing suits some of them appeared almost grotesque, not glamorous as one would expect from models. One folder contained heavy middle-aged women wrestlers.

He asked her to pirouette so he could get a good look at her.

"I think I can use you," he said. "What size are you?"

He flicked ash into a small ashtray crammed with cigarette butts and handed her a shoebox from a stack on the floor. He rummaged through a pile of shortie pajamas on the bed.

"Could you pose in these?"

In an unadorned white bathroom, she changed into

the pale pink baby-doll pajamas. She kept her under-wear on. She remembered seeing pictures of movie stars posing in baby-dolls, so she thought it was all right. She left her black slim-jims and green Ban-lon sweater on a hook on the bathroom door and emerged awkwardly, the red high heels catching on the carpet.

"What do you do with the pictures?" she asked.

"I work with several magazines. Freelance."

She wondered how she could stand around in high heels for an hour. Still, ten dollars was stupendous pay for one hour. She had earned seventy-five cents an hour when she worked one summer at a dress shop.

He placed her in front of the blank screen. Preoccu-pied with getting the shot right, he hardly spoke. The cigarette dangled from the corner of his mouth while he adjusted his tripod and his camera settings. His rig-ging seemed professional enough, she thought, not that she would know. The room was small, with just a bed, a desk, and a tiny kitchenette. Two shabby duffel bags were squeezed into a space between the bed and the closet.

He spoke vaguely of traveling around. He once worked in a zoo and before that in a photo lab with the famous Hotshot Hansen, whoever that was. In *Blow-Up*, David Hemmings had a nice pad and lived the high life.

"That's good," the photographer said, after shooting several photos. "Anybody ever tell you you look like Natalie Wood?"

"No."

"Well, you do."

"Really? She's pretty."

"Could you change into this outfit?"

More baby dolls, a different color, a different cut—cheap, not nice like she would wear. She changed, and when she came out of the bathroom, he went in.

She waited, wishing she could get dressed and be gone, but her clothes were in the bathroom. And she had committed herself to earning ten dollars.

He emerged finally. The water gurgled. He shut the door.

"Now where were we?" he said.

He fiddled with his camera, then lifted it from the tripod. He asked her to move along an imaginary line while he shot pictures rapidly. He had her raise her arms as though she were holding a volleyball. "Pout," he said. "Do a rosebud with your mouth."

"How much longer will this take?"

"Almost finished, babe."

Babe. She pouted a rosebud.

"Hold still. There! That's a good one."

When she returned to the bathroom to get dressed,

she peered out the window at a playground. A quartet of small girls was seesawing behind a school. As she dressed, she realized that her slim-jims were slightly damp. The room was stifling. His shaving kit was on the windowsill. The seesawing girls still went up and down. Ann saw her face in the mirror. Caption: *Chick from Sticks in over Head.*

He removed his billfold from his hip pocket and peeled out a ten.

"As promised."

She snatched the bill and hurtled into the sunshine. She sped home and into the gloomy shower. She should have been reading *Humphry Clinker.*

Ann glided in shadow through the cool arcades alongside the Main Quad, out of the sun. She had forgotten her sunglasses. She wore low heels, a dark flared skirt, and a blue cotton blouse with a Macmillan collar. She had ironed the blouse without scorching it. It was cold in the daytime in Palo Alto, and she wore a wool cardigan. From her large leather handbag with double handles, attached by small brass horseshoes, her Emily Dickinson paperback rose upright, the name visible.

Ann almost bumped into Yvor Winters as he turned to enter his corner office. She recognized him from the photograph on his book jacket. She fled upstairs to the restroom, where she waited until the precise time of her appointment. She combed her hair and freshened her lipstick—Persian melon. It was really too orange for her, she thought. She tucked in her blouse.

"Come in, come in," he said, not lifting his eyes from a paper he was reading.

She waited until he motioned her to the chair facing his desk.

He was a round man in a donkey-gray suit, his wire-rimmed glasses like owl eyes. He appeared to be ill, his face saggy and pale.

"Welcome to the graduate program," he said, without emphasis. His voice was low and somber. "What are your plans with us here?"

"Well, I'm here to study toward the PhD." She was self-conscious about her accent.

"That goes without saying." He made a dismissive gesture, as if he were swishing off a fly. "Why? What are your research interests?"

"I love to read," she said, with a strong effort at perkiness. "I'm tackling the long list."

"The canon and then some," he said, as if making a joke. An off rhyme? He tapped his pencil and fumbled through some papers.

"I see from your transcript here that you are lacking in early studies. You'll need to take Old English. Can't get away from that. It won't include *Beowulf.* You'll need that too. And you should start out with the poetics course. That's a good range of theory."

"I want to take your modern poetry seminar."

"Better sign up now. There won't be space."

He shuffled through some papers and marked something she thought was a sign-up sheet for the seminar.

"Take these to registration," he said, shoving two cards into her hand.

"What poets are you reading now?" he asked abruptly.

She nudged Emily Dickinson forward. "I might like

to write my dissertation on her," she said. A mouse talking. She straightened up.

"Humph. I don't know if you'll get away with that here." He scratched his nose and readjusted his glasses. "You'll find some other enthusiasm by this time next year. It would be wrong if you didn't."

Her armpits felt sweaty, unusual for her. Her face was hot. Had he actually said "humph," or was it "harrumph"?

A student in khakis and an Ivy League shirt waylaid her in the arcade outside the English department. "So you're going to work with the celebrated Yvor Winters."

"He's my adviser," she said.

"Did you get any good advice?"

"Not really."

"Aha," he said, glancing at Emily Dickinson. "Looking for brownie points, I see. He loves Dickinson. What do you think of his poem to her?"

"I didn't know he wrote one."

"He nods to tradition with the Spenserian stanzas but reaffirms his modernist penchant by twisting the scheme."

Ann crammed the book down into her bag. "I think she's funny."

"I'm Peter," he said. "Second year, seventeenth-century British. If you need me to show you around, let me know."

Although Peter had the slick, well-groomed appearance of a frat pledge, Ann was indifferent to seventeenth-century British. "You're a little late for Winters," he added when she didn't reply. "They say he was at his best a few years ago. It was the heyday of Yvor Winters."

The heyday of Yvor Winters. The phrase lodged in her mind. It would be nice to have a heyday, she thought. Not mousy, she told herself as she scurried home. She stood in her studio room in her slip, then searched for something comfortable to wear. She pulled on an old pair of tan slacks and a light sweater. She could not imagine holding an exalted position of professional authority, much less having a heyday at it.

Those Stanford boys! Young gods with money and smart talk and khaki pants. She feared them and lusted after them. What was she doing here?

Pixie Katsaros, her neighbor who lived downstairs next to Sanjay, had a lava lamp on her desk and a beaded curtain between her kitchen and the main room. She was in her second year at Stanford, and her apartment came with a stray cat, Nicodemus, who swished through the bead strings with the flair of a fan dancer. Pixie filled Ann in on the landlady, Maria Sokolov.

"Her circus name was Jingles. Her husband died years ago, and she made a shrine to him. You've seen that awful living room?"

"A funeral parlor."

"I was expecting to see him laid out in a goddamn casket in that alcove to the left."

"Ooh." The cat brushed against Ann's leg. She said, "With all the flowers in California, why a houseful of false flowers?"

"Did you see the floral bower with the swing? And the trapeze overhead?"

"No."

"Her husband died falling from a trapeze. They were a famous high-wire duo."

Pixie was studying psychology on a Broadbent Fellowship. She was from New York and had a degree from Brooklyn College. They became friendly, even though Ann found Pixie's abruptness disconcerting. Pixie could peel an orange with her teeth and eat it in twenty seconds. Her favorite musicians were Donovan, the Mamas and the Papas, and the Who. She said Herman's Hermits were shit.

———

Meredith and John, a couple from Kentucky who were relatives of Ann's college roommate, Josie, had promised to watch out for her in California. Meredith and John's modern bungalow in Menlo Park was decorated with African market baskets and tribal masks they had bought in Kenya. Ann thought of the pair as urban sophisticates.

John, tall with a limber frame like a teenager, explained his research with mice in a lab.

"Killed two hundred today," he said. "You finish the experiment and you can't use them for another experiment. They're contaminated."

"You have to start with fresh, pure mice?" Ann asked. "Newborns?"

"Not newborns."

"No, that would mean bottle-feeding, I guess." Her wit escaped unnoticed.

"Want a cocktail?" John asked.

"A Kentucky girl might rather have iced tea," said Meredith to John. "Wouldn't you, Ann?"

"I guess so. Yes. Iced tea, please."

Meredith, a slim blonde in a short pleated floral dress with a dropped waist, a style popular when Ann was a freshman, said, "When Josie told me about you, I was so thrilled. It's hard to get to know people here. I think I had more friends in Africa."

"I had a pet monkey in Africa," John said. "I don't mean Meredith."

They made faces at each other.

"He called his monkey Lucille Ball," Meredith said. "I was so jealous."

Their two little boys darted about in matching cowboy pajamas.

"No cavorting before bedtime," Meredith said. "Calm down."

She tugged at the taller boy's pajama top. "Take a deep breath, William," she said. "Your face is red."

"Your face is red!" taunted the other boy, Christopher.

Christopher and William, Ann repeated to herself. She wasn't used to kids. Meredith spoke to the two boys in the tone of a college professor. Later, Ann observed that when Meredith said good night to them, she packed them tightly into their beds and folded the covers straight across their chests, leaving their arms stranded outside. The boys' room had red curtains printed with cowboys. Ann still had no curtains, just the ugly old shades on rollers. Out in the hall, Meredith said to Ann, "I definitely don't want them to have their hands under the covers."

John opened a bottle of pink wine. Meredith and John used cloth napkins, with napkin rings. *Lah-dee-*

dah. Dinner was a casserole of shrimp and rice with mandarin oranges, avocado slices, and hulled pistachios arranged on top.

"I've never had avocados," Ann said.

"You should take some to Kentucky next time you go," Meredith said, smiling. "A bit of California."

Ann was sure her mother would have no use for such tasteless green pulp.

"I'm rosy . . . like the wine," she said, feeling her cheeks flush.

"Heavens, you can't be drunk on a little rosé." Meredith tittered and dabbed her napkin to her lips.

As he escorted her to her car later, John said, "The friends you make in graduate school are the ones you will always have. Remember that."

He opened the door for her. "Anything you need, Ann, please let us know. I promised Josie I'd look after you if you ever get in trouble or need something."

What could she need from John and Meredith? A hangover remedy? They had hinted that graduate school was a great place to find a compatible mate, as if they thought she was desperate. When she got home, she flopped on her bed, still dressed, and woke up when the bedsprings next door began squeaking. Her head buzzed from the rosé.

Meredith had gone into detail about her wedding,

with her sorority sisters as bridesmaids. Ann had never even been to a large wedding because she hadn't been in a sorority. She couldn't imagine a bridal shower or a gaggle of giggling bridesmaids in identical dresses. She seemed to be blazing a trail that forked off from the wedding march. What good would Eliot's *Four Quartets* do a bride? How would reading Emily Dickinson help her? Apparently Emily had been stuck in a house, not venturing far, but she probably didn't have to do all the housework herself, so she had time to fool around with poems. Ann did not want to waste her time on domestic detail, so what could she offer in a marriage? Prince Charming would walk right past her. She wanted to be married, but not like Meredith and John. She thought about her Kentucky professor Albert, and his wife, Pat. They didn't appear to be tied down. They had a camaraderie she admired. They seemed bohemian, open to surprise. Pat was a potter.

Berea, Kentucky
June 3, 1966

Dear Ann,
*   If you go to Stanford, I want you to find El Palo*
Alto, the tall tree. It is a big redwood the Spanish
explorer Portola camped under in 1769. Eventually
the name of the tree became the city of Palo Alto.
1769 was the same year Daniel Boone first set foot
in Kentucky. Think about the parallel movements
of these explorers. It would give me pleasure to
imagine you looking up at that great tree and con-
templating how you as a Kentuckian are now in
California, taking part in history.
*   I want you to meet my old pals at La Honda.*
They know just how to open up your head.

                                                    Albert

Although Albert was full of loosey-goosey advice, she
couldn't argue over the tree. In California she would
learn all those flowers and strange trees. Maybe she
would trip the light fantastic with his acid-head soul-
mates. She might bunk in a woodland commune.

Pixie's parents ran a little grocery in Brooklyn and had saved to send Pixie to college. Then a prestigious award propelled her to apply to Stanford. She was going into research rather than therapy because she didn't want to listen to people talk about their problems. Ann could see that Pixie would easily have the patients diagnosed and out the door before the hour was up.

Ann made a Southern meal for Pixie, who had never had fried chicken, but the chicken was tough and the cornbread burned. Pixie complained that the food was too heavy and that she couldn't imagine eating like that every day. She zipped down to her apartment for her jug of Chianti nestled in its cute basket. Used to drinking milk or iced tea with meals, Ann hadn't thought of wine.

"Wine is the one thing I splurge on," Pixie said. "That and Kleenex."

Ann rarely bought Kleenex and had never bought wine. Pixie was just getting over a boyfriend and now had the hots for Sanjay, who had fed her biryani with dal paneer and naan and something with lentils. "I could become a vegetarian with somebody like him!" she said. "He grinds his own spices."

"I had Indian food once in Louisville." Ann was aware that Pixie was claiming Sanjay out from under her.

Pixie shook her dark, bushy hair like a madwoman. "He is so sexy. I'm so hot and bothered I can't study. Jesus shit."

Ann had heard people say "Jesus wept." That had seemed an innocuous thing to say. But apparently people from New York were bold in their speech.

School began. The quiet did not burst into noisy throngs. It murmured into life. The flower-rimmed paths were not crowded. Except for the occasional swish of a bicycle, the atmosphere on campus was subdued. Stanford was a large, confident place, with a high-class history hidden to Ann. Among her fellow literary students were a Taiwanese girl with freckles, a California girl who always wore a gardenia brooch, a girl who cultivated her image of the model Twiggy, and a charming Irishman who was married with a baby. One of the lecturers was said to have a venereal disease; a former Stegner fellow had disappeared in the Amazon the year before. A couple named Jodie and Michael had fallen in love the day of orientation and were already shacking up in a little house on University Avenue. They discovered they had both written undergraduate papers with the same title: "Seeing and Perspective at Walden Pond." Ann thought Henry David Thoreau would have easily belonged with her parents in Kentucky, hoeing beans and fishing. Ann had had enough beans and wanted something loftier. Everybody said the place to go for a carnal weekend was the hot springs at Big Sur. Jodie and Michael went there the first weekend of the term.

Ann had expected Yvor Winters to be haughty and condescending, but in the modern poetry seminar he was mild-mannered, with an affable detachment. The seven other students, all male with show-off vocabularies, seemed more imposing and opinionated than he was. She observed how they thrust themselves forward. Where she had curiosity, they expressed glib certainties. She kept quiet, on edge. The poetics class was more fun. The elderly professor, Dr. Parker, had Xeroxed his own translation of Aristotle's *Poetics*. At each class meeting, they pored over the translation, bit by bit, sometimes accomplishing whole paragraphs in one class period. "That word is not a happy choice," he would say. Or, "I am still debating whether *catharsis* is the correct word."

"It seems tragic that Aristotle's work on comedy was lost and all we have is his tragedy," Ann said in class one day. Nobody laughed at what she meant to be funny.

Pity and terror, she thought. Aristotelian basics.

Old English was better. The words were dazzling. *Mōd, ēagan, brēost, heorte, lufu*: mind, eyes, breast, heart, love. Vital words. She loved their casual resemblance to modern words—a drunken typist hitting the wrong keys. It was amusing to imagine people centuries ago, in robes and tights, declaiming their *heortes* and *mōds*. She spent hours translating Aelfric and other literati of early England. She liked to imagine monks copying manuscripts in fancy lettering, with colorful little drawings. She had put her stamps away, but now she recognized her monkishness. She could see her future—absorbed in ancient texts, whispering the words to herself. She got chill bumps.

It was clear to her that she needed a husband if she was ever to have a house and any measure of comfort. Otherwise, she was going to have to earn her own living, and unless she could conquer and thrash a PhD, that probably meant office work. But the thought of John and Meredith's marriage gave her the heebie-jeebies.

To avoid the need for a roommate, Ann advertised for typing jobs and soon found herself typing term papers for fifty cents a page. It was easy money. She could type a page lickety-split. She typed on floating-cloud-like erasable paper. Her blue-and-white Smith Corona electric had large, clear pica letters and a satisfying hum. During the first week of classes, she typed a novel about the explorers Lewis and Clark written in blank verse, and a long biographical essay on Stephen Crane. "Thank God that son of a bitch died when he was twenty-eight," the Crane biographer said. "I spent two years on this thing."

Before typing a science paper about pepper-plant experiments, she drove to the Stanford Shopping Center to buy a ream of typing paper. Outside the variety store she ran into the baby-doll-pajamas photographer. His cigarette was still stuck to his lip like a growth. He recognized her.

"Hey, babe. Boy, did I have a run of bad luck. Somebody broke into my car and made off with my gear bag and two cameras. I lost ten rolls of film I hadn't developed yet. I got robbed."

"All your display folders? And the pictures you took of me?"

"Yeah. Negatives. Rolls of film." He shrugged. "I've told the police, but I don't expect to get anything back."

"That's too bad." Ann suppressed a spurt of glee. "Good luck," she said, waving a little bye as she entered the store. Her knees were shaking. She imagined her photo showing up in a sleazy magazine, although probably no one would ever know it was her. They might think it was Natalie Wood.

When the author of the pepper-plant paper, an undergraduate in red Little Orphan Annie curls, came to pick up the finished typing job, she asked to use the bathroom.

When she emerged, she said, "Wow! That bathroom is so neat!"

"It drives me up the wall," Ann said.

"You wouldn't be looking for a roommate, would you?"

Ann declined. The pepper-plant paper was thoroughly boring. After the student left, Ann sang with the radio.

"Woolly Bully, Woolly Bully!"

She did a little dance.

"Watch it now, watch it now!"

Hopewell, Ky.
September 25, 1966

Dear Ann,
    We got a laugh out of your trouble frying chicken.
The way I do it, you cut up a young fryer, and in a
skillet you melt Crisco or use Wesson oil about an
inch deep. Coat the pieces with flour on a plate.
Fry on one side, then turn it, cover, turn down the
heat and cook till it's done. Uncover when you go to
brown it. . . .

Love,
Mama

"**Ann, you** really should be on the Pill," Pixie said. "Saving yourself for somebody special? That's a scream."

Pixie had a cowlick, deep-set eyes, and a hefty but curvaceous shape. Ann learned to shrug artfully at her judgments, but she thought Pixie was harsh and manipulative. The cat, Nicodemus, was similar in temperament.

"Sanjay brought me biryani the other night, and I gave him some baklava," said Pixie, propping her feet on her brass-bound steamer trunk—her coffee table. "His family sent him here to become a doctor, but they have a wife lined up for him at home. That was arranged when he was a child. Imagine? Now he's in love with this undergrad history major from Wyoming, and he doesn't know what to do."

"Do you want to marry him?"

"Hell no. I just want to sleep with him."

"I've known too many girls who had to get married," Ann said. "I'd be terrified of ending up with the wrong person."

Pixie rose from the table and scooped the ragged cat into her lap.

"Let me recommend a really good gynecologist," she said.

"For me or for the cat?"

"The cat has been taken care of."

"I heard the Pill causes heart attacks."

"The gynecologist told me they've fixed that."

"I don't know."

"Think about it."

Pixie's bathroom was burgundy like Ann's, but it had a window, with a view of the parking strip. The light brightened the murky tile. A swath of lace curtain material was slung across a brass rod. The lace edges were raw. All that time Mama had spent hemming curtains and working those metal hooks into drape tops, Ann thought. So much work. Why bother? This hank of lace cut straight from the bolt made a more interesting aesthetic statement. Pixie was saying she wasn't a slave to conformity or pointless labor.

You didn't have to hem curtains! Or mess with drape hooks! Ann felt a little tug in her chest, like the loosening of a tight bra strap.

Hopewell, Ky.
October 7, 1966

Dear Ann,
  I hope you make a go of it with that teacher you're so worried about. You always were smart and your daddy says they'll be paying you forty thousand dollars a year someday just to think. . . .

Love,
Mama

———

Someone had said Yvor Winters was a puppy dog beneath his classroom mask, but Ann wondered about that. She had seen him crossing the Main Quad, stumbling along obliviously, a frown twisting his face. In his class, students did not raise their hands to speak and they were not called on. It was supposed to be a conversation. Ann watched the seven males carefully, studying their deliberate, assertive gestures—the way they interrupted one another and didn't take turns. The vigor of their debate reminded her of a Punch and Judy show—comic and terrifying. She could not squeeze a word in edgewise.

In the poetics class, Ann felt bolder. One afternoon Professor Parker probed William Blake's visions of heaven and hell in humorless tones that seemed at odds with the riot of images on the page. After listening to thirteen ways of looking at a silly line—"The cut worm forgives the plow"—from *Proverbs of Hell*, Ann impulsively raised her hand.

"If you cut a worm in two, it will grow into two worms. So the worm may not merely forgive the plow, but be indifferent to it, or even thankful. Two for one."

Professor Parker stared at her as if she had wandered in from the remote reaches of the zoology lab. A student who seemed to be about sixteen years old said,

"The worm, of course, is the nameless objectification of the poet's embrace of the universe. It is a rationalization, a feeble foray into the mystery of life eternal. It has nothing to do with the actual worm writhing in dirt."

"That's bullshit, Annie," Stephen Chancery said to her after class. "Don't you know bullshit when you hear it?"

"I ought to," she said. "I've stepped in enough of it. Cow shit anyway."

"Shit"—could she really say that? Pixie said it all the time. Stephen didn't bat an eye. How could he call her Annie?

She had had her eye on Stephen, a second-year grad student who rode a motorcycle and who was rumored to be Yvor Winters's star pupil the previous year. He was good-looking, tall and sturdy, with an appealing aloofness. Nobody called him Steve.

Now they became acquainted over Blake's apologetic worm. They brought beer and pizza to his apartment. He rented a basement apartment from a dancer whose jetés jarred the ceiling. Stephen had an Australian sheepskin rug, a Navajo blanket, an Indian water pipe, a Chinese hookah, a fat stone Buddha, and a large plaster statue of a Siberian tiger. They seemed to be decorative objects, of no significance. Ann wondered if he was an atheist who was nevertheless covering the bases, in case. The narrow bed was made up hospital style, with a fuzzy blanket folded neatly at the foot. Ann had not followed Pixie's advice about the gynecologist.

But Stephen spoke of the thrill of riding his motorcycle over the mountains, how it felt transcendent, even quiet. Ann told him about Albert's friends out in the Santa Cruz Mountains.

"I feel obligated to go and make their acquaintance, but I've put it off." Ann expected them to be a dazed circle of potheads and girls in gingham frontier dresses. Albert had called them "freaks," as if to be odd and offbeat were the highest aims.

"That would be a whacking good ride," Stephen said.

They set out on Saturday afternoon. She had talked to someone—a soft-spoken man called Hal—at the number Albert had given her.

"I don't have a helmet for you." Stephen shrugged. "But you wanted a ride."

The motorcycle was bright red, so huge and heavy she didn't see how anybody could keep it upright. She sat behind Stephen, holding on to his hard stomach. She wondered if he was ticklish. The whirl of the wheels hummed through her body.

He screeched to a stop at traffic lights and zoomed

off when the light changed, reaching high speed in seconds. She wore her prescription sunglasses and no contact lenses. The wind burned her eyes. She had tied her hair back in a knotty little ponytail, but her head was cold in a madras kerchief with string ties. The wind cut through her wool cardigan. Her teeth chattered.

The highway over the mountains was narrow and shoulderless, with trees hugging the sides. Ann rocked behind Stephen as they careened around the curves toward La Honda. She held her legs ajar to avoid burning her calves on the hot pipes. They passed through small settlements as they climbed into the mountains. Tall redwoods lined the road for dark intervals, and then the view opened for a stretch. The motorcycle lurched around curves. She held on tightly but wondered if she clutched too hard, she would cause him to lose control.

I'm going to die.

Ann imagined her breakfast streaming behind her at fifty miles an hour. The vigor of vomiting might even throw her from the bike.

They were climbing higher. The road was narrow, and the curves were switchbacks. The forest was dense and at times dark. The redwoods were regal, several times the height of telephone poles.

Then patches of ranch land opened up. The road

kept going. They flew on through La Honda, past the turnoffs into town, and shortly afterwards they found the entrance to the private lane. A large hand-painted sign on stilts greeted them.

WELCOME, WORLD.
DO YOUR OWN THING,
THE TREES WILL SMILE

The bumpy lane led across a bridge to a long ranch-style house. Stephen cut the engine, and they could hear a Motown tune tootling from a distant radio.

"Redwoods in the front yard," she cried. "Get a load of that stump! Big enough to dance on."

He was not agog. Redwoods were a dime a dozen.

It was shadowy among the trees, and some laughing children were running along, hiding behind them.

"Hide-'n'-go-seek must be really interesting here," Ann said. "You could circle around a tree like a squirrel, always out of view."

That was the sort of comment that people often ignored, she thought. When she tried to make small talk, they didn't notice.

Several people lived there, Albert had told her. You never knew who might be around. A friendly girl greeted them and left quickly to get the Chief from his studio.

The children were squealing, invisible monkeys in the woods.

A different girl, wearing a long skirt patterned with parrots, brought a pot of herb tea and a tray of mugs outside to the gigantic stump.

"He'll be here in a minute," she said. "He knows Albert. I just came here two months ago."

Ann, still staggering from the ride, asked for the bathroom. Removing her sunglasses, she tried to tackle her tangled hair in the dim mirror. She could find no electric light, but a squat scented candle was burning on a rickety table.

The girl in the parrot skirt set a plate of misshapen cookies on a patch of moss on the stump. She was humming "Good Day Sunshine."

"I love the sunrise here," she said. "I never miss it."

Ann and Stephen each ate a cookie while the girl poured the tea.

"The cookies are supposed to be the shape of California, but the batter was runny."

The Chief appeared. He owned the house and let friends live there rent-free if they did chores. He was a large, red-bearded man, whose voice reverberated through the trees. He had been in class with Albert, and for a while they spoke of Albert and his job in Kentucky and his gregarious personality and how Ann knew him.

"I didn't really know Albert that well," the Chief said. "Buzz knew him. Buzz moved to Santa Cruz last year."

"Albert mentioned Buzz," said Ann.

"Albert wrote such funny stories," the Chief said with a blast of laughter. "We laughed and laughed. He wrote about his Granny and her bean patch and his Uncle Rooster who got his nickname because he carried around a red chicken when he was a kid. We never heard anything like his stories."

"He sounds like a redneck," said Stephen.

"What do you mean by 'redneck'?" Ann asked.

"Oh, farmers. Rubes, hayseeds."

"My father is a farmer," Ann said. "Albert is not a farmer, and my father is not a hayseed either."

"Hayseeds are my favorite people," the Chief said, staring at Stephen. "Albert is an original, always full of entertaining ideas. I'd love to see him again."

He spoke of Albert as if he were a curiosity, Ann thought.

"What do you people do here?" Stephen blurted. "Is this a commune?"

"Nothing that requires labels," said the Chief. He pressed his lips together and turned his head.

Ann thought Stephen must be thinking that these seemed like people whose time had come and gone, the party over, the leaders drifting away into myth.

They seemed kind, but she couldn't find what Albert had so urgently wanted her to experience here. He had stressed how he had been there at the beginning— when the bohemians of Perry Lane discovered LSD through Ken Kesey when he was a guinea pig at the Veterans Hospital. Albert claimed he had "tripped" probably fifty times. He spoke of that time as if it was the dawn of an era, like the Industrial Revolution or the Romantic period.

After a while, Stephen announced that they were leaving. "I have an important paper to write on *The Divine Comedy.*"

He rolled his helmet in his hands as if it were a skull of someone he had personally slain. When he was out of earshot, Ann apologized to the Chief. "I don't really know him."

"Don't mention it. We're all on the path of learning."

He gazed into her face too long. She craned her neck to see the redwood tops.

"I've gone back to school to study physics," he said. "I'm studying the patterns of brain waves in meditative states. There's a new frontier of consciousness that begs our attention."

Ann thought he must mean acid, but he seemed serious and thoughtful.

The girl in the parrot skirt was admiring the motorcycle.

"My favorite color," she said. "This is snazzy."

Ann observed that Stephen was flattered and would have taken the girl riding on the bike and left Ann there.

"It's an Electra Glide. A Panhead," Stephen said to the girl.

"Why's it called a Panhead?" As if she cared deeply.

"Because the rocker-arm covers resemble pie pans, see?"

"Oh."

She twisted around in her skirt, and the parrots seemed to move, at a loss for words. The girl would have trouble riding the bike in that skirt, Ann thought.

"I never met such a bunch of phonies," Stephen said as they were leaving. "Vapid, pretentious! 'The world will smile!' What a bunch of fakes!"

He cranked the engine before Ann could reply.

The ride back was milder, more familiar. Gripping his hard waist now was like hugging a fence post. Her anger dispelled her fear. She had never been sure what a redneck was, but now the sound of it made her bridle.

At his house, he removed his jacket and then his motorcycle boots. In the bathroom, she removed the madras kerchief and tried to figure out her matted hair.

Apparently it was in a permanent state, so she retied the kerchief. She blamed Stephen for preventing her from relaxing in the shade of the redwoods with some people she might have enjoyed, although she admitted that she was disappointed with them. Albert would hear from her.

When Ann emerged from the bathroom, Stephen was standing there in his undershirt. He cocked his head toward the absurdly neat bed, which was sandwiched between the Buddha and the tiger statue.

"I'm going home," she said, glad that her car was in his driveway.

"Don't you want to stay?"

Stephen was fumbling with her sweater button.

"Didn't we have a nice ride?" he said, rubbing her shoulder.

She pulled away and aimed for the door.

"I have to go," she said. "I have to write an important paper myself."

He stared at her for a moment—incredulous or contemptuous, or both.

"Do you know what you need?" he said, his voice rising as she slipped out the door. "What you need is a good, royal fucking."

Hopewell, Ky.
October 14, 1966

Dear Ann,
    Oh, me, those trees you wrote about! You'd get a crick in your neck just looking up at them.
    What you asked about the worm is true. If you cut a worm in two, both parts will grow into a new worm, with a head and tail. . . .

Love,
Mama

Ann felt as if she herself had been cut in two and left to grow in two directions. In Yvor Winters's seminar room one late afternoon, she couldn't help interrupting the class to point out the astonishing sunset. They were considering Wordsworth's Lucy poems as a point of departure for a discussion of the bifurcation of the modern voice. Wordsworth was somehow deemed an antiquated revolutionary.

"We should honor Wordsworth by noticing this beautiful sunset," Ann said.

It was Ann's impression that she could not have uttered a more naive, girlish, unprofessional remark. The seven male students chuckled and nodded knowingly as their mentor glanced at the window, made a brief sweep of his left arm at the sight—both acknowledgment and dismissal—and returned quickly to the text.

Bob Dylan was singing "Like a Rolling Stone" on the radio.

LBJ had ordered five thousand more troops to Vietnam.

The day was cloudy and warm. There had been no rain since Ann's arrival in California.

Pixie brought Ann a brownie in a cocktail napkin.

The brownie was round and tiny, like a Swedish meat-ball.

"It's good for you," she said. She had brought one for herself in a separate napkin.

Ann turned off the radio and set her Dylan album on the stereo. Dylan sang incomprehensibly while they watched flickering candles Pixie had brought. Her new Beatle haircut looked raw. Some curly tufts wouldn't lie flat, and sprigs stuck out over her ears.

"I think Sanjay is used to long hair on women," said Pixie. "Just my luck. I'm always on the wrong train."

"But he probably thinks short hair is alluring. The girl from Wyoming probably has short hair."

"I've seen her—long, blond, straight. Face like an apple pie. She probably irons her hair."

The taste and texture of the brownie were exaggerated, too rich to eat quickly. Ann nibbled at it.

The Dylan album played loudly—strange and nasal wailing, like a preacher on a street corner addressing passersby. The music was both whiny and vigorous, a sort of contradiction. Ann stared at the candles, trying to count the flickerings.

"Is Dylan a poet or merely a songster? What are these words? What would I do with words like this in a graduate poetry class? What would Yvor Winters say?"

"You're getting paranoid about that professor," Pixie said.

Ann tried to explain. She was awkward in class, her memory stopping up when she was put on the spot.

"Then why are you at Stanford?" Pixie said sharply.

"I won't have to get a job as long as I'm in school."

"That sounds like a draft deferment. Are you afraid of getting drafted?"

Ann wouldn't answer. She ate the rest of the brownie. It was chewy and unusual.

"What's in this brownie? It's crunchy like cow feed."

"Oh, it's a Mary Jane brownie. My specialty."

"What?"

"Oh, Ann, you're so naive." Pixie laughed, crunching her napkin in a brisk move. "And for God's sake, Ann, everybody's fucking everybody. It doesn't matter. You don't have to feel guilty. Go on and get the Pill."

"Isn't it against the law if you're not married?"

"Just say you are—or will be next week. Or say you need it to regulate your period."

Random sex was slutty. Ann felt undone, flattened like the Wyoming girl's ironed hair.

Ann did have a pill for special occasions—half a bottle of Preludin, a diet pill, saved from senior year.

Whenever she had to write a term paper, a quarter of a pill set her ablaze and kept her up all night in a raging fit of clarity. Crazed with concentration, bursting with focused energy, she shuffled her jumbled notes. Normally she didn't think linearly or logically. Her thoughts tumbled around chaotically, but with pep pills, her ideas became orderly, like a tree, with all the supporting material hung like ornaments on the branches. Writing a paper was like diagramming sentences.

She spewed out a paper for poetics class on Ovid's hilarious love elegy about the unattainable Corinna and her dead parrot. Ann always found it fascinating when something repeated itself—the girl's parrot skirt at La Honda and Corinna's dead parrot. It was only coincidence, but she liked the pattern such overlaps made. In his elegy, Ovid complains when Corinna dyes her hair or has an abortion. Ann wondered how an abortion worked in Ovid's day. They probably didn't have coat hangers. Toga hooks. An old song, "Corinna, Corinna," played in her head.

She lingered on Ovid's poem about cosmetics, with its ancient beauty tips. She pictured Ovid's toga-clad Roman girlfriends at a beauty parlor, getting their hair treated while they complained about the plumbing and gossiped about laundresses and handsome serving boys. In elegiac couplets, they mourned lost loves.

"Won't coffee do the same thing?" Pixie demanded after Ann had spent the night enlarging her paper to include Ovid's letters from heroines to the lovers who had abandoned them.

"I hate the taste. How can anybody drink that stuff?"

Pixie ran her hand through her unruly hair. She said, "If you're trying to catch a guy, why don't you learn how to make a pot of coffee?"

Ann was still mad at Pixie over the Mary Jane brownie. She recalled reading about a girl who drank acid-laced Tab and went berserk on a roller coaster.

Pixie said, "If you could make someone a passable cup of java, your fortunes might change."

Nicodemus suddenly landed on Ann's lap as if for emphasis.

Obtaining the birth-control pill was easy, and at first opportunity Ann found herself spending the night with an eighteenth-century enthusiast named Ben. The next morning, she realized their dabblings meant nothing, and she knew that he felt the same. Empty sex was distasteful, she thought, remembering certain grating textures and smells.

Although she was eager to finish a typing job, she waited while Ben made breakfast. He cracked four eggs into a simmering skillet of water. He covered the pan and turned off the heat.

"There. Twenty minutes."

"Twenty minutes?" She would die of boredom. "There are faster ways to cook an egg."

"This is the way I do it."

She perused his bookshelf. His science-fiction books were grouped with studies of Milton's *Paradise Lost*. When she asked if there was a connection, he expounded on his theory of *Paradise Lost* as the original science fiction. Although blind, Milton had a vision of Eden that outshone any science-fiction movie today. Ben's ambition was to make a film of *Paradise Lost*.

"I can just see Lucifer in the flames and Adam and Eve being cast out." He was folding a tea towel fussily.

Surely twenty minutes had passed. The coffee smelled like motor oil. She survived three sips. Soon after the slowpoke, slow-poached eggs, she left.

She didn't see Ben again. There was no fire. She wanted something sparkier. If she had to grade it, it would be a C-minus.

Paradise Lost was on her reading list. It was chilling

to visualize earnest Ben making a Technicolor extravaganza from the outlandish imaginings of a blind poet.

Her cavernous bathroom was so dark, and California should be so light, she thought.

Ben and the eggs. That was exactly what happened. Why can't she imagine that scene differently?

Hopewell, Ky.
November 15, 1966

Dear Ann,

Remember Mrs. Slocum's boy Tommy? She got word this week that he got killed over there. Oh, she'll be to bury. She loved that boy. She waited on him hand and foot. Raising him without a daddy and now this. Several on our road are going to make up for flowers if they ever get him home. Tommy aimed to go to the junior college and learn a trade, but he went off to fight.

He helped hay here summer before last.

I hope they get this thing over with before your brother's old enough to go. What you said about him going to college and getting out of being drafted—I don't know if he could go to a college. He won't study. He just wants to play ball. He couldn't get a scholarship like you did.

Love,
Mama

Ann's first quarter at Stanford tumbled along swiftly. The schoolwork was demanding, like pulling an all-nighter eight days a week. In retrospect, Yvor Winters's seminar seemed ludicrous. He was sometimes gruff and touchy, with a scowl and odd literary prejudices that Ann quickly learned to ignore. He admired Emily Dickinson but didn't see her humor.

Ann said to the class, "'I heard a Fly buzz—when I died.' How can you fail to snicker?"

Although several of the students in the seminar dismissed Dickinson as a minor versifier, Ann thought death to Dickinson was like a pet, or a mascot—a thing always looking over your shoulder, waiting for you to finish some trivial task. Death was a comic figure. A sidekick, like Smiley Burnette to Gene Autry. You could take a broom to Death, sweep it under the rug, talk to it, play jokes on it, pretend it wasn't in the room. Even though you were too busy to stop for it, Death was ridiculously patient and polite. Ann was drawn to the spinster waif of Amherst, who was undoubtedly a victim of sexual repression—not because she was neurotic, as the Freudians would have it, but because she was afraid of getting knocked up.

Ann no longer feared such shame. She could explore possibilities with dear devil-may-care Enovid. The wheel design of the little compact of twenty-eight pills both pleased and alarmed her. Ovid's ancient girlfriend should have had such a cosmetics case, Ann thought.

"Did you read Ovid's poem about makeup?" she said after class to the girl who resembled Twiggy. "Ancient beauty tips."

The Twiggy girl, whose name was Elise, ran her fingers through her short hair.

"Did he mention aerosol spray?" she asked.

After the lackluster, lackadaisical night with Ben and that interminable breakfast, Ann proceeded with care. She wanted something more glorious. To take something just because it was free was a bad habit of country people, she thought. She was restless and uneasy. She had a habit of jumping in over her head. She was scared.

Some songs on the radio the autumn of Yvor Winters's seminar in modern poetry:

"You Can't Hurry Love"
"96 Tears"
"Just Like a Woman"
"Lady Godiva"
"How Sweet It Is"

Yvor Winters summoned Ann to his office for a conference. He was scribbling notes on a paper, and when he raised his head he stared hard at her. "Why are you wearing sunglasses?"

"They're prescription." Her contacts had been irritating her eyes.

"But I can't see you."

Didn't he see they were chic Italian sunglasses? She wore a miniskirt, white go-go boots, and Mary Quant makeup. Already those styles were passé, she realized.

"What are you hoping to get from the program here?"

Ann remembered her fourth-grade teacher smacking her upside the head for an innocent impertinence—sticking her tongue out at a boy. Haltingly, she tried to explain to Yvor Winters how she had been a big reader all her life. Her mother always said Ann had her nose in a book, lost in stories. She felt like a child talking this way, her face flushing.

"For example, take Heathcliff in *Wuthering Heights.* I'm enamored of Heathcliff."

Professor Winters hooted. "He is only a fictive creature on the page. Would you really love someone so monstrous in real life?"

She was stymied. She pictured Heathcliff rising

thrillingly out of the mist on the moor. She wondered if a heath and a moor were the same.

"I don't know," she said, fumbling with her sunglasses. When she removed them, Yvor Winters shimmered in the form of a turtle.

"We don't know what to make of you," he said. "We can't tell how serious you are as a scholar. We don't know what you think."

Her head was stopped up. She was sure her own peculiar ideas were of little value to people like him. She wondered if he thought she was a redneck. Although she rarely spoke up in class, she took notes with dedication and always read her assignments. She loved literature but didn't see the need to argue about it. Her classes were full of know-it-all pedants competing like Quiz Kids, each trying to sound more professorial than the professor. Their talk seemed to freeze her brain. She thought Yvor Winters expected her to explain herself in lit-crit jargon and to take sides on the New Criticism. She didn't care about the New Criticism. She liked the pleasure of verbal oddities, the mouth-feel of Anglo-Saxon words, the exhilaration of *Moby-Dick*, the lustiness of the Wife of Bath and Molly Bloom, the swooning rhythms of Woolf's *Orlando*. Old English filled her with joy because it was so intricate and strange. Sometimes a poem was so beautiful it would make her head shoot smoke. But she was no judge.

"Don't worry," Yvor Winters said, the first note of kindness she had heard from him. "Your papers have been commendable, even original, and we know it sometimes takes some adjustment in graduate school, but remember, we do expect great things from you."

She felt jumpy. She stumbled to the bookstore and bought a ream of typing paper and a box of blue ink cartridges for her fountain pen. She could never remember to say what was in her mind. She felt ashamed that she would allow Yvor Winters to intimidate her. But he had said her work was original.

She typed all evening, a political-science student's dissertation on the rise of fascism in England. Her typing was swift and purposeful, while the Beatles' *Revolver* played full blast on her stereo. Now that she was charging sixty cents a page, she could earn almost ten dollars an hour—as good as modeling baby-doll pajamas for a vagabond pervert. She didn't think the scholar of fascism would mind if she corrected his dangling references. At eleven, she paused to eat a hard-boiled egg and some saltines with a large bottle of Coca-Cola.

Berea, Kentucky
November 22, 1966 (Three years gone by!)

Dear Ann,

I couldn't make any sense of your letter. Are you in some kind of trouble, or are you just overcome by stultifying academic voices?

Whatever is bothering you, let me remind you that a major thing is for you to develop a truer sense of Kentucky, for one day you will return and you will see it, as Buddha or somebody says, for the first time. You must always remember where you came from. You will need to know that one day.

For now, you need to shake loose. Introduce yourself to a jazz musician and learn about improvisation. Listen to Bob Dylan's Highway 61 Revisited and seduce that Indian guy. Explain Highway 61 to him. I mean the real highway, the one that cuts down through the U.S. like an arrow. Go out and talk to a tree. Ask yourself, what is important? Go to Walden.

By the way, I heard that Yvor Winters wrote a mean letter to the Kenyon Review.

Your pal,
Albert

A few times Sanjay invited Pixie and Ann to eat with him and the girl from Wyoming, Paula, who was often there on weekends. Ann enjoyed their company but thought it odd that he would invite two girls besides his girlfriend. Paula didn't seem jealous, though. She teased him affectionately. She had long blond hair and wore dungarees and mannish sandals with socks. Sanjay cooked kimchiri, a kind of spicy mush, and something with spinach and cheese. Pixie, realizing that Sanjay was off-limits, had been trying on boyfriends as if she were shopping at Macy's. Ann glimpsed them coming and going at dusk and dawn. Pixie had apologized for the brownie while pointing out that Ann had not complained about its salubrious effects. Ann could see how attractive Sanjay was now that Paula from Wyoming was there, indulging him with hand-fed bites of naan and laughing at his gentle humor. Paula was taller than Sanjay.

Ann attended a few grad-student gatherings, and she was friendly with Elise, who bleached her hair to resemble Twiggy and complained that she couldn't get thin enough. (Cupcakes.) Ann had heard that she was a pet of Yvor Winters. Ann saw Meredith and John again but had trouble placing herself in their realm, where they seemed guided by the stern certainties of adulthood. On campus, Ann saw the undergrads acting silly. She had never gone in for frivolous group behavior, yet she didn't want to be a grown-up. Grown-ups were serious in the wrong ways. She felt most herself when she was alone, in a strange place. She thought about returning to La Honda to see Albert's friends, but she didn't want to sit around watching people trip. Somebody said LSD was out of favor, but she knew Pixie had taken it, and the Twiggy girl had too. Ann was aware that she was casting lines in all directions and not finding a clear path for herself.

Instead of returning to La Honda, one Saturday Ann drove to Monterey—a long way to drive without music—and walked out on the pier. She gazed at the sky and felt a nothingness. The whole day was blank. She could not have reported a thing about it. She watched the pelicans swoop in and land with their mouth-loads of fish. They reminded her of her mother lugging a load of wash.

The round trip to Monterey had taken most of the day. With half a pep pill, Ann stayed up all night in a euphoric rush, writing a paper on Dylan Thomas. She ate nothing but a packet of graham crackers in a bowl of milk—dipping them one by one so they wouldn't get soggy. Toward dawn, when she was trying to sleep at last, her heart turned a somersault. It stirred and fluttered like a butterfly and then revved up. It began to beat loudly, as if someone had turned the volume knob. When she switched on the lamp, she could see her nightgown pulsating. Pulling it up, she observed her stomach jumping with the force of her wild heartbeat.

Before eight on Sunday morning, Ann bounded into the infirmary with her runaway heart. She hadn't slept all night. A skinny intern asked her to run in place for one minute and then switch to jumping jacks. He watched her as she bounced until she was breathing heavily. He listened to her chest again.

"Aren't you afraid I'll have a heart attack jumping like that?"

"You're all right," he said.

She wasn't sure. Why would her heart do that? What if the pep pills had harmed her heart? Or could it be the birth-control pill? Embarrassed, she mentioned Enovid but got no reaction. She didn't volunteer that she had taken Preludin.

Wanting someone to know what had happened in case she did have a heart attack, she stopped in at Pixie's. Pixie came to the door with a hair-dryer bonnet on her head.

Handheld blow dryers weren't in general use yet.

"Why don't you just drink coffee instead of taking those diet pills?" Pixie asked. "Coffee will wake you up."

"Maybe I will. But I need some sleep now."

"You won't smoke a joint and you turn your nose up at wine, but you'll take speed like it's candy. I don't think that's very smart."

"I'm not very smart," Ann snapped. She left abruptly.

Her heart had calmed down after the jumping jacks. Somehow they seemed to recalibrate the rhythm.

In the bathroom, the dark sea of tile accentuated the blankness of her face in the mirror. Would she recognize herself on the street? Possibly not.

Ann thought she was having an identity crisis. Was she a farm girl raising a calf for the county fair, a typist, a wallflower, a Stanford scholar, a budding spinster? On the one hand, she sank in obedience to trends and class syllabi, flustered by academic challenges, and on the other, she remained resistant, perverse, willful. Mistress Contrary.

She stared at her vacant face in the mirror. Was she defined by others, or was she behind a plow, shoving her way through muddy furrows? She could hear her father saying to her, "You gee when you oughter haw." She couldn't remember now if gee was right or left. Her mother was saying, "Do it this a-way; that's not the way to do it. Hold the paring knife like this. You're a-grabbing it Annie Godlin."

Mistress Contrary.

She listened to "Tomorrow Never Knows" from *Revolver* over and over until she could feel sleep coming. Some of the words were from the Tibetan *Book of the Dead*. She wondered what it would feel like to be dead. Maybe it would feel like this—anonymous, blank, colorless.

The following morning, Pixie brought a pot of coffee. Smiling brightly, she said, "I know you can learn to like it."

Ann gave in. Pixie was trying to be a friend.

"I have to put milk and sugar in it," Ann said.

"I expected that. Southerner."

Ann shrugged and removed the milk bottle from the refrigerator. She plopped two spoons of sugar in the cup and added milk to the coffee Pixie had poured.

Ann sipped the coffee.

"How is it?" Pixie asked.

"Bearable."

Pixie laughed. "I get a kick out of you," she said.

"You're a student of psychology. You can probably figure out my problems." Ann sipped more coffee. It wasn't bad.

"You're depressed and repressed," Pixie pronounced. "You need a cat."

She told Ann about a psychologist she had heard was good. She had heard this from a girl who had tried to commit suicide but who had conquered her negative impulses through therapy and was getting married in June. Ann didn't like Pixie judging her this way, but school insurance covered the cost, and she was curious.

The psychologist was a behaviorist of an obscure variety with roots in Europe. Pixie said he was influenced by the Bandura school of thought, which had something to do with redirecting aggression and involved punching a doll. When Ann protested, Pixie claimed that everybody was aggressive in some way, whether they knew it or not.

The psychologist's office was a pleasant walk from Ann's apartment. Nobody walked, but Ann decided to save gas. Besides, her engine was knocking. As she set out, she dropped off her rent check with the landlady and as usual peered into the dim, forbidding house. The overhead trapeze bar was an odd touch, for Jingles had a dumpy, middle-aged body, not the svelte form of an acrobat. Ann wondered if Pixie had only imagined Jingles doing flips in the parlor. After leaving, Ann noticed the landlady acrobat peering out the window at her from behind her heavy, velvet-roped drapery.

The psychologist, a natty dresser in a blue blazer, wanted to be called by his first name, Frank.

"Everybody's talking about relationships," Ann said, getting straight to the point. "That and their identity crises."

"Do you have an identity crisis?"

"I don't know." She confessed the envy she felt when she saw young people in pairs flirting and holding hands. All her life, she had been told that a woman had to trap a man. Her dentist had called lipstick "man-bait." What was she doing wrong? How could she grab hold of a boy and make him care about her?

Frank curled his fists and flexed his fingers.

"You've come to the right place," he said. "We can fix your problem."

"And can you fix my car?"

His little chuckle made her relax. She couldn't have made such a remark in class. People were too quick to pounce. But Frank seemed concerned.

She told him about three attractive boys in her seminars, not including Stephen or Ben. One by one, she had met the other three at Tresidder Union, where she gushed her excitement about Eliot's use of literary allusion or the beauty of "The Seafarer" in the original. All three had traded quips about Yvor Winters with her.

One of them, named Dennis, defended Yvor Winters and even seemed to be on his level. The second one, Wayne, didn't take Winters seriously and wasn't at all threatened by him. The third one, whatever his name was, found the modernist poets boring and seemed to feel the same about her.

After listening to her laments, the psychologist, Frank, said, "Maybe you shouldn't be talking shop with these guys."

"But we're all students, studying literature."

"Maybe you threaten them."

"But they act so superior with all their knowledge," she said.

"Men don't expect women to be smart."

"Really? Well, yes, I know that." She rambled on longer about the challenge of sophisticated flirtation and then found herself on a detour to La Honda with Stephen the bad-tempered motorcyclist.

Toward the end of the hour, Frank the psychologist said, "From the way you're talking about these guys, I don't think I know them. You speak of them like abstractions, like fantasies."

"I want to know how to act when the real thing comes along," she said.

"The real thing?"

"Yes, the Real Thing."

Frank stared at her, as if she had just asserted her belief in Santa Claus.

"I want to be in love with someone," she said. "I want someone to be in love with me. That's what I mean, for it to work both ways. That would be romantic love, the Real Thing."

She bought a small aluminum percolator and experimented with coffee strength and additives. She added more milk and sugar. She soon became accustomed to sitting down to work at her long table with her coffee on a cork coaster. Coffee made her buzzy and alert, but it wasn't as strong as Preludin, which transformed her into a whirligig. Now her heart was behaving itself.

The couple next door performed regularly, usually late in the evening, around midnight—not every night but always on weekends. She heard them in their bathroom. She wondered about the color scheme there. Sometimes in the mornings she saw them, moving swiftly down the exterior stairway. They were older than students, and they dressed in drab brown uniforms with yellow piping.

Once in a while, she heard them quarrel, but usually

after a time she would hear the bedsprings squeaking. For a few weeks, she didn't hear them. Then one day their door was open and she glanced into their apartment. She saw that the bed was on the far side of the room. They had simply moved the bed. Their walls glowed bright orange.

Frank the psychologist listened to her, but he wouldn't answer her questions about his methods. He wouldn't tell her about the Bandura voodoo doll, or the cult-like origins of the particular school of behaviorism. He was treating Ann the individual, he said; he wasn't checking off a list of regulation procedures. "Relax," he said.

"And it's not a voodoo doll," he said.

He was wearing a blue Oxford shirt and love beads like those in Pixie's curtain. If Ann's parents knew she was seeing a head doctor, especially a man who wore beads, they would go crazy with worry. Her life was mostly a secret from them, but it occurred to her as she told Frank the psychologist about them that perhaps her life was a secret to everyone, even herself. People often said she was standoffish and didn't reveal her thoughts. Frank himself had observed that she didn't show her feelings to people she sought approval from, those fantasy boyfriends. And Yvor Winters had accused her of mysterious reticence. Yet when she did manage to express her feelings, people didn't always take her seriously. Earnestly, she laid her thoughts out for the psychologist, waiting for directions.

He sat there like a knot on a log.

"Why haven't you asked me about my beads?" he asked.

"Why don't you answer my questions?"

She felt satisfaction in resisting him. Although the psychologist stirred up troublesome thoughts, sometimes Ann felt a little glow of optimism as she left his cool bower, with the greenery in his waiting room. Since the flowing ferns and cacti and jungle flora required three different climates, their cohabitation was intriguing. But that was appropriate, she thought, for a therapist who could accommodate extremes. Lost persons, with varying degrees of damage, found a home here. It was California. She was really there. One day she spotted an intact pomegranate under the tree in front of his building and dropped it in her bag.

Ann had never picked up a date in her own car, but all the old rules were shot. Leonard, a second-year student who was immersed in the poetry of Ezra Pound, asked her to go with him to the city to an exhibition of erotic sculptures fashioned from the metal of junked cars. And then he said, "You'll have to drive. Unless you want to ride on my bicycle."

It took an hour to drive into San Francisco. They should have taken the train.

Going there was fine, breezy. Ann knew the roads by now. She chatted with Leonard about architecture and cars. She didn't challenge his ideas on Ezra Pound. Ezra Pound made her spine crack and made her head feel waterlogged, but she didn't pursue shoptalk. She asked about Leonard's background in Rhode Island. He had never heard of the chickens known as Rhode Island Reds. No, not a sports team. She listened to him explain the art they were going to see, and on the way back, she listened to the same observations.

The streets were wrapped in fog then. She could hardly see to drive.

"This is super!" Leonard cried. "I love this. We might just roll out to sea. Look how the light shimmers. You couldn't get this from poetry!"

"I can't see where I'm going," she said, slowing to a crawl. "Where is the turn? Is this the right highway? Should I get off?"

"Just go with it!" he said. "Man! Man oh man. You couldn't get this on psychedelics!"

She had the strange feeling that Leonard had just reached a climax.

She recalls the end of that year, going home to Kentucky. It was balmy on Christmas Day, and then came an ice storm. Remembering, she feels she is riding a seesaw of weather, but that is the tremble of the ship, behaving like a spirit level. She should head for the stateroom to make the tea. Domestic duties make her angry, and the calm blue sea seems spiteful in its placidity.

1967

It rained. The Quad was puddles. The rain felt icy. Ann pulled up the collar of her trench coat and clutched her books against her chest.

"Join me in jail! Refuse to fight!"

A large crowd had gathered in White Plaza, and a tall student in an army fatigue jacket was hoisting a poster high on a stick. RESIST THE DRAFT. He twirled the sign around. The back read, SAVE AMERICA FROM VIOLENCE. Ann squeezed through the crowd and trudged toward the parking lot with her armload of books. Loudspeakers began to blare.

Even though it was midday, cars were turning on their headlights. Ann's windshield wipers, long out of use, scraped hoarsely, and she drove slowly through the unaccustomed gloom. The eucalyptus trees waved, as if signaling for help.

The radio news that evening did not mention the protest, but the next day the *Stanford Daily* gave it front-page, above-the-fold coverage. The student-body president was calling for massive resistance to the draft. Ann had heard some students say they would go to Canada before they would comply with the draft, but now they were being urged to go to jail instead.

A jumpy mood was spreading over campus—louder voices and more desperate questions. To Ann, immersed in Victorian novels and the Irish Renaissance, the antiwar talk seemed disorienting. Sometimes she felt as if she had been tossed into a snowbank. Or she was sledding on a cafeteria tray down the hill behind the dorm.

But this is California.

In February, Vice President Hubert Humphrey spoke on campus. The auditorium was packed, and Ann could not enter. She listened to the loudspeakers outside in a noisy crowd. While Humphrey was still speaking, dozens of people began walking out of the auditorium. Ann saw a group of faculty members emerge from the side exit. They were all wearing white armbands. Yvor Winters? Was that Yvor Winters? He wore a white armband. It was passing strange that he should be in that crowd, she thought. He looked ill. Ann felt she hadn't known him at all. She had been in his presence only twice since his seminar ended before Christmas. Outside the English department door, she had overheard him say to Wallace Stegner, "Now, Wally, you know that's pure twaddle."

Dozens more in white armbands streamed out. Eventually she had a glimpse of the vice president, who was being hurried to a car. Humphrey, his struggling potato face turning red, had not expected this hullabaloo.

"Humpty Dumpty!" someone shouted.

"Shame, shame!"

"Why don't you stop killing children in Vietnam?"

Ann had thought it was a privilege to be at a university—a self-contained world, like the Vatican or a Pacific island. She couldn't remember the difference between Viet Cong and Viet Minh or which side Ho Chi Minh was on, and the tumult on campus made her feel guilty. She was glad she didn't know anyone in the military.

In late March, just after turning in her paper on *The Playboy of the Western World*, she flew to Kentucky.

Hopewell, Ky.
March 30, 1967

Dear Ann,
    We were tickled to see you here for a whole week. Sorry we had to put you to work in the garden, but we were behind this year. It come a heavy rain and washed out some of those beans, but I'll get some more in. We still have black seeded Simpson lettuce and plenty of reddishes. Wish I could send you some wilted lettuce with bacon grease! . . .

                                        Love,
                                        Mama

What her mother didn't know wouldn't hurt her, Ann thought. Pixie was thinking of going to a nude encounter group. The Twiggy girl was having her own personal be-ins on weekends at her family property in Woodside. Even Sanjay bought a pair of blue-jeans.

And then Jimmy appeared.

He isn't supposed to be here. She feels a trace of vertigo from an almost imperceptible wobble of the cruise ship. But they are in California, she thinks, clutching the rail. It can be a different story.

Jimmy sat across from Ann in the Kelly and Sheets class. That's what he called the seminar on the poetry of Keats and Shelley. (That was probably an old joke, she thought later.) Whenever she glanced up from her notebook, he was gazing across the oval table at her, but he lowered his eyes when she noticed him. Her heart did a butterfly caffeine flutter, then revved up. He had long, shaggy hair like a poodle dog. Random ringlets framed his face.

At the end of the class, he shoved his books into a green canvas bag and slung it over his shoulder before he moved in her direction.

"Which is your favorite, Kelly or Sheets?" he asked.

"Keats, of course. How can that be a question?" She was trembling.

"Touché." He grinned. He had nice, even teeth.

He was smoking a cigarette. They headed down the stairs.

"Where do you come from? I like your accent."

"Kentucky. Can you hear my accent?"

"Yeah, can you hear mine?"

"Hmm. A little northern—Detroit?"

"Chicago." He sucked in his cigarette and then blew little contrails out his nostrils. "Tell me everything about yourself," he said.

"Everything?"

"Sure. What was your first word? First tooth. Stuff from your baby book."

The sunlight on the Main Quad was blazing. As if they had a destination, they headed up Lasuen Mall toward Hoover Tower. She was glad it was her heretofore embarrassing accent he had mentioned instead of the fatuous remarks she had made in class about Shelley's wind poems. Sitting on the steps of Hoover Tower, she told Jimmy things about her childhood she wouldn't have expected to tell—about milking cows and cleaning manure from the barn. His childhood was Boy Scouts and Cubs games in suburban Dullsville, Illinois. He apologized for his humdrum history, which sounded alien to her. He smoked another cigarette.

"Let's walk," he said after a while. He stubbed out his cigarette on the sidewalk. "Give me your books."

He stuffed her Keats and Shelley paperbacks and her

notebook into his bag, then hoisted it over his shoulder. She thought of Johnny Appleseed.

"Where are we going?"

"Nowhere, just walking around."

They meandered around the library and back to the Quad. He zigzagged in and out of the archways. She was wearing the wrong shoes.

Ann asked him if he had been at any of the protests.

"No, but there's going to be a big one in the city in a couple of weeks."

"Are you going?"

"Yeah. I hate this goddamn war." He pointed to a bird high in a palm tree. "Hark! Keats's nightingale! Come on, Florence Nightingale, take my arm."

They passed the bookstore and the crazy green fountain. Jimmy crooked his elbow for her to take his arm. She liked touching him. He was tall but not towering. He wore a nondescript brown duffel coat, a blue Oxford shirt, and twill khakis with an ink stain on one knee. His clothes seemed to be an undergraduate wardrobe he hadn't worn out yet.

She liked his long, messy hair and the unselfconscious way he walked, a walk that meant confidence. And he wasn't toplofty, like so many Stanford boys.

Her car was in the parking area below Tresidder Union. When they reached her car, he handed over her books. "I'm going the other way," he said. "See you in class."

He waved a little goodbye.

Ann was stunned. She felt as though an actor had stepped off the screen and taken her for a vigorous stroll through a make-believe El Dorado before slipping back into the celluloid. What movie? What actor? Actors were all suave, with molded hair. Jimmy was something new.

She bought an ashtray in case he ever came to her apartment.

Would he really wear that old duffel coat? It is seventy-one degrees and sunny in Palo Alto.

She read "Ode to a Nightingale" carefully and tried to think up something interesting to say. Frank the psychologist had warned against shoptalk, but she fancied that she and Jimmy shared a sense of irony and a willing flippancy about their reading. She hardly ate. She wanted to touch Jimmy again. She wanted to play footsie with him under the seminar table. She imagined walking with him under one umbrella, with his arm around her, pulling her out of the rain. That was at least one half-remembered movie ending.

When she said in class that Keats's nightingale made her think of a drugged banshee—a tamed, benign counterpoint to the Irish banshee, the horrifying scream in the night—she could sense Jimmy's amusement.

"Banshee?" he said afterwards. "It was all I could do to keep from whooping out! Man, what a thought." He laughed. "Come on, my little banshee. I mean nightingale. Sing to me over coffee. We'll have coffee and you can chirp to me."

Ovid again! His chirpless Philomela turned into a nightingale. Ann felt tongue-tied.

They sat outside Tresidder, on the plaza, an area where affinity groups often showed up to fulminate or perform. A student was yelling his head off about Robert McNamara, and a group of girls in leotards was performing silent ballet-like exercises. The table was shaded by a canopy that resembled a hovering flying saucer. Jimmy smoked Marlboros and drank his coffee black. Ann had hers with milk and two sugars. While she fiddled with the sugar packet, a bit nervously, he was observing her intently. Her heart was not jumping enough to show through her sweater.

"Do you have banshees in Kentucky?" he asked.

"My mother thinks we do!"

Laughing at herself, she told him about the worm in the Blake poem and the Wordsworth sunset. "The other students were so high and mighty!"

"They're just polishing apples, you know," Jimmy said.

"Thank you."

He reached over and lifted her chin with his fingertip. "I like that way you have of lowering your head and mumbling."

"Do I do that? That's terrible."

"It's nice. It's humble."

"Oh, I should be more direct."

"But you are, in your own way." He stubbed his cigarette out. "Do you want some more coffee?"

"No, thank you. I mostly drink it to write papers. Coffee helps me focus."

"You've got an unusual kind of mind." He moved his cup around on the table.

"Really?"

"Want to walk?"

She had to go to the restroom first but didn't want to say, then realized she had to say it even though it was awkward. She left her books with him, and when she returned, he slid them into his book bag and they set off. She was wearing Capezio lace-ups instead of ballet flats today.

The day was soft, mizzly. They ambled through the campus, between the library and Hoover Tower. The grandeur of the campus was still stupefying. The giant oak by the library seemed like an ancient ruler, an ultimate authority. They didn't speak for a while. As they were passing a parking lot on Galvez Street, near the stadium, Jimmy stopped suddenly.

"This is my car," he said. "Want to go for a ride?"

The car was a sleek blue Mustang.

"Neat!" She was surprised.

"My dad gave it to me for graduation, but I'm embarrassed by it."

"Why? It's nice."

"I like the color, but what a crock. He didn't even let me pick it out. He just had an idea of the image he wanted for me."

"Why would your dad want you be a wild horse?"

"He was a big fraternity man, and he believes in levels—that is, you stay in your social class, and you meet the right sort of chicks if you drive the right car or wear the right thing. I wouldn't even join a fraternity in college." Jimmy laughed. "If the war keeps up, I'll wind up in the Mekong Delta frat."

"I hope not!" She laughed, but that wasn't funny.

"He thought I'd be a doctor like him. He's a proctologist. Imagine, poking your finger up men's asses all day for a living."

Ann couldn't imagine that.

He opened the passenger door for her, then tossed a worn Chaucer paperback into the back. The car had bucket seats, like chairs.

"Where to?" he asked, starting the engine.

On an impulse, she said, "The park by San Francisquito Creek. There's something there I want to see."

"I'm all yours," he said.

The car *was* like a wild horse, the way it seemed so alive, kicking into gear.

The park entrance was not obvious, and Jimmy had to backtrack and turn a few times to cross the railroad tracks by the deep, barren creek. They left the car on Alma Street and headed into the park.

"What are we looking for?"

"Surprise. Follow me."

They walked some distance without speaking. Then she could see the sequoia ahead.

"That's the tree Palo Alto is named for. El Palo Alto—the tall tree."

"It's magnelephant!" cried Jimmy, his arms wide, head cranked back.

"My freshman English teacher wanted me to find it, but I've never been over here."

The tree was scruffy with a thin topknot.

"It's seen better days," Jimmy said, picking at the bark. "Why did he want you to see this?"

"He wanted me to know about the history of the settlement of this place by Portola, the Spanish explorer."

They found the plaque and Jimmy read it aloud.

"'Under this giant redwood, the Palo Alto, November 6–11, 1769, camped Portola and his band on the expedition that discovered San Francisco Bay.'"

"Far out," said Jimmy.

"The year," Ann said. "It's the same year Daniel Boone explored Kentucky for the first time. That's important to my teacher. He was out here on a Stegner, and now he teaches in Kentucky."

"I've never been to Kentucky. I bet you come from a beautiful place."

"It's a small farm. My dad grows a little of everything. Cows."

"Horses?"

"No. Sorry, no mustangs."

"I want to see Kentucky!"

"I was just there last week on the break."

Now at least she could tell Albert she had seen the

tall tree where Portola the explorer had camped. He would be pleased.

You saw El Palo Alto years later, during a summer residency at Stanford. You drove to the park and admired the tree on the deep, dry creek bed by the railroad trestle. The tree had been rescued and refurbished, with a new plaque on a large boulder. A water pipe ran gallantly up the trunk. The tree once had twin trunks, but it was thriving. You had never really understood until then what the tree had meant to Albert. It was like the mast of a magnelephant ancient ship, a grand pole crowned with a crow's nest. A whaling ship or a slave ship? Either way, history can be so brutal.

Jimmy turned onto Sand Hill Road. In front of the shopping center, a man was guiding sacks of groceries on a rolling wooden platform to a car in front of the supermarket. A woman in high heels waited by her open trunk. Ann glanced at Jimmy, his strong hands guiding the wheel. She was stuck in a moment.

Then Ann led Jimmy up the metal stairs to her door.

He seized the quilt on Ann's studio bed.

"This is beautiful! Wow." He rubbed the quilt between his fingers. "Magnolious."

"My mother made it."

"It must have taken years. Look at that stitch work!"

"I helped her piece it when I was little."

The quilt was supposed to be a traditional marriage quilt, but Ann had gone to college instead, and her mother gave it to her then, saying, "You'll need some cover in that dorm room."

Jimmy traced a finger along a star in which she recognized the print of a blue dress she had worn in first grade.

"I like this star," he said. "Far, far out." He laughed. "The things we say. I must eschew clichés! Of course a star is far out. That's an astronomical term."

Jimmy had a sort of long face and intense blue eyes that were a little droopy. His untamed hair fell in clusters onto his forehead. She was breathless just looking at him.

"I want to know your mother," he said. "What would it be like if you took me there, to your farm?"

"It's nothing special. About seventy-five acres—some fields, a creek, an old farmhouse that didn't have indoor plumbing until I was five years old."

"Could I ride a tractor? Or would it be mules? Did you wear a hoopskirt?"

"How would I get a hoopskirt into the outhouse?"

He laughed. She was pleased to see him use her new ashtray.

"I'm kidding," she said. "We didn't have an out-house. At least not after I was five. And nobody wore hoopskirts. Too hot!"

Jimmy surveyed her tiny apartment—her piles of books, the cabbage-rose rug, the fuzzy, rough arm-chair.

"Why don't you have a TV?"

"It costs money. And why do I need a TV?"

He shrugged. "I'm sorry. I was making assump-tions. I thought everybody had one."

"We got a television when I was in high school and then later I'd watch it with my daddy and little brother when I came home on breaks."

"Didn't your mom watch it?"

"She couldn't see it from the kitchen."

After they had retrieved her car from campus, they saw a Bergman film, *Persona*, at the little theater where she had often gone alone. Jimmy bought two boxes of popcorn and two Cokes, but she forgot to eat her popcorn. The movie was slow and artful, the kind of movie you were supposed to take seriously, but she could hardly concentrate for the electricity between her and Jimmy. Touching casually. His hand filching her popcorn.

"Did you like the flick?"

"Yeah. Confusing at times."

"That's Bergman for you."

At her door, he said good night and kissed her awkwardly. "May I see you again?"

"That would be nice."

He hugged her tightly.

It was impossible to concentrate on the reading for class. An innocent word would spin her off into a daydream of passion. Instead of showering efficiently, she luxuriated in the hard, hot stream, soaping herself and imagining Jimmy there.

You are such a mooncalf. You can't help it. You would think no one had ever fallen in love before. You know what will happen. But you can revise it. You can X out all the awkward constructions and wrong turns. The setting will change everything—those trees, the sun, the red roofs of academe. California paradise. You can keep the good parts.

They drove one afternoon later that week to San Gregorio Beach. The day was damp and windy, colder than Palo Alto, and as they walked along, Jimmy curved his arm around her, shielding her from the wind. They didn't stay long among the dramatic cliffs.

The Pacific Ocean seemed anything but peaceful, she thought. They retreated to a café. Jimmy ate half her tuna-fish sandwich and smoked several cigarettes. Fog smudged the window beside their booth. The ocean disappeared. The fog shut out everything around them. All afternoon, they kept up a conversation about themselves, their backgrounds, their schooling, their ideas. Jimmy seemed intensely interested in everything about Ann's family and what it was like to grow up on a dairy farm. He dismissed his own family in a few words—conventional, straight, uptight, patriotic, the kind of people who would buy their kid a Mustang but never ask him an important question. His father, who had avoided World War II—4-F—was paying for grad school so Jimmy wouldn't get drafted.

They spoke little of the present war. Ann didn't have to know the fine points of President Johnson's thinking to realize how wrong the war was, how misguided the United States was, what a delusion the domino theory had to be. It was all evident in the tone, the sound in the air. It was in the music on the car radio as they drove away from the coast, in the clearing fog. Ann let the window down a few inches and breathed the sea smell of birds and fish and decay. The radio played Smokey Robinson and the Miracles, the Spencer Davis Group, Aretha Franklin, Jefferson Airplane. Jimmy turned the radio up loud and they didn't speak for a long while. Ann felt as though they were driving down a remote road in the dark, not knowing their destination or whether they would arrive together.

"I'll show you my place," Jimmy said, when they reached Palo Alto.

Ann realized what she had been missing by not having a TV. The war. There it was, on the network news.

"That's infuriating," Jimmy said, pointing to the screen. "Sending more and more kids. For what? Westmoreland's on a rampage."

"It all seems for nothing," she murmured. Seeing the war news made her anxious. She should have read more newspapers. She wasn't even sure why the United States was in Vietnam, what had started it all.

The news ended, and Jimmy turned off the TV.

"Do you want some tea? I can make tea."

"O.K." She still wasn't used to hot tea.

His small house, in a quiet neighborhood of woodframe houses, was luxurious compared to her place. Four rooms and a bath (plain, white). And he had more belongings—books, record albums, a tape recorder. His bookshelves were fashioned from concrete blocks and unpainted boards. A dartboard hung beside a poster of the Rolling Stones.

Jimmy ran water into a small aluminum stewer. It heated quickly on a gas flame, and he poured the bubbling water over tea bags in mismatched ceramic mugs. One was striped, and the other had Porky Pig on it. As they waited for their tea to cool, Jimmy was drawing invisible patterns on the maple table with his finger. His hair fell into his eyes, and he brushed it aside. It fell again, and when she reached to push it back for him, he grasped her hand and held it tightly.

"Can't wait for this tea to cool," he said. "That might take all night."

"It might take till tomorrow," she said with a slight gasp as he jumped up, pulling her by the hand.

His bed was piled with laundry. He threw the laundry on a chair and bounced onto the bed, dragging her down onto the blue comforter with him.

"I've been wanting you so long," he said. "Every minute."

"Jimmy," she murmured.

"Turn off your mind and float downstream," he half hummed.

They shed their clothes slowly and deliberately, exploring a little more as they went along, closer and closer, skin on skin, toward a quiet frenzy. With Jimmy, there was a grand difference from those other jabs and gropes, she kept thinking. Those fantasy guys, according to Frank the psychologist. This was real. The depth, the luxury, the rhythm.

The cut worm forgives the plow, she thought suddenly and almost laughed. Again and again, and more and more. Then time disappeared and they were traveling into space.

She wondered why he didn't use a rubber or why he hadn't asked her about the Pill. She didn't tell him. They had plunged into each other without any thought to consequences. She thought he must have trusted her wholly to be prepared, but nothing would have stopped her.

Holding each other, the intensity of the pleasure, was beyond anything described in her books, wasn't in any poem in the world.

"Here we have naming of the parts," Jimmy said, as they explored each other in his big bed. Touching her breast, he said, "Bubble."

"What do you call this?"

"Oh, that's my pogo stick."

She smiled. "That sounds like something you'd say in grade school."

"No, I didn't have such a powerful pogo then. It couldn't do tricks." He sneaked his hand up her thigh. "And what do you call this?"

"My bandersnatch. The dreaded bandersnatch will snatch you up."

"No, you're defenseless. My pogo stick is going to invade your velvet box."

"My silk tunnel," she corrected him. "And what are these?"

"Dog toys," he said.

This was so adolescent, she thought. They were teenagers, shameless and silly. They were the first explorers. They sat cross-legged, two lotus blossoms, facing each other. Four naked knees nudging. She had never been this close with a boy, eyes open, staring at each other's nakedness. In truth, she had never gotten a really good look at the mystery parts.

He touched her cheek and gazed straight at her. "That first day when we walked, I ran off. I was too shy with you, but I really wanted to stay. I couldn't take my eyes off you in class."

"I caught you staring at me."

"I didn't mean to. I just liked to look at you."

"Why would you notice somebody like me?"

"There's nobody like you. I didn't notice anybody else." Running his hand along her cheek, he said, "I thought you seemed so mature, you might look down on me. You were quiet. I thought you were so confident you would never take me seriously."

"No. God, no, just the opposite. I was afraid you'd think I wasn't good enough for you."

"Don't talk like that. You're so classy."

She laughed. "I never thought I'd hear that word."

"You are a classy chick." He grinned and rumpled her hair. "See. You don't even need a tiara or a crown to be a queen. Why, you don't even need clothes! You're beautiful, just the natural way you are. *Au naturel!*"

He picked up his underwear from the floor.

"Your shorts are pink!"

"Like them?"

"They're the color of Pepto-Bismol!"

"I washed the red bathroom rug with them and they turned pink. I have eleven pairs of deep-pink underpants."

She was seized with mirth. Then she couldn't stop, and giggles overcame her.

"I'm not laughing at you!" she sputtered. She laughed because he didn't seem at all embarrassed. They laughed together, and they couldn't stop. She was laughing that a boy would wash his underwear with a red rug, and he was laughing with her, laughing with her laughter. She was letting loose at last.

"I'm having such a good time," she said eventually. "This is better than the Tilt-A-Whirl."

"I love to see your face like that, all puffed up and red."

He gazed directly into her eyes, and she was searching his face. She didn't remember anything so close and warm.

She never had an actual date with Jimmy, as she used to know the practice. They just fell in together. She couldn't wait to see him and he seemed thrilled to see her. He called her Snooks. With Jimmy, she felt she was really with someone, not hiding behind questions, not assessing how she looked or acted. It always startled her when they were peering straight into each other's eyes. His bright blue eyes.

"You're really here," she murmured.

She isn't inventing him. But there is no snow. The sandstone buildings shine brightly in the sun. Something new will happen here.

In those first weeks with Jimmy, they had fun just acting crazy, laughing together. She believed that falling in love could happen only once in life. Jimmy had a good voice, and he had a knack for remembering song lyrics. He could do Gilbert-and-Sullivan patter. He had played a policeman in a high-school production of "The Pirates of Penzance." In the car, he sang Beatles songs, stomping his left foot so vigorously in time with the tune that the car seemed to bounce. "I could have been a Beatle," he would say with mock braggadocio. He was unfailingly polite, always pausing at a threshold for her to enter before him and always opening the car door for her. He even had the money to take her out to eat. At the International House of Pancakes, she ordered Swedish pancakes with lingonberry syrup because she had never had lingonberries. He seemed charmed by her delight over such simple indulgences, and he let her drive his Mustang, which thrilled her, especially the way it zoomed so quickly after takeoff.

Jimmy had read widely in Freud, Wittgenstein, and Heidegger, giants of the mind, but he wasn't a show-off in class. He didn't even find the Twiggy girl attractive. She was trying too hard to be cool, he observed.

He swam laps daily at the university pool, where he had to pack his tumble of hair into a rubber cap. His body was limber and strong. He had a soft blue shirt that Ann admired. She loved to touch it and smell it.

At Half Moon Bay, Jimmy was standing in the sand, his toes in the water. "What do you think the ancients thought clouds were? What did they think they were seeing?"

Ann and Jimmy were gazing at layers of marshmallows, some with raised heads and some with pink cloaks.

"They told stories," Ann said. "They made up things, just like we do. See that turtle? It's going to bump into that warthog over there."

"That's not a warthog."

"Isn't it? It's covered with warts."

"I see moles."

On a love cloud, with a pot of coffee, Ann stayed up late, writing a paper on Percy Bysshe Shelley. She asserted that if Shelley hadn't drowned at twenty-four he would have died inside anyway, at the rate he was going. He couldn't have topped "Ozymandias," she declared.

"Bysshe," Jimmy said, when he read her paper. "Percy Bysshe Shelley. Snake sounds. Don't you love that name?"

Jimmy had the faintest lisp, she realized. It was a subtle feature she found endearing.

She tickled his feet with a feather.

"Where did you get a feather?"

"At the beach—the day we went, remember?"

"That feels good."

"What about this?"

"That feels nice."

"Do you like this?"

"That's good—that's *really* good!" He pulled her hand to him. "What about this?"

"Oh, I like this texture, like a baby's skin."

"Are you coming with me? Hold on. There. Mm."

"I could do this all night."

"Oh, Ann, you're so . . ."

There were zero words for this.

She was giddy and silly. She told Frank the psychologist that she felt happy, no longer confused, but he kept asking her, "What do you mean?"

What it was like. They were in on it at the beginning, Albert had said of his acid-freak pals. That was how Ann felt about falling in love. Everybody had a first time.

Ann and Jimmy swapped confessions of adolescent sex experiments. Jimmy told Ann about discovering girls at the swimming pool in junior high. By swimming stealthily underwater like a shark and zooming up behind an innocent swimmer, he could yank down a strap of her swim top, sometimes revealing a glimpse of nipple.

"I was such an ignoramus," he said.

Ann told Jimmy about the time Billie Jean Maddox in fourth grade coached her in the secrets of the private parts of boys. They were at the playground at lunchtime, under the tall hickory trees. The swings and slides were in the woods, and the ground was scattered with large ripening hickory nuts the size of peaches, the outer husks brown and hard. Billie Jean informed Ann that boys had things in their pants approximately that size, two of them, and she talked Ann into putting a couple of the hickory nuts in her pants to see what it would feel like to be a boy. They sat at their desks in the afternoon with hickory nuts in their pants. It was uncomfortable, and Ann squirmed until the nuts rolled out from beneath her dress. One hit the floor. She reached for it and raised her desk lid and deposited it inside before the teacher saw. Billie Jean was on the far side of the room, coping more confidently with her own hickory nuts. Neither of the girls ever mentioned the nuts again.

Jimmy told Ann about his high-school initiation. Two of the older boys escorted a group of four into Chicago, a thirty-minute train ride. They planned to see a concert at the Chicago Theatre, Dave Brubeck in his prime. After the show, the older boys took the younger four to a hotel to visit someone—a fancy woman who initiated each of them, in turn. She was in a suite with a bedroom, where she entertained each privately. She wore a slinky outfit, very high heels, and a flashy necklace. She had short hair puffed up on top and bulbous red-purple lips that she repainted after each seduction. Afterwards, Jimmy questioned whether she could have been a regular downtown Chicago prostitute. She could have been arrested, especially for entertaining boys so young. It didn't make sense, but who was she? Jimmy thought she must have been someone the older boys knew, maybe a relative. He never found out, but he confessed that what she had taught him had been useful.

"Brubeck was fantastic," Jimmy added.

In New York, war protestors were marching to the United Nations, and on the same day in San Francisco protestors were marching down Market Street to Golden Gate Park. The Stanford campus was quivering with spontaneous demonstrations and teach-ins. With the antiwar movement intensifying, Ann, who had never been a joiner, felt she had changed direction. Without Jimmy, she would have still been floundering among her stacks of books, with her coffee, her judgmental neighbor Pixie, and her threatening professors. But now she saw herself as one of many earnest young people, in jeans and long hair, who were out to change the world. Enter the clichés of fashion. She had flung most of her college wardrobe at the Salvation Army. With a flurry of new typing jobs, she was able to buy some embroidered blouses and a pair of bell-bottomed jeans. She liked the artistic way the flared sleeves paralleled the bell-bottoms. The clothing style sent a complex message, she thought, a shared sentiment against the war, in favor of youthful energy and honesty and against the conventionality of people like Jimmy's parents. Her own parents lived in another world entirely and were not at all responsible for the war or the buttoned-down mentality of those in their generation who had more privileges. Jimmy said once that he hated his parents. She thought that was extreme, but she began to understand valid reasons to rebel against the materialism they represented. Jimmy often referred to them as WASPs, and he tossed the word *phony* around. He seemed to idealize Ann's parents, because they lived close to the land and worked with their hands at something real. Still, his respect for them didn't make her want to put out a corn crop.

On the way into the city in the Mustang they picked up Jimmy's friend Chip, a grad student in computer sciences. Jimmy, who had roomed with Chip at the University of Chicago, told Ann that Chip was brilliant, a man of vision.

Long-legged, bushy-headed, mustachioed Chip folded himself into the back seat after declining Ann's offer to sit in front. "Ann, you are a beautiful girl. Jimmy is lucky."

Jimmy eased into the traffic toward Highway 101.

"Jimmy's always been shy with the ladies," Chip said, thumping Jimmy's shoulder playfully.

"Knock it off," said Jimmy.

"He's not shy," said Ann, twisting around to see Chip, who was sitting directly behind her. His hair, dark and unkempt, shot in all directions.

"He wants to talk about poetry, and that scares off most girls."

"I talk about poetry," said Ann.

"You're his dream girl if you can talk poetry."

Traffic was slow and thick. They passed several Volkswagens emblazoned with peace signs and daisy decals.

Chip shrieked. "Look at all these freaks going to the march! You can tell they are."

Chip kept up a descriptive monologue about the traffic, and then Jimmy stopped for a pair of hitchhikers. Ann got out and pulled the seat back forward for them, but when she saw that the woman was pregnant, Ann let her have the front. Chip scooted over, and Ann clambered into the back.

"Thanks a million," the hitchhiker said, squeezing

in next to Ann. "Katie is seven months along, but I couldn't make her stay home."

"I'll take the risk," Katie said. "If we can stop the war, it will be worth bringing a new life into the world. Otherwise, I don't know."

"Of course we all know this country is the most corrupt in the world," said the guy, Larry. "And LBJ is a warmonger."

Chip said. "Shit, I'd go live in a truck in the Yucatán before I'd go in the army. But look on the bright side. This is April fifteenth. Twenty years ago on this day, Jackie Robinson played his first game in the major leagues."

"Did you hear Martin Luther King on campus yesterday?" Larry asked. "He said Vietnam and racism are all about the same thing."

"I heard it on the radio," said Jimmy.

Ann hadn't heard it. She had spent the evening on a typing job. Chip had a class he couldn't miss, but he said he knew the "I Have a Dream" speech by heart. He kept talking, his flamboyant mustache twitching with every word. He covered LBJ's myriad abuses of power, the virtues of passive resistance. Wedged uncomfortably between the two guys, Ann felt the rough presence of the male sex—their breath and loud voices—and regarded the pregnant woman rocking in the bucket seat. Jimmy and Katie were chatting, but Ann couldn't hear what they said. She was squeezed in so tightly that her elbows met. Her purse ground into her lap.

"I went to the protest at the napalm factory in Redwood City last spring," Larry said.

"I was there too!" Chip said.

"Man, that was awful. All those pictures of burned children."

"If you don't mind," Katie said from the front.

"She hates to hear about that," Larry said.

Since traffic was heavy, Jimmy parked in a lot far from where the march began, and it was on the move by the time they reached Market Street. They soon lost sight of the expectant couple, who had thanked Jimmy profusely and assured him they would find another ride home.

Chip was muttering as they walked along. "This would be better if we all started out stoned, but as they say, there's a time and a place."

"You might just end up in Leavenworth," Jimmy said with a playful jab at his friend's arm.

"Don't listen to him, Ann. Jimmy exaggerates. But I ask you, if you had to choose between war and getting stoned, which would you prefer? Slog through jungle mud with a gun and chiggers, or go on a head trip that's so intense and beautiful you feel about to burst? Think about it. That's the choice they're offering us."

The crowd dazzled Ann. All kinds of people, all ages. Babies in strollers. Gray-haired couples. Bearded men. Men wearing ties. Children scampering. She saw placards from the AFL-CIO and the GIs Against the War. Ann half expected to spot Yvor Winters in his new career as war protestor.

The throng rambled along Market Street. Among these impassioned people, Ann felt secure with Jimmy.

"Hang on," he said.

"Where's your friend?"

"Don't worry about Chip. He has to check out the scene."

For a time, the flood of protestors carried them uphill. The crowd was moving counter to the stern steps of a military formation. The signs people were carrying told the story.

MAKE LOVE NOT WAR

DROP ACID NOT BOMBS

Bitter labels floated in the air—napalm, Dow Chemical, Ho Chi Minh. But people were smiling and waving at the policemen they passed. Now and then shouts and roars turned into a full chorus.

"Historic day," someone said.

Ann liked the energy, the righteousness. Some of the sounds and antics were undergraduate fraternity party style—whistles and yelps of fun—but mostly it was a fervent, directed passion, a deliberate march over the hills toward the Golden Gate, like a journey to heaven, if there was such a place, which she doubted. Ann was indifferent to the question of heaven. But she doubted the United States was the most corrupt country on earth, as the hitchhiker had claimed.

Hi ho, Ho Chi Minh, the NLF is gonna win.

The zeal of the demonstration surprised her. She held on to Jimmy, feeling proud of their small part in a huge movement. Her chest pounded.

Hell no, we won't go!

She chanted along with the crowd.

One, two, three, four, we don't want your fucking war.

The rhyme was satisfying. But she wouldn't say *fucking*. Jimmy didn't chant. He seemed to be more of an observer of the scene, not a participant, although he kept an affectionate hold on her hand, as if she might stray. He wore a faraway look, like a visionary who could see the big picture, how it fit into history. She

thought he was wise. He was always reading philosophers. He seemed amused by her enthusiasm at the
march. She herself was amused at her own behavior,
not what a bookish person like her would expect to do.
Back in Kentucky, people her age were having babies
and working at soul-destroying jobs. But she was still
a student, a Beatles fan, an idealist determined to stop
the war. She had the Pill—and a boyfriend—and she
was free.

As the marchers turned from Market Street toward
the stadium, she thought of the cows on the farm
coming home to be milked—eager but patient, plod-
ding together with a single purpose, ready to burst,
they were so full. She was a little girl with a dog, herd-
ing cows, sure that she was in control of her destiny.

Ann thought she had never seen so many people together in all her life. She and Jimmy couldn't find seats
and had to stand off to the side. They were too far
away from the stage to hear the speeches clearly. The
ebullient crowd jostled her, and now and then someone tromped on her feet. It was hard to fathom that she
had known Jimmy such a short time. Everything had
fallen into place. She hardly heard the speeches. The
sound roared, the crowd chanted exuberantly, and she
surrendered to the emotion. Judy Collins's sweet, pure

voice seemed to echo her own feelings, and then Big Brother and the Holding Company churned the crowd with raw urgency. During Dick Gregory's speech, Ann was waiting in a long line at the restroom, and she could not distinguish his words.

Jimmy was supposed to be waiting by the bottom of the bleachers, but when she emerged from the restroom she didn't see him anywhere. A band she didn't know was playing. After she had waited a minute, checking her watch, she began to wonder. She didn't want to leave the spot. Maybe she had misunderstood. As she turned, Jimmy stepped out from behind the column. He was laughing.

She gasped. "Were you hiding from me?"

"I was watching you." He grinned.

"Why?"

"It's all right. Don't worry. I wasn't going to abandon you."

They left before the program was over. Jimmy wanted to beat the traffic. They were a long way from the car, but Jimmy knew some shortcuts through less crowded side streets.

"Shouldn't we find Chip?" She had been scanning the crowd for him.

"Don't worry. He'll find a way back."

Ann was glad when they arrived at the blue Mustang—

familiar now, like a cozy home. Jimmy reached across her and found some almonds he had stashed in the glove compartment.

"I wonder if anything will come of this day," he said, in an almost bitter tone, as he tore open the package. He poured almonds into her hand.

"Don't you think it will?" Ann had been impressed by the optimism of the demonstrators but sobered by the words on the placards and the fury of some of the speakers.

"I don't know. It's awfully hard to stop a war machine."

Ann pictured a John Deere combine, a behemoth harvester sucking up a wheat crop.

They were hungry when they arrived at Jimmy's. He set two sirloin steaks and two potatoes in the oven. The steaks were done long before the potatoes, so they decided to have the potatoes later, like dessert. Ann pieced together a salad out of some odds and ends from the bottom refrigerator drawer. The drawer had a label: vegetable crisper. Everything had a label, she thought. People labeled one another. Heads, peaceniks, freaks, straights, warmongers, baby killers, draft dodgers.

The national TV news came on as they ate. The march to the United Nations in New York was first, but the San Francisco march was also prominently featured. The crowd was said to be sixty thousand.

"I remember that guy," Ann said, pointing to a long-haired man with a sign, *Out of Vietnam*.

"You couldn't miss him," Jimmy said.

"I wonder where Chip wound up." She was scanning the crowd scene. It was a thrill to see something she had been part of materialize on the screen.

"How did you find the day?" Jimmy asked, finishing his steak. "What did you think?"

"It felt important," she said, not having a ready response. "I know for sure I don't want you to have to go to Vietnam."

"Thanks, Snooks." Jimmy lit a cigarette, blowing smoke hard from his nose.

A commercial about a floor wax finished, and then Ann was staring at dead, mud-soaked bodies, with the sound of chopper blades beating, a distinctive reverb familiar now that she often heard it on the TV news at Jimmy's.

"What would it be like over there?" Ann asked. "What are they going through? How can they do it?"

She used to ask herself, hypothetically, what bare necessities she would need if stranded on a desert island. Lipstick and some face moisturizer. A comb. But she was a silly girl then. What was really important? The thought of anyone's boyfriend or husband sent to a jungle war seemed painfully real now. And wrong.

"Chip said he'd go to the Yucatán if he was drafted," she said. "What would you do?"

"I try not to think about it."

"Wouldn't you work in an office or something, or would you be an officer commanding troops?"

"I wouldn't be an officer. I wasn't in ROTC. You have to go to officer school." Jimmy flicked his cigarette into an overloaded ashtray. "I'd be a grunt."

"I can't believe they'd send you off to a rice paddy."

"Do you think McNamara would care? You think he would put me in charge of the Romantic poetry study group? The Keats Brigade?" He laughed and patted her head. "The Byronic division of Napoleonic complexes."

"That's not funny."

"Don't worry." He hugged her.

"But people get special assignments, don't they?" she said. "Like singers who entertain at bases?"

Jimmy crossed the room to switch off the TV. He turned in an exaggerated pose of insight, slapping his forehead. "I just had the most awful thought. Poor John Keats, writing those letters to his sweetheart, Fanny Brawne, and never getting to marry her, probably never even getting to sleep with her."

"It wasn't allowed, was it? Do you imagine they ever even kissed?"

"But all that intensity and joy could be contained in a few words, wouldn't it, if you were a poet like Keats? Instead of a kiss, he'd give her a line like 'Truth is beauty.'"

"Not enough! Do you imagine I'd be happy if that's all I got from you?"

"You would if I were Keats, or, say, Shakespeare."

"Oh, no, you'd have to put your pogo where your mouth is."

"That sounds dirty."

"I bet Keats and his Fanny talked dirty."

"Fanny? That sounds even dirtier!" He reached to smack Ann on the fanny. "Say *fuck*. I dare you."

"No! I can't."

"But that's what we do—in bed."

"No," she said. "We're making love."

"Of course. But in order to make love, we have to fuck."

"No, it's screwing."

"No, it's not."

"Yes, it is."

"No, it's not!"

They made each other laugh, and before long they

flopped onto the bed. Then, after a while, they could smell the potatoes burning.

When she first told Frank the psychologist about Jimmy, Ann was full of self-congratulation. With Jimmy, everything seemed real, no longer a scheme to get a boy to like her. She expected Frank to be proud of her progress, and she was surprised that he didn't say whether he found her exultant reports of Jimmy just as fantastical as he had her descriptions of earlier boyfriends. But now talking to Frank seemed futile. The war wasn't a psychological problem she could consult him about. A raw note had been struck. She couldn't articulate how disturbing the war had become now, and Frank didn't press her.

Hopewell, Ky.
April 15, 1967

Dear Ann,
    This Jimmy sounds like he's serious about you. I haven't heard you talk about a boy you liked that much before.
    I hope he respects you and takes good care of you. What kind of work is he aiming to do when he gets out of school? . . .

Love,
Mama

But Ann wasn't sure of Jimmy, really. Sometimes she didn't see him for days. He rarely telephoned, preferring to drop in unannounced. He hadn't actually said "I love you." He didn't always speak directly. When he called her "my little tulip of the tundra" or "my rosebud of the Rubicon," she could not measure the depth of his affection. He had a way of teasing her, she thought, a way of leaving her hanging. Walking across campus together, he would suddenly disappear, just as he had at the march. She would turn, bewildered, then realize that once again, he was hiding from her. He found this hilarious, but she felt ridiculous hunting for him behind doorways and trees, then finding him hunched behind a bush, or in a shadow of an arcade, and once up in a tree. Or he might be peering through the frosted glass panes of a classroom door. Once, he was crouched like a tiger behind some lush grasses in an area of plantings beneath some tall tropical trees. She noticed that he invariably called the game hide-and-seek, while as a child she always heard it as hide-'n'-go-seek. The same with May I. He insisted the game was Mother, May I. No, it was May I, she said.

Chip had given Jimmy some grass. Ann watched Jimmy roll it in a crisp little paper, not spilling a crumb. His carefulness and confidence inspired her to try it. The smoke was choking and vile, but she held it in as Jimmy instructed. Then, after a bit, it felt nice. It was a caffeine antidote, she thought. It was smooth, like pudding.

"What are you reading?" she asked Jimmy.

"Snorri Sturluson and the Icelandic Eddas."

"Aren't they a music group?"

"No, that's Martha and the Vandellas."

"I can't tell the difference."

"'Eleanor Rigby' could have been a poem in the *Norton Anthology*," Jimmy said. "It's as good as any edda you could name."

Ann loved the way he spouted things out of the blue that she had thought of herself. She and Jimmy stared at the photo of the Beatles on the cover of *Rubber Soul*. The Beatles obviously had had their hair set on big brush rollers at a beauty parlor.

"It's teased," she said. "In college I had a bouffant. A beehive do."

"I bet you were cute. I want to see a picture of you in a beehive."

"Take my word for it. You don't want to see it."

"You're the most," he said. "You're tops."

She grinned. "You're stoned."

Ann hoped for a future in which Jimmy would provide for her. They would be together, married. She would escape the persistent fear of becoming a cliché, an "old maid," the caricature in the card game. They would have enough money to buy a few things. Maybe they could have a house someday. She hardly dared fill out this picture in her mind. They didn't need matched furniture. They could drape lace over curtain rods, paint the woodwork red if they wanted to. Nothing had to be what it was supposed to be.

Her eyes roved his small house. He was surprisingly neat. His desk was clear, except for a pencil jar and a stack of *Newsweeks*. A photograph of an army general on the top cover caused her to choke back tears.

Hopewell, Ky.
April 25, 1967

Dear Ann,

We had a scare the other day. Your daddy's big
Jersey he calls Hortense got out. He missed her and
thought she probably went to the creek to find a
place to have her calf, but come to find out she had
got through the fence and was over in Mr. Martin's
field, down in the creek below. Sure enough, she
had a little calf with her. He got them back to the
barn and the next day she went right back to that
fence. He had tried to fix it but she broke through.
She was bound and determined. He followed her
and if she didn't have another little calf back there,
I'm not here! It was still living and he's feeding it
with a nipple bucket. He felt bad that he didn't realize she had two twins. I don't know if he'll keep
dairy cows much longer. There just ain't no living
in it. . . .

Love,
Mama

One night they drove up to Skyline Boulevard, to look at the stars. Jimmy seemed to be driving a little recklessly—sometimes too fast, sometimes too slow. He tailgated. And he hummed the whole way. She held her breath, made tiny moans. Curves were the worst. But if she was going to die, there she was with him, not on a motorcycle with stuck-up Stephen.

Jimmy parked at an overlook and shut off the light and engine. He came around to the passenger door to open it for her. The night sky was bold and black.

"Behold, the Milky Way!" he said, his arm around her shoulders.

Ann didn't remember anyone on the farm in Kentucky ever paying attention to the night sky. In grade school, she had learned that the moon revolved around the earth and the nine spinning planets traveled around the sun, but she recalled nothing of delight or wonder, no amazement from teachers. Why was this? It occurred to her that children had nothing to compare the stars to. Her own sense of wonder seemed to have increased with time, mostly through poetry. Now, beholding the universe with Jimmy was wondrous. The stars, flung across the sky willy-nilly, were beyond comprehension.

Pointing out Orion's Belt, Jimmy said, "I used to

think Orion's Belt came from a prize in a cereal box. When I was a kid, I pretended I could go to the stars if I had a magic belt. It didn't have to be a belt. It could be a ring. Or a bicycle."

"I didn't have a bicycle," Ann said.

"Have you ever tried acid?" Jimmy asked.

"Of course not. Have you?"

"Once. I wanted to see what it was like."

"What was it like?"

"There are zero words for that." He tightened his grasp on her shoulder.

"You always say that."

Ann had thought of taking Jimmy out to La Honda, but she recalled Stephen's disdain. Albert had once described to her an "acid test," where people unwittingly drank acid-laced Kool-Aid from a punch bowl. That scared her.

Jimmy was moving his free hand slightly, trying to summon the words to describe acid but giving up in one small gesture. Then he said, "You might try it, just to know."

"That's what my English teacher in Kentucky said. You know, the one who wanted me to see El Palo Alto, that tree."

"Really? Your teacher wanted you to take acid? Well, it wasn't against the law then, I guess."

"No, he was just telling me about it. He was out here on a Stegner, several years ago, and he hung out with Ken Kesey and that bunch. He said the same thing as you—take it once and you'll never be the same, he said."

Jimmy loosened his grip on her and turned to face her. In the dim light, he seemed older.

"That's true. It changed me."

"How were you before? Was your hair curly? Did you have a habit of humming?"

"I don't know. It's just a way of seeing. It helped me get out of a mess in my head once."

He was a million miles away, a distant star.

Yvor Winters retired from teaching, and Ann had to get another adviser.

"Who are you going to work with?" Jimmy asked when he came over after swimming.

"Whom," she said.

"We live in English-major hell," he said. "Whom, then, my little cabbage flower of the Carpathians, with whom do you choose to work?"

"I don't know. I haven't decided my specialty yet."

"What do you think you'll do with your degree?"

"I don't know. I can't imagine." His hair was wet on her face.

Jimmy had expressed doubts about the study of literature. He believed that reading literature deepened the human experience, but that critical study of it was a false direction. She agreed, but she had committed herself to that path.

"When I read a critic like Northrop Frye, I feel lost in molasses," Jimmy said now.

"Well, I don't want to work in a factory—or milk cows."

"You'll be all right teaching, but I don't see it for me. I need to get out into the real world. I don't know much about tools. I can barely change a tire. I can ride a bicycle, though."

"You could get a paper route."

"Why am I in school? I think I should dig ditches."

"Why don't you get yourself sent to prison? You could go out to work on a chain gang."

"They make music," he said. "That might be tolerable, yes."

"You're good with a camera."

"Construction work would be satisfying. I never had a chance to work with my hands in any real way."

She couldn't tell if he was serious. But it seemed that everybody was working with their hands these days— pottery, découpage, clothing. Ann had tried macramé a few weeks before and made a plant hanger for her mother.

Dear Ann,

Oh, that contraption you sent! I had a time a-swinging it from the window frame. It wants to hang Annie Godlin.

"What does she mean—Annie Godlin?" asked Jimmy when Ann read him the passage. "Is that you?"

"It's one of her sayings. *Anti-* something. It means whopper-jawed or catywampus. I don't think it's a real word. Anti-Godling, maybe?"

He had a laughing fit. "I want to meet your mama! She's a poet."

The night Jimmy brought Chip over to meet Pixie was a turning point, Ann thought. They arrived with a pizza and two cartons of bottled beer. Ann had been keenly attuned lately to how people dressed and what their clothing said about them. She was devoted to blue-jeans and sandals now, feeling a liberation from every kind of dress code. Jimmy was thoughtless about the way he dressed, joking that "a handsome man looks good in any old thing he just happens to throw on." That evening Pixie was wearing floral bell-bottoms and a fringed top. Her jumpy bob had grown out, and she had straightened it. But Chip's attire seemed inexplicable to Ann. He was wearing an army surplus military paratroop suit.

"I'm just identifying with the GIs!" he said, handing her the pizza.

"You shaved off your mustache." His face was less exaggerated now.

"I wanted to look my best to visit your girlfriend," Chip said to Jimmy. "I see you have two of them." He grinned widely when introduced to Pixie.

"I told him they'd pick him up for impersonating a military man," Jimmy said.

"I want to remind everybody," Chip said, tugging at

the breast pocket flaps. "Here it is. War, war, war. We can't forget it."

"It's a mockery," Jimmy said, teasing.

Ann, rummaging in the kitchen drawer for her bottle flip, remembered seeing the GIs against the war at the march.

"I think it's far out," said Pixie, stroking the arm of Chip's suit.

"I get some crazy looks," Chip said, eyeing her. "Some mean looks if they think I'm really a paratrooper. Like I'm going to jump down from the sky and grab their babies."

"Picture that," Jimmy said, handing Pixie a beer. Chip opened one for himself.

"Anything can happen in a war," Chip said. "And worse." He slugged his beer.

Ann made a space for the pizza on her long desk. Jimmy pulled over her heavy reading chair and her desk chair and her only kitchen chair, so Pixie and Chip went downstairs to get another. They returned with that and Pixie's Mamas and Papas album. Pixie wanted them to hear "Go Where You Wanna Go." After they had eaten most of the pizza and opened more beers, Chip rolled a joint. Ann was drinking a Coca-Cola. Beer could be dishwater. She managed to take the smoke in without coughing. She didn't hold it in long enough for the full effect, but it made her relaxed and giddy.

"Chip has a fine head of hair, don't you think, Jimmy?"

"A veritable Liverpool moptop."

"And you're a moptop yourself," she said, tousling Jimmy's curls, which were already permanently tousled.

"Lassie," said Pixie.

Ann saw Pixie's imperious glance at Jimmy and remembered that Pixie had said recently that Jimmy reminded her of Holden Caulfield. Now she was startled to realize that Pixie saw Jimmy as an innocent, a kid, a shaggy dog. Ann did not understand how anyone could look down on Jimmy. But she was not good at reading people. Why would Chip wear a military jumpsuit? She pictured him jumping from an airplane, holding on to an umbrella. A Magritte image.

Chip spoke of a book he was reading about French Indochina, the Warren Commission, where music would go next, companion crops for corn, the myriad uses of cornstarch.

"I could listen to you for hours!" Pixie cried.

Chip wasn't usually a motormouth. He was a good listener. Maybe the grass triggered logorrhea, Ann thought. He raced along from one thing to another until someone interrupted. He seemed glad to be interrupted.

Ann cleared the table and wiped it with a wet dishrag. Chip was going on about binary code, how words and even thoughts could be reduced to ones and zeroes.

"It comes from Chinese math," he said.

"Yeah, you can do Chinese math," Jimmy said with a grin.

"It's the principle of the I Ching," said Pixie.

"Itching?" Chip said, flirting.

"I think of throwing the Ching as hopscotch," Pixie said, deadpan. "It's the idea of chance, the meaning in it."

Chip swigged his beer. "Tell me more."

Pixie went on in a Bacall-to-Bogart tone, "The random can be revealing. Out of the unexpected comes a weird order."

Chip said, "In statistics class we're studying patterns in randomness, so this makes sense!"

"You're a *science* major, Chip!" said Jimmy.

"It's the same in physics on a deeper level," Chip said. His eyes had not strayed from Pixie.

Ann remembered the Chief at La Honda speaking of physics and meditation. She said, "But it sounds a little like speed, in a contradictory way." She thought of how

Preludin made her scoop up all her random thoughts into a new arrangement.

Pixie described how the Chinese originally used yarrow stalks that fell in patterns.

"Pickup sticks!" cried Ann.

Chip, growing excited, began a spiel about the wonders of Stanford University. The greatest minds were on a cusp, change was afoot, breakthroughs were in the offing; radical shifts in thinking were in exploratory stages, in the union of the intellect with technology and ancient wisdom. The I Ching was startlingly relevant.

"Industrialization is old hat," he said. "Computer science is in the ascendancy! We're on the verge of postmodern, technological radical spiritual utopia! Remember that we are on a cusp. *Cusp* is the word."

"I like cusps," Ann said. "They're like lisps."

As if making an announcement, Chip said, "Here is my question for the I Ching: What is the alternative life of a military jumpsuit?"

"Should I go get the Ching?" Pixie asked.

No one answered, and Pixie didn't budge from the deep reading chair she had claimed.

"Let's do horoscopes next," Jimmy said to Chip.

"But the I Ching is about how coincidence mirrors the subjective," Pixie said, glaring at Jimmy.

Jimmy shook his head. "It's like hearing a song on

the radio and you realize it is your song. It is saying exactly what you're feeling. It's subjective. That's no mystery. But any song that comes on the radio would work. You can make something out of it." He pointed to the stereo. "California Dreamin'" was playing. "There. Isn't that a song for all of us?"

"I don't believe in magic," Ann said. The conversation was going oddly. Although Pixie was being disdainful, Chip seemed attracted to her.

"It's synchronicity," Pixie said. "When things come together for no real reason and they reflect the unconscious."

"There's a function on your slide rule for that," Jimmy said to Chip.

"You can't quantify everything," Pixie snapped at Jimmy. "Serendipity is out of bounds."

"Let's decorate my jumpsuit," Chip said suddenly, as if the I Ching had just ordered an art project.

Much later, Ann reflected that a string of pivotal events began on the night they decorated Chip's jumpsuit. It would take her years to piece together a patchwork perspective on the breakdown of her innocence. But recalling Pixie's snottiness that evening was illuminating. That night, absorbed in a frivolous pastime, lulled by just a little tangy dried grass—it contained some seeds that popped—and blinded by her adoration of her precious Jimmy, Ann began to feel like a chick pecking its way into the world. A hatchling. She would have to tell Albert. The paratroop jumpsuit was like a wrong note in a tune.

Chip had worn the jumpsuit over a plaid shirt and jeans. He unzipped the suit, stepped out of it, and spread it on Ann's desk. He had come prepared with an assortment of Magic Markers—blue, red, and black. He drew a peace sign on the left backside in black ink, and on the right he wrote, "Synchronicity. Out of Vietnam." On a sleeve, Ann wrote, "I heard a Fly buzz—when I died—" Jimmy drew a fly beneath, like a signature.

They must have spent two hours decorating the jumpsuit.

"I'm a peace freak in a hand-me-down war suit," Chip said.

Pixie was engrossed in drawing flowers on the leg pockets, and Chip was leaning onto her shoulder, scribbling close to her hand.

Ann wrote, "The cut worm forgives the plow" and Jimmy wrote, "Three cheers for the objective correlative."

"What's that?" asked Chip.

"The fly and the worm," said Jimmy. He drew a

halved worm, like a mustache, beneath Ann's Blake quote.

The Mamas and the Papas were dancing in the street.

On the right leg of the jumpsuit, Chip wrote, "The random is not random." Pixie nodded knowingly and brushed her hand down his arm.

Ann wrote, "'Poetry is NOT conversation'—Yvor Winters."

"Yvor Winters said that?" Jimmy glanced up from an Escher-like drawing he was attempting.

"He said it in class. I think he meant Robert Frost. He hates Robert Frost."

"You English majors," said Pixie, rolling her eyes. "Living in your ivory tower."

"Hoover Tower, you mean," Jimmy said.

"Oh, you know who I saw at Hoo Tow?" said Chip. "Alexander Kerensky."

"Who's Alexander Kerensky?" Ann wanted to know.

"He was prime minister of Russia and the Bolsheviks exiled him," Jimmy said.

Chip said, "I've seen him, big as life, walking along Sand Hill Road with his walking stick."

"Our landlady knows him," said Pixie. "She said he's half-blind but he walks everywhere."

"How in the world does Jingles know the prime minister of Russia?" Ann demanded.

"She's Russian."

Jimmy was humming "Music! Music! Music!" He sang,

Khrushchev, Pravda, Mikoyan,
Lenin, Trotsky, Bulganin,
Dostoevsky, Nabokov,
And Pushkin! Pushkin! Pushkin!

"Would you be a Bolshevik if you lived in czarist Russia?" he asked Chip.

Chip grinned and laid down his marker. Then he declared that he would wear his jumpsuit everywhere, every day, until the war ended. "Oh, wow, look at my suit! I'm going to parade across campus in this."

"No one will notice," said Pixie, busy coloring the flaps of the leg pockets.

Jimmy had abandoned the Escher drawing. The thick markers were the wrong tools. He used the word "tools" often, Ann noticed. He drew Porky Pig on the back of the jumpsuit. They flipped the suit over when they turned the album over. They lost track of time. Ann decided she was going with the flow, the warm camaraderie enveloping her like a bed of marshmallows. She hadn't known Jingles was Russian. Chip yammered on, a cauldron of grand ideas bubbling out of his head.

"You're a good artist," Ann said, admiring Jimmy's abstract scribbles. He seemed very patient, dedicated to doing a job well. "What is that?"

"Pluto the dog is baying at Pluto the planet."

"I should have recognized the Plutos." She touched the blue circle with little rays coming from it.

"I think Pluto is blue," Jimmy said. "And the dog would know. They're on the same wavelength."

Sounds were mixed with colors. Words moved like waves, peeking from the folds of the jumpsuit. Bolsheviks quoted Emily Dickinson, and Yvor Winters was on Pluto, where there was no conversation, only poetry.

Chip, his jumpsuit flapped over his arm, left with Pixie and her chair. She took her album with her. She said she'd drive Chip home. Ann was glad; that meant Jimmy didn't have to leave. They were sharing the last piece of pizza, which was delicious, even cold.

Jimmy touched a smear of tomato on her face and licked it from his finger. They kissed, sharing pizza flavors.

"Pixie and Chip sure hit it off," Ann said.

"I don't know about those two."

"She wasn't nice to you."

"She could tell I think the I Ching is crap." He

smoothed his hair and fingered a ringlet. "I should have apologized to her."

Ann couldn't figure people out, why Pixie was so judgmental, why Chip meandered intensely in all directions. And why Jimmy was often remote, as if he were trying to solve a grand philosophical problem. He wasn't bothered by Pixie calling him Lassie.

"Pixie has a Chip on her shoulder," Ann burst out, but Jimmy didn't laugh.

He drained his beer and set the bottle on the sink drain.

"She's always critical," Ann said. "And she called you Lassie!"

"I like Lassie!"

"Well, me too. You're a nice Lassie, but she didn't mean it that way. She says insulting things and sometimes I don't realize they're insulting till later."

"Don't let her put you down."

Ann crammed the pizza packaging into her garbage bin.

"Will he really wear that jumpsuit in public?" she asked. "He said he would."

"Probably. He has no self-consciousness. The funny thing about Chip—he's not after attention. He's so full of ideas he can't keep up with them."

For a while, they parsed Pixie and Chip and the jumpsuit. Jimmy didn't want to assign profound meaning to the jumpsuit. Ann thought there must be something she didn't know.

Was this being stoned? Her mind was in outer space, on a blue astral plane, when through the wall, bedsprings began jangling to the tune of "Mr. Tambourine Man." Apparently the couple next door had returned their bed to the wall between the apartments.

"Shh! They'll hear us!"

"They won't notice if we do it at the same time," Jimmy said. "We'll all come together," he said. "That's synchronicity."

"Making love," she whispered at the end. She had throbbed with mirth throughout. "I love making love."

"I love you," he said, or she thought he said.

Hopewell, Ky.
May 1, 1967

Dear Ann,
    Had to take your daddy to the doctor yesterday.
He was wheezing, couldn't hardly breathe. I thought
it might be azma, but the doctor said it was just
something in the air. He had been out cultivating
all day. He wouldn't have gone to the doctor, but I
was afraid he was going to lose his breath. He feels
better now, and the planting is over with. . . .

                                        Love,
                                        Mama

"That's a relief," Ann said to Jimmy, after reading him the letter. The letter was longer, with details about the garden and her brother's eighth-grade graduation.

Jimmy was lying on her bed, staring at the ceiling. He had been reading *The Portable Nietzsche*, which was not an assignment. He sat up and swung his legs to the side of the bed. It was dim in the room, and he went to the window to raise the shade. He didn't hold the edge precisely, and it suddenly flew up on its roller with a snap.

"Can I trust you?" Jimmy asked her.

"Of course."

"Do you trust me?"

"Yes. Why wouldn't I?"

"I'm trying to understand what is meant by *trust*."

"I think with trust you don't ask questions."

"But that might be naive. How do you know you can trust in someone or something? And how does a person earn trust?"

"You're full of questions."

She brought him a peach and a paring knife on a saucer.

"Do I dare to eat a peach?"

"Unless you'd rather not disturb the universe."

He sat in her reading chair, with the saucer set on the wide arm.

"Wouldn't just touching this peach be a disturbance of its own?" He held the peach up to the light. "Say there's another universe that's identical to ours except for one small detail—this peach. There's a universe where this peach is not ripe, another one where there is no peach, one where you eat the peach, and one where I eat it. And it's true for everything right on down to variation at the atomic level. The mind can't hold this!"

He laid the peach on the saucer and ran his hands through his hair.

"There! That loosened up my brain. Now, where was I? Infinite peaches, infinite universes. And maybe each universe is only a mote—"

"I know—in God's eye. How many peaches could you fit on the head of a pin?"

"With or without dancing angels?"

"Try it both ways."

"Infinite. Infinite would be the same number, regardless of peaches or angels. If the angels ate the peaches, would they still count?"

Ann gave Jimmy an affectionate bop on the head.

"Isn't this the stuff you think of when you're ten?"

she asked. "Don't tell me this is the nitty-gritty of Nietzsche."

"Is this a true peach or only an illusion?" he asked. He bit into the peach. "I'm baffled. That old question makes me really uncomfortable."

"You're eating the peeling! It's fuzzy!"

"Its delicate beard delights my lips." He chomped again. "Oh, I think there's a worm in it! Is that a worm?"

"Don't worry, the cut worm forgives the gnashing molars."

"What about the canines?"

She patted him on the head. "Nice doggie."

Jimmy had been tantalized by the concept of the multiverse, she remembers. In one alternate universe, she never met him. In another, they strolled easily down an entirely different path towards the sunset. The road not taken could well lead to California.

"You're wiggly," he said.

"I can't keep still. My back is killing me."

She was thinking about the baby-doll-pajamas photographer and how different *this* was. Not for money but for art. And private, for Jimmy. She still shuddered whenever she remembered changing in that rooming-house bathroom, stepping forth in high heels and little Dacron shorties with elastic hems, the frilly chemise like a maternity top. It was the pastel colors that seemed so indecent, she thought now.

But she was surprised by how boring it was to stand nude before someone she was intimate with. Sitting fully clothed, Jimmy was being thoughtful, even meditative, as he sketched meticulously, filling in tiny details of her body. She was reminded of her mother examining a bolt of material at a fabric store—feeling its texture, searching for flaws in the weave. Mama would hold out a length of material from her fingertips to her nose. That made a yard. Ann felt Jimmy's eyes exploring her body, measuring it. He kept saying this or that line of her body was beautiful.

She told Jimmy about the photographer, how she was attracted by the offer of ten dollars an hour and thought she would be fashion modeling.

"He was a creep," she said.

"Were you in danger?" Jimmy asked, laying down his pad.

"No, I think he was just somebody trying to make money. But so was I. I don't know why I did that. I jump into things."

"Sometimes that's good. I like that in you—mostly."

Maybe she shouldn't have blurted out the baby-doll-pajamas incident. But Jimmy did like her impulsiveness, he said.

Jimmy smudged his sketch with a thin piece of charcoal, then lifted his drawing pencil again. He said, "If you knew you were going to die, what book would you want to read first?"

"*Ulysses*," she said.

"I'd read *War and Peace* if there was time."

"It's not on the exam," she said. "Aren't you going to take it?"

"I won't have to take it if I'm going to die!" he said. "What a relief! What would you miss most—if you knew you were going to die?"

"I'd miss you. What would you miss?"

"Riding the cable cars."

"That's ridiculous."

She would miss home, of course.

She said, "How could you miss anything before it's gone? And if you were dead, you wouldn't miss anything."

Jimmy said, "The question is how do we value an experience? What is important?" He held his pencil aloft and stared at it, as if it might provide the answer.

She said, "There's too much that's important. I can't hold it all."

Jimmy worked on his drawing, as if in deep thought.

Then, raising his head, he gazed directly at her. "Is *Ulysses* something you really want to read or something you feel you should read?"

"It's hard to tell the difference."

"You can't go through life on *should*," he said. "Sometimes you just have to grab a moment. And sometimes you just have to leave it. Otherwise, you're only a consumer, taking in everything indiscriminately. Ingest, regurgitate." Nibbling the end of his pencil, he stared at his drawing and then closed the sketchbook.

She pulled on the long blue plaid shirt he had given her.

She liked Jimmy's patience, his dedication to doing something well, but he said he felt most alive when he was roaming around with no particular purpose. Riding the cable cars made him feel receptive, open to possibility. Ann began thinking that she might devalue the wrong things. Cable cars—too many people, too much time, unpleasant sensations. But Jimmy said he liked the sounds and gravity-defying movements of the cars. He liked watching the people. She'd rather read a book than be in any kind of uncomfortable situation.

At the Laundromat, waiting for her clothes, she attempted to sit and watch, leaving her Shelley text in her purse. A woman and a little girl came in, pushing a cartload of laundry. The woman had light brown skin and wore a bandana twisted around her dark, wavy hair. The child began banging on the vending machines. The woman tossed laundry into the washer indifferently, mixing colors and whites. She poured detergent from a box without measuring. She called to the child in Spanish and then sat her down. They sat, side by side, the child swinging her feet against the chair rung. Opening a magazine, the woman fingered a glossy picture and showed it to the child. Ann retrieved her Shelley book and began to read "Ode to the West Wind" for the hundredth time.

She was at Jimmy's place. He had been swimming, and his hair was still wet. Chip was there, unloading some new ideas. He had brought a stock of stiff white textured cloth on a roll like her window shade.

"This is called photo linen," he explained. "You can print pictures on it. See this? I made it in the darkroom in the art building."

He held up an eight-by-ten photograph of Mick Jagger, his rubber pout larger than life.

"It's a silk-screening process, à la Warhol. Wouldn't it be fun to wear a shirt with Mick on it?"

Jimmy said, "That would be even better than the designs on your jumpsuit."

"The Beatles," Ann said. "Or T. S. Eliot."

"Sheets and Kelly!" said Jimmy.

"You could wear your own picture," Ann said.

They were laughing. She imagined Yvor Winters wearing his own photo. Or Emily Dickinson's.

"A million possibilities," Chip said. "You can sew, can't you, Ann? We could make a sample and offer it to a big company."

"This material is too stiff. It's for tents. How could you wear it?"

"This will just be a prototype," Chip said. "Science will follow."

He left the roll of photo linen and biked off to class. He hadn't mentioned Pixie or his jumpsuit.

Ann liked showering at Jimmy's. His bathroom was bright white, not the gloomy color of stale blood. When she emerged and grabbed an extra towel for her hair, Jimmy was standing in the doorway with his camera.

"I want to photograph you," Jimmy said in a quiet tone that sounded almost worried.

"Like this?"

"I like the way you look, just coming out of the

shower. I want to photograph you like this—clean, pure. But we should go outside."

"Outside?" She toweled a thigh.

"No one can see back there, with all the trees. I go out and pee there all the time. There's a fence."

She rubbed her hair with the towel. "My mama told me never to go outside with a wet head."

He doubled over laughing, as though he were suddenly naked, trying to hide his dog toys, or whatever he wanted to call his things.

They stayed indoors. Posing for photographs was easier than standing stock-still and stark naked for a drawing. She thought her hair looked good. She was growing it long and straight, so she didn't need brush rollers. Jimmy had waited while she fixed it. She wouldn't have wanted to be photographed with stringy hair.

Jimmy complained about her makeup—powder to reduce shine and liner to accentuate her eyes. Artificial, he said.

"You don't need lipstick," he said, jabbing his finger at her mouth. "It's not natural."

When Jimmy began aiming his camera she stuck her tongue out at him. She made faces. She marched around like a wooden soldier. She did deep lunges and pirouettes. She balanced Shakespeare's tragedies on her head.

Jimmy said. "That's good."

"I've got good balance."

She clowned in the buff while Jimmy clicked his camera. He had a way with it, she thought, admiring his quick moves. He was adept with his hands. He was meticulous and delicate. Click-click-click. His hands were graceful but strong. She thought about her father's hands—rough and hardened. She had seen him dehorn a cow.

Besides photographs, Jimmy was experimenting with tape loops, making a sound collage of forties radio comedies and bubblegum rock tunes. Everyone seemed to be making things—and using the word *authentic.* Ceramic pots, furniture, clothing. The Twiggy girl was making bird sculptures out of thin wire. Ann tried making a collage from magazine illustrations. She realized she had a phallic theme in the display—lipsticks, rockets, bombs—all pointing away from the spiraling center of an oxeye daisy.

Later in the week, Jimmy brought his photographs to show her. He had printed four of them on photo linen and displayed them on her worktable. They were grainy. She was pleased, because her figure showed to advantage, and her pubic hair was light, not bushy.

Her breasts were suggestive shapes. The photos seemed almost like drawings.

"I like that they're not literal," he said, tracing the lines. "Do you think they're artistic?"

"Yes, very." She was rather thrilled, thinking of some nude drawings by French artists she had seen in an art museum in San Francisco.

Jimmy teased her about wearing one of the photos in public.

"You could put them on a skirt—the front view on the front and the back view on the back."

"Or vice versa? Then I could twirl."

She was remembering the sign at the protest rally on White Plaza. It showed different messages on the front and back.

"You wouldn't really do this," he said.

"In the Quad, maybe. But not at the pancake place, for instance."

Of course she wouldn't, but it was silly fun to imagine. The shock, the utter abandonment of self-consciousness. She pictured herself in a scene in a French movie.

She excavated a dress from her closet—a plain black sheath that she had worn to a cocktail party senior year. Because her mother had made it, it had survived her Salvation Army purge. Now she showed Jimmy how the photos would fit. She basted them onto the dress and then modeled it while he snapped pictures of her.

He folded a copy of the *Oracle* for her to use as a fan. It rattled and flapped clumsily as she tried to wave it provocatively.

She said, "Artists in the twenties would have done this. Zelda."

They laughed and laughed, holding each other. They might have been stoned, but they weren't. She felt so reckless. She didn't know what she would do next. What she would do for Jimmy. She glimpsed the familiar mole on her breast in one of the photographs. What was happening to her?

Over the years, she has been filled with questions about the photo dress, most of them beginning with why. *She has, shockingly, imagined it as a wedding dress.*

At Jimmy's, they made omelets and opened a can of tomato soup and ate on his couch with the stereo playing *Peer Gynt.* During "The Hall of the Mountain King," Jimmy said, "I was thinking—you're always typing and typing. And you leaped at the chance to model for ten dollars an hour."

"Ha. One hour. Then I got cold feet."

Jimmy suggested that instead of typing, she could earn money making photo shirts.

"People wouldn't have to be in their birthday suits! You'd be making something with your hands. Like that macramé stuff you did."

But Ann didn't want to sew. It was women's work. So was typing, but she liked that better.

"You know I don't want anyone else to see your picture on that dress," he said.

"No, it's for you. It's just something between us."

Jimmy finished his omelet and set the plate on the coffee table, a red octagonal stop sign, a curb discard he had salvaged and screwed legs on. The trolls and gnomes had finished their wild dance and now were creeping through the Mountain King's castle. At least that was what Ann pictured. She was roaming through Jimmy's *Newsweek* and *Ramparts* magazines. She admired his bookshelves made from concrete blocks and raw pine planks.

"Where did you get concrete blocks?" she asked.

"That builders' supply place out on El Camino."

She fingered the rough texture of one of the blocks. "I can't get over how simple it is." It wouldn't have occurred to Ann to stack up some scraps of wood and blocks. "Authentic," she said, testing the word.

And then she felt ingenuous, seeing how conventional it was to think books had to be shelved in regulation bookcases. The Troll Kings were frisky again, going at top speed before collapsing.

Ann was troubled by Jimmy's suggestion about sewing. For the most part, this feeling was vague, nothing that could stop the train she was on. She didn't feel a sense of danger, yet she often felt that nothing was ever for sure with Jimmy. Sometimes she felt a momentary foreboding, a fear that they would not end up together, but then he would suddenly thrust his face in hers and grab her and pull her into the pillow of his shaggy hair and hold her close with what genuinely felt like love and affection. And kindness.

Pixie had covered the floor of her burgundy bathroom with pink pebbles, a layer two inches deep. She must have lost her mind, Ann thought.

"The tiles will be all scratched up. Jingles will have a fit!"

"I knew just what you'd say!" Pixie laughed, chortled in fact. It was as if she had staged the scene just to hear Ann fuss.

Pixie said, "This is so sensuous. I put lotion on my feet and then saunter around in here. The pebbles buff the feet!"

"How can you clean the floor?"

"Oh, Ann, you're so practical."

Ann figured Pixie would get bored with the novelty by the time the floor got dirty. The surface would be covered with scratch marks, making an accidental artwork.

"Jingles will kick you out!" Ann said.

She wondered why she was incapable of thinking up something so outrageous, unless the photo dress counted. But that was Jimmy's idea. She wondered if she should get a load of pebbles for her bathroom. It was an original thing to do, and she rather liked the effect, just as she had liked Pixie's bathroom lace swath. But she couldn't chance having to pay the cost of replacing floor tiles. And she felt that Pixie had been laughing at her.

Jimmy banged on Ann's door the next afternoon. She had just finished reading and underlining some passages in a critical essay about Keats's odes. Poor Keats, dead from TB in his twenties. A spunky redhead with a spicy sense of humor and a love of cats and a tragic awareness of his fate.

"Special delivery," said Jimmy, with a grin. "I'm the Bookshelf Man."

He carried several bricks in his arms. He set them

near the wall where Ann's books languished and tee-tered in random piles. The pristine white bricks were like slices of cake.

She helped him haul twenty-four more white bricks and three redwood planks up the stairway. He stacked the bricks and laid the planks, making four complete shelves, counting the floor.

The bookshelves were beautiful—Danish modern, Ann thought. Jimmy began placing her books on the shelves.

"Do you want them in alphabetical order?"

"No. Groups—Old English, Victorian novels, Romantic poets."

"How about color? The blue ones here and the yellow ones. I could make a color wheel."

"You're weird."

Together they organized her books, with running commentary on whether they had both read a given book. Ann pointed out Norman O. Brown's exhilarating *Life Against Death*.

"I read this, but Pixie thought it was drivel. 'Pop pap,' she called it."

"Pixie pooh-poohed it as pop pap? Stop the presses!"

Jimmy always made Ann laugh. She hadn't mentioned the book to Frank the psychologist.

With satisfaction, she surveyed the small unit of

Old English texts and the large Irish section. Jimmy devised new subcategories such as Modernist Poets and Scribner Editions. Her art books were too tall, so he laid them horizontally on the open end of the lowest shelf. On the top shelf, he made a bookend by setting her large volumes of Freud and Jung horizontally next to the books on mythology. They seemed to belong together.

"There," said Jimmy, standing back to admire his work. "See, I'm good for something."

Ann wore blue bell-bottoms, a peasant blouse, and water buffalo sandals the night she brought Jimmy to Meredith and John's for dinner. Meredith had insisted that Ann bring her new boyfriend over. Ann felt she would be bringing him on approval, and she was watchful, a little nervous, seeing Jimmy through their eyes—overly serious, too shaggy. And she saw them through Jimmy's eyes—straight and prissy, fatally conventional. Jimmy was eager to meet Kentuckians, although Ann had insisted they were not at all like her parents.

John had smoked a salmon in an outdoor contraption like a baby spaceship, and Meredith made a complicated sauce, which she explained in detail to Ann in the kitchen. Ann doubted that she would ever make such a sauce or smoke a fish. As Meredith neatly fitted a Tupperware container together and burped it, Ann tried to describe how she and Jimmy were suited for each other, free to imagine something new together.

Meredith said, "Wait till you have kids." The two little boys had been put to bed, but they reappeared in the kitchen, underfoot.

"You may *not* have a cookie," she said to the older one. "You've already brushed your teeth. Now go to your room and read. In five minutes, I'm coming to tuck you in."

Ann recalled the way Meredith had swaddled the little boys into bed. She had asked Jimmy at what age boys started to play with themselves, and he didn't remember. He thought it was always, probably even in the womb. "Why not?" he said.

Jimmy sat between a rubber plant and a dieffenbachia, and Ann sat across from him on a striped love seat. John installed himself in a high-backed chair like a king on a throne. Meredith was looking at Jimmy as if he were an overgrown kid. She must have been thinking she would like to take her scissors to his hair, Ann thought. Jimmy was smoking more cigarettes than usual.

They drank Manhattans and tackled bowls of pistachios peeping like clams from their bright green shells. Ann was aware of the color-coordinated family of furniture. Small lights beamed up like admirers at some reproductions of abstract expressionism on the walls. The surroundings struck her as strange—the pale green shag rug, the orange drapes pulled shut across the sunset. It was more luxurious than any place she had ever lived, but she saw it now through Jimmy's eyes—ordinary, artificial, meaningless. She realized that the African market baskets had been seized from their source like elephants or lions—for show. These insights made her feel a bit smug.

John served the salmon. It lay on its side, staring at the ceiling, on a fish-shaped platter, with sprigs of greenery adorning it.

"Sprigs of greenery, like it's caught on seaweed when you reeled it in," said Ann, the cocktail clogging her brain.

John laughed. "I doubt if the seaweed would have made it upriver."

Strains of unidentifiable classical music played low on the stereo in the living room. As they ate, in the bay-windowed dining room, John and Jimmy picked up an earlier conversation about the war. They wandered down several obscure trails. The salmon was delicious.

John said, "I don't agree with you, Jimmy. Johnson has to escalate. I don't like this war any more than you do, but he can't leave the others there to take all the risk. With more troops, it will be over sooner." He waved his fork in the air.

"But why send these yokels who have no idea where Vietnam is?" Jimmy was louder than usual. "That's not fair. It's a con, a trap, the draft."

Ann recognized Jimmy's style of argument.

"John, Ann's glass is empty." Meredith gestured at the bottle.

Ann hadn't realized she had drained the glass. Time had slipped away during this perplexing gabfest about the war.

John filled Ann's glass, saying, "I would call for a volunteer army."

"Would you go, then?" Jimmy asked.

"I'm over thirty. They wouldn't want me."

"Then you can argue anything you want to since you wouldn't have to be part of it." Jimmy forked a hefty chunk of salmon. "All the old guys in charge can just decide whatever they want to make young guys do. They could have us dig a canal from here to San Francisco Bay if they wanted to. They could make us build highways. But they'd rather send us to war. To get us to be patriotic and fight for our country, they set up a bogeyman—communism."

"Oh, we have to have communism to be against!" John laughed, as if communism were a joke.

"I'm not sure about the domino theory," Ann piped up, but no one noticed.

Meredith sent around the basket of bread. With the basket poised above his plate, John said, "If Johnson doesn't send more troops, then it will be dribs and drabs for years—one step up and two steps back. I think we need to end it fast. Johnson needs to send more or risk losing the ones he's already sent."

"But it's not fair to protect the kids in college," Jimmy said.

"Kids like you shouldn't go. You need to take advantage of your privilege."

"But I'm able-bodied."

John laughed. "Did you hear that, Meredith?"

Meredith said, "Most kids would be aiming for a 4-F."

Ann was alarmed. "Jimmy, your education gets you out of the draft!"

Jimmy stared across the table at her. "Does that mean people who haven't been to college are expendable?"

"No. I didn't mean that." Ann was confused.

John said, "If it was a volunteer army, you wouldn't have so much ruckus. It would be a job that some people agreed to do. And it would be like any job."

"Not like *any* job," said Jimmy, wide-eyed. "You can't be serious."

"Well, no, I take that back. But it would be efficient."

"The army right now is two-thirds volunteers anyway," said Jimmy. "That still doesn't make the war right, and it doesn't stop the protests."

"But the problem is the draft, that other third. That's the reason for the protests."

Jimmy, to Ann's surprise, argued against draft deferment. She always admired how natural and at ease with himself he was when he got passionate about an idea, but it seemed now that he must be playing devil's advocate.

"It's not right that mostly lower-class guys are drafted while students get off scot-free," he said. "Read the CORE report."

Jimmy had never mentioned the CORE report before.

"You suburban kids aren't good draft prospects. You've been sheltered," John said. "They give you the deferment because they know you wouldn't last over there. If you're scared enough you'll stay in school. And if you drop out of school, then you're a risk taker, more likely to make a good soldier."

"That's screwy reasoning," Ann said. She wondered how John could tell Jimmy was from the suburbs.

Jimmy and John continued down a wilderness path. Secretary of State Dean Rusk. Congress. Ann never knew how to argue with men. Meredith wasn't making a peep.

Ann ventured, "Maybe student protestors can have an effect. People working in factories don't have the time."

"Students aren't going to end the war," John said. "That's foolish."

"How do students have the time?" Jimmy asked Ann.

"You said yourself you didn't have time to pay attention to the news."

Ann knew her face was so red from the wine that nobody could tell she was blushing. But she felt angry. Men always ganged up on her, she realized then. Men decided wars.

"The fish is delicious," she said to Meredith. "Maybe I should learn how to make that sauce." Meredith was eyeing the plates and offering seconds. *The fish is delicious*, Ann thought. A ridiculous rhyme.

"Here's what bothers me personally," Jimmy said later in the car as they were heading up University Avenue to his house. "Those guys going over there, they know how to do things. They know how to clean their rifles, they can carry a hundred pounds on their backs, they know what it means to risk everything."

"I can't imagine going to the jungle and living in that heat with all the bugs and wild animals." Ann spoke with unaccustomed sharpness.

"But you grew up on a farm."

"I know about bugs and mud, and I had to do chores, but that's just what I want to get away from. And I wouldn't want a gun."

"I didn't even have chores. I got an allowance and there were things I was supposed to do, like take out the garbage, and once I helped paint the garage, but that's about it. I don't know how to do anything."

"Well, that's just not true. Who made me bookshelves? And you do artistic things. You draw. You're a wizard with a camera."

"Maybe I should just get a wizard suit and a wand," he said, pounding the steering wheel.

The streetlights made the bushy tops of the palm trees silvery like old men.

They fell into bed, dazed, too sleepy to make love. Ann awoke before dawn, her head cracking. She regretted taking Jimmy to visit her Kentucky friends. The war argument was discombobulating. And Meredith was a drip. Ann and Jimmy shouldn't be in disagreement. They should both be out protesting, but the exam was coming up and Jimmy couldn't afford to lose his draft deferment. It hit her even more deeply than before what a looming monster the draft was for people who couldn't afford college or keep up their grades. Jimmy had been so quiet about it, but she realized that he must be torn with both guilt and fear about the draft. He would be nervous about it all the time. His imagination would be full of the possibilities, and he would be questioning continually whether his deferment made sense.

Jimmy's hair made a halo on the pillow. He had wound the sheet tightly around his shoulders and clasped it tightly to his neck. Ann pictured him sleeping on an army cot in a barracks full of snoring young men. She thought of Meredith and John's boys, trapped in their chaste little beds. Through the half-open Venetian blinds, the headlights from a passing car made film-noir stripes on the wall. The clock said three past six. She eased herself from the bed. She needed to do some reading for class but couldn't find her book. It was still dark outside. She accidentally clattered the soap dish in the bathroom, but Jimmy didn't stir. She slipped back into bed and tried to sleep, but her head hurt and she was thirsty. She got up and drank a glass of water, but that made her feel worse. Meredith and John and their wine and their fancy fish. Now Ann realized that Jimmy had been standing up for people like her and her family in Kentucky. She felt grateful and proud, even closer to him.

Finally she slept again, and they awoke at the same time. As they struggled awake, they squeezed each other tightly, half in a dream. It was a luxurious feeling, as they squeezed deeper and deeper in mutual need. They clutched each other like long-separated lovers reunited.

Jimmy's battered aluminum skillet appeared to be an antique from Conestoga wagon days, but his percolator was new.

"Chow's on," he said. He had made a complete breakfast—bacon, scrambled eggs, toast, and coffee. He gave her his Porky Pig cup.

"This is good." She laughed. "I'm trying to imagine my dad cooking an egg."

"Or mine," he said.

He stubbed out a cigarette, half-smoked.

He wasn't eating. She had finished her eggs and a piece of toast when she realized that he was crying.

"What? What's wrong?" She touched his face, dabbing the tear.

"I'm told a man never cries," he said, rubbing his face with a wad of his hair.

"What's wrong, Jimmy?"

"I feel so worthless," he said. "You're not the only one without confidence. I may seem to you like I know what I'm doing, but it's not true. I feel like I have an empty bucket right in the center of my being."

"That's so strange," she said. "A bucket."

"I'm hollow," he said. "There's just nothing in there."

"That can't be true, Jimmy."

He really was crying. She stood up and held his head

in her arms. "I don't believe it," she said. "You are full; you are overflowing. You're good, kind, true."

"You've been reading too much Christian bullshit in Western Civ. If there's anything in the bucket, it *is* bullshit."

"That's not true."

"Maybe you don't really know me."

A bad image—like the snake in Eden—was about to spill out their happiness into a sour slop bucket of hog swill. The empty bucket was a cockamamie metaphor, she thought.

"You're so much better than me," he said, pushing her away. "I don't deserve you."

"What are you talking about?"

"I try so hard," he said. "I always want to do what's right, but sometimes I feel so inadequate."

She sat down again at the table, and Jimmy forced a playful grin. He was no longer crying, but this wasn't a joke. Ann tried to assure him that his fears were unfounded, that most people were shallow compared to him. How could he feel so empty? But she realized that his self-doubts were nothing she could simply shoo away.

"Listen, we've got each other. Tell me what I can do. I'm here. I'm listening." She touched his cheek, but he wouldn't turn toward her.

He told her a few things—his lack of direction, the absence of encouragement from his family—but she wasn't convinced. She knew he was smart, he found school easy, he saw through sham and pretension, he possessed a critical mind that was always busy and alert. Why wasn't that enough?

"I guess I'm a spoiled brat."

"Jimmy," she said, holding him as closely as she could. "You saved me, you know. I don't know what I would have done without you." She thought that saying this would give him confidence.

But she was worried about him, that he would cry over a scary emptiness that he couldn't tell her about.

The sun blazed hot, the water burned, the breeze died down. After the pointless days on deck come the casual-chic evenings, the ceaseless vulgarity of the buffet table, the sunsets crowded with ooh-ahs, champagne, and shouting.

The silence of the sea. The thought of the norovirus spreading like nuclear fallout.

Railings lower than you'd expect.

Writing a paper is beside the point," she said. "*These* are the words that count." She ruffled the pages of her Riverside edition of Keats's poetry, which she had found peeking from under the sofa skirt at Jimmy's.

They were at her apartment that evening, writing their papers on Keats and Shelley. They had eaten some food she had made—broiled burgers, peas, baked potatoes. Jimmy didn't want any ice cream. He was writing about Shelley's clouds and idealism, and she was playing around with Keats's birds. The memory of her banter with Jimmy about the banshee was an inspiration. Its demonic, wailing shriek made a counterpoint to Keats's chipper chirper, the nightingale. She thought Jimmy had shown her that she had a choice—she could let the backwoods banshee of superstition stifle her own voice or she could soar with the nightingale. She wondered if Keats could see birds from his window as he lay dying in Rome. Probably he saw pigeons on the Spanish Steps. One of the last things he saw could have been bird shit spattered on those steps. Shelley's last sight might have been clouds reflected in the Gulf of La Spezia as he went under, gurgling.

Jimmy closed his notebook and thrust it into his book bag. "I have to go home to write this. I can't think with you sitting there tempting me—just like someone I saw in a picture on a dress once."

"Jimmy," she said, reaching for him at the door. "I

meant what I said this morning. You saved me. You really did."

He faced her and put his hands on her shoulders. "Remember what you told me about the cut worm and the Wordsworth sunset? You were right—what you said to the class. That's what I love about you. I told you the day I met you what I thought of those brown-nose apple-polishing sycophants, sick elephants." He touched her cheek. "We saved each other," he said. He kissed her nose and gave her a long hug. "Adios, Snooks. See you tomorrow." He held the door open for a second, then added, with a little grin, "My Daisy of the Dardanelles."

From the door, she watched him skip down the stairs in a hurry, his book bag over his shoulder, his footfalls ringing on the metal mesh steps. The hollowness he had spoken of, the empty bucket, frightened her. She thought of her father emptying the coal scuttle into the stove. How could Jimmy say she had saved him? Had she really?

As the sound of his car faded down the street, she remembered an evening when her father had not come home, and she had to help her mother milk the cows. Mama, although sick with worry, would not go to the police until nearly midnight, for fear of learning that he had had a wreck. And he had. He had hit ice, and the car rolled four times down an embankment. He spent a week in the hospital while Ann and her mother milked the cows every day—at five in the morning and five in the evening. Now she thought of her mother's churning worry that night when Ann's father had not come home.

"O.K., Miss Snooks. Listen to this." Jimmy crossed the living room and searched among his record albums. In two days, he seemed to have jumped headlong out of his depression. "Forget Keats and Shelley. The greatest poem in the English language had already been written when they were still talking baby talk."

She sat down on the couch. He placed a record on his turntable and dropped the needle into the groove.

"Listen to this."

"Sounds like 'Eleanor Rigby'—the violins. What is it?"

"Saint-Saëns—'Danse Macabre.'"

"That's the greatest poem?"

"No. Listen." He lowered the volume and stood holding an imaginary microphone like a lounge crooner. He began reciting.

In Xanadu did Kubla Khan
A stately pleasure-dome decree:
Where Alph, the sacred river, ran
Through caverns measureless to man
Down to a sunless sea.

Jimmy recited the entire poem. Ann was thrilled that he knew the whole of "Kubla Khan" by heart. He was handsome, irresistible, his shaggy head aglow with the slanting light from his pole lamp, his faint lisp echoing like a subtle motif throughout. She could see Jimmy's "flashing eyes, his floating hair." At the end, she cried.

"That's so beautiful."

"Coleridge had already done it," Jimmy said, flopping down on the couch. "Neither Keats nor Shelley, and certainly not Byron, could do better than 'Kubla Khan.' And that includes Wordsworth."

"What's all this about an empty bucket?" she said. "You've got that poem in it. What else do you need?"

Blotting her face with his shirttail, he said softly, "And which Romantic poet is the most quoted to this day, I ask you?"

"It's Coleridge, isn't it? 'Water, water, every-where . . .'"

"And the albatross! You can't even walk across campus without stumbling over the fucking albatross."

"The ancient mariner had an albatross around his neck, and you've got an empty bucket inside. Water, water, everywhere, but nothing in your bucket, Jimmy? That's absurd."

"Yeah." A grin broke out. "You make me feel better."

"You make *me* feel better."

"You know, if Coleridge suddenly came back to life in the twentieth century, he would fit right in. He'd be so hip he'd be collaborating with the Beatles."

"I heard that a new Beatles album is coming out the first of June."

"Yeah, I heard. I love the Beatles. They could end the war."

"Maybe they'll know what to do about the albatross."

They held each other tightly, and Ann felt sure he loved her. She would fill his bucket with love, although she knew that seemed soppy.

Jimmy said, "Did you hear what happened to Blankenship?"

"No, what?"

"He flunked an undergrad who begged him to change his grade because if he flunked out he'd be drafted. But Blankenship refused, said he had to abide by the rules. He had his principles. Well, Blankenship just the other day got word that this student was killed in Vietnam."

"That's terrible. He must feel awful."

"But somebody else didn't die. It evens out."

"Oh, good, we're supposed to be glad this prof condemned a student to his death."

"Blankenship probably feels bad but rationalized his part in it. But there he is—prof in ivory tower demoting lowly minion to the battlefield because he wasn't good enough for college."

Ann had her eyes fixed on a bougainvillea vine—the rampant flowers devouring light and air.

They stopped talking about the war when *Sgt. Pep-per's Lonely Hearts Club Band* arrived with the force of a church tent revival. It was the first week of June, and spring quarter exams loomed. The pervasive smell of citrus blossoms gave the campus a mellow, dreamy air, while the Beatles provided a whimsical yet revolutionary soundtrack. The new album overturned what Ann had been thinking about the study of litera-ture, her background, her future. It seemed to throw everything onto a smiling, self-congratulatory merry-go-round of in-jokes and jests. She and Jimmy lis-tened to the album over and over, discussing it as if it were on a level with Chaucer or Joyce. They analyzed the four thousand holes in Blackburn, Lancashire, at length. The holes symbolized alienated individuals, pitfalls, potholes. Empty buckets, Ann understood but did not say.

"Nobody has ever done anything like this," Jimmy said. "The Beatles were stoned. Acid. I bet you any-thing."

He scrutinized the collage of figures on the album cover. "Here we have the leaders of the world. Bob Dylan. Marlon Brando. Edgar Allan Poe."

"Marilyn Monroe," Ann said.

As the album played on Jimmy's stereo, they were

smoking a joint together and trying to identify each figure. Oscar Wilde, Marlene Dietrich, Fred Astaire. Most of them they didn't recognize. The figures were portrayed like a crowd of mourners at a funeral. Ann thought the Beatles could have been English majors, like her and Jimmy.

"I wish I'd seen them at Candlestick Park last summer," she said. "I got here two days later."

"I know a couple of people who went," said Jimmy. "They said you couldn't hear them for the screams."

Ann took another drag on the joint. She was getting more accustomed to the harsh smoke.

She cut out the pictures that came with the album—Sgt. Pepper, the two badges (the band logo and the head of Sgt. Pepper), the mustache, the sergeant's stripes, and the stand-up card of the Beatles in their satin Day-Glo band uniforms. Jingles the landlady was ahead of her time with her Day-Glo decor.

Jimmy placed the mustache under his nose.

"I'm Sergeant Pepper," he said. "I am here for the benefit of Mr. Kite. He and I see eye to eye. We know who is going to die."

Ann heard the songs at Tresidder Union. At the gas station, lovely Rita, the meter maid, was coming to life, and when Ann arrived at her building, the songs were wafting from the apartments downstairs. Pixie and Sanjay were playing opposite sides of the album. When Ann went to her appointment with Frank the psychologist—who was exploring her mind, fixing a hole in it—she heard the song "Within You Without You" coming from behind the door that said MENLO PARK DEAF SOCIETY. Each encounter with one of the songs seemed to have a meaning—the power of co-incidence, the continuity of a theme, a motif in the novel that was her life in the sixties. Or that was how it would seem decades hence. Synchronicity.

"Something is happening that is bigger than us," Ann ventured to say. She had no idea what she meant.

"Yeah. The military-industrial complex, for instance," said Jimmy. "My car is bigger than us."

He was teasing. But there was a feeling in the air, Ann thought. Chip reported that he had heard the Beatles blaring from every doorway when he walked through the Haight-Ashbury district.

"That place is harder and harder to get through," he said. "Don't ask me what I was doing in the Haight. Pixie wanted to go."

Chip had just come from downstairs, after spending the night with Pixie. He complained that her pink pebbles hurt his arches.

"That gal is a madwoman," he said.

In the car Ann and Jimmy talked about *Sgt. Pepper* all the way to the beach at Half Moon Bay. The radio was playing the album over and over. Jimmy sang along happily as if his "bucket" was filled with music now.

Ann saw the Lonely Hearts Club Band as an old vaudeville act telling stories to the future. "Billy Shears the band singer and his friends," she told Jimmy. "Maybe they're going to help him with a barn raising. The girl with kaleidoscope eyes is going boating. The girl running away from home. Rita the meter maid. Even the guy imagining his old age."

She imagined that the meandering strains of the long song George Harrison played on the sitar was about a Buddhist monk.

Jimmy pointed out that the characters were all ordinary people except for the last one on the record. "Look what happens at the end. The lucky man blew his mind out in his car. The successful man—maybe he was even in the House of Lords."

"He couldn't face reality," she said.

"And these stories are all interior," Jimmy said. "That's what acid is like."

"Are you still trying to get me to take that?"

"Sometimes I try to explain something to you in acid terms and I can't because you haven't been there."

Ann thought Jimmy was suggesting that she wouldn't be so uptight if she took acid. He and Frank had both used the word *repression* several times. Albert had said the same thing.

Chip, holding up the album cover, said, "I've identified more mourners."

"Who?"

"Aubrey Beardsley. Here. And Aldous Huxley. Aleister Crowley."

"I found Lewis Carroll," Ann said.

"Dope fiends all," said Chip.

Ann heard something new each time she listened to the album, and hearing it everywhere made her feel she was part of a vital movement that was grabbing the future. So when Jimmy again suggested they take LSD together, she consented.

"Sex on acid," he said. "I'm tingling just thinking about it."

"What will it be like?"

"You'll come for about five hours," he promised. "We will. Together."

"How do you know?"

"Just imagining."

She knew he had once had a girlfriend named Martha, but except for their comical adolescent confessions, Ann and Jimmy never mentioned their sexual history. Although she knew people had bad trips, she trusted Jimmy and thought sharing an acid trip would bring them even closer together. It would be an adventure into a dreamworld of new stories.

Chip arrived at Jimmy's early on the chosen Tuesday, wearing his jumpsuit like an official uniform.

"Sergeant Pepper here, reporting for duty," he said. "Are you ready, Ann?"

"I guess so."

"Are you sure?" Jimmy said, for the fifteenth time.

"I'm ready. Yes!"

Chip, their guide for the trip, had assembled some special items—a kaleidoscope, a book of Escher drawings, a Stockhausen album. He patted Ann on the head.

"Remember, if you freak out, I'll be here. Jimmy will be here. This woolly blanket will be right here if you're cold. I will make hot, soothing tea. I will bring giant sandwiches and milkshakes. Your wish is my command."

"Oh, cut it out, Chip," said Jimmy, laughing. "It will

be a nice, quiet, loose day—very ungrammatical. You'll be bored out of your gourd. You can sit there with your slide rule and calculate the universe." He mimicked Chip working his slide rule like a guitar. Jimmy said to Ann, "And at the end you can sleep with Chip if you want to."

"Don't be absurd." She laughed.

"Why not? Chip's a good guy. He's taking care of us. I can share."

"You're teasing. You're teasing, aren't you?"

Jimmy grinned and fluffed her hair. "I'm just kidding."

"Don't be a prude, Ann," she remembered someone saying. Pixie?

Ann had been holding in her mind the thought of sex on acid with Jimmy. Jimmy had spruced up his bedroom. From the overhead light fixture and along the walls he had draped an orange-and-white silk emergency parachute he had gotten from army surplus. He had anchored the billowy silk along the walls with chairs, books on the bookshelves, and safety pins on the blinds. It was a haphazard canopy over a love nest. And he had scattered some colorful pillows on the bed.

Chip disappeared for half an hour, returning with a lavish bouquet from the florist. Jimmy found a milk jug for the flowers. The bouquet was a grand assortment, like a Flemish still life.

"For texture and color," Chip said.

Jimmy made bacon and eggs for the three of them.

"Start out with a good breakfast," Chip said. "My mom always said start every day with a good breakfast."

"One thing I do know is how to make breakfast," Jimmy said.

"I'm just going to hang out here and work on some data analyses till you feel like going to the redwoods," Chip said later.

The acid was on postage stamps, one for Ann and one for Jimmy. She licked the stamp, rolled her tongue around her mouth as Chip instructed, sipped some water.

"I want to save the stamp for my collection," she said. She set it on a shelf above the bathroom sink to dry. She wondered why the stamp was a ten-cent stamp and not a penny stamp. It seemed extravagant.

Jimmy swished water in his mouth.

"Anything happening?" he asked.

"So soon?"

He held her close to him. "I'm right here. It's going to be superlative, magnolious! I'm here all the way."

Jimmy was good to her. She would do something about that emptiness of his. She felt herself letting go.

But Jimmy's arm was shrinking. His shirt was falling off, its shape turning into a cloud shifting in a fast wind. It slithered to the floor, a white formless thing.

Then, a surprise heave. Her breakfast shot to the floor, barely altered. Chip was sopping it with paper towels.

"A Pollock painting," he said, as Ann watched yellow and brown colors mix and disappear. The colors were fascinating, rich in their transmogrification.

"Are you all right?" Jimmy said. "Let's steady ourselves. Sit here. Do you feel better?"

"I'm just ducky."

Jimmy's face was a frog staring at her bug-eyed. Then the big eyes were those of a cat, smiling knowingly like the slyboots Cheshire.

"Let's study the flowers," he said.

"Is there a quiz?"

California flowers! A mountain of them, grand and intricate, multiple jigsaw puzzles, like a millefiori paperweight. She was lost on the petal of a daisy. A drop of water glistened on it. Tiny flecks of pollen had dispersed on the surface of the petal and their absorption by the drop of water was imminent. She would wait to observe this phenomenon from her perch in eternity. Knowing she had all of time, she relaxed, flooded with euphoria.

Suddenly the Lonely Hearts Club Band appeared through the doorway, marching in place, then marching forward. Sgt. Pepper was directing the band with his slide rule.

"Billy Shears sounds just like Ringo," she said. Her words seemed yellow and brown, like her eggs and bacon.

She would get by with a little help from her friends! They were looking out for her. She had never felt so secure, so loved. It was like being in a bassinet with a baby rattler. A toy rattle, not a snake! The rattler coiled into a tight little comfortable pillow—lovely, pink, benign. She was not afraid.

John, Paul, and George sang behind Ringo in a high-pitched refrain, loving and innocent. They sang out of another age, when there were bandstands and Sousa tubas and kind neighbors. At the end of the song, Jimmy stood and gave Sgt. Pepper a military salute. Chip, saluting too, retreated into the kitchen. The word *synchronicity* waggled on his butt, and "Poetry is not conversation" hovered above. Ann smirked. Jimmy rocked her on the bed in his arms. They were beneath the parachute, drifting.

During "Lucy in the Sky with Diamonds," Chip handed Ann the kaleidoscope and she watched the geometric dazzle through Lucy's eyes. He lit a strobe candle on the bedside table. Ann and Jimmy were lying on the bed, eyes to the flickering canopy. A spherical paper lantern that had covered the light fixture rolled on the bed like a tumbleweed. Inside it, dust fluttered in strings. Shadows roamed the silk walls.

"I'm burning a strobe candle at both ends," Jimmy said.

"She's Leaving Home" was ineffably sad. It was effably Ann. She had left home. On a Wednesday morning, very early, tiptoeing out of the house with her handkerchief, her parents finding her note and blaming themselves. What could they have done better? Didn't they know her? How could they have misunderstood? She felt tears—for the girl in the song, for the bereft parents, for the man in the motor trade. But then it was clear that this man would treat her badly—use, rob, jilt, abandon, hurt. The parents were right. The girl went with the man to the carnival, of course. Mr. Kite was the headliner, jumping, sailing through hogsheads, hoops of fire, which Ann could clearly envision, but Mr. Henderson's ten somersets would be a true wonder. She loved doing somersets when she was little. In college she learned that people did somersaults, not somersets. But now it thrilled her to realize that the Beatles had no doubt done somersets as children and played hide-'n'-go-seek. The record seemed to turn itself over. "Within You Without You" ambled slowly, a brittle sound, with sparkles. The song lasted for about two months. Her eyes ranged through every pore and fold of the silk ceiling, a mere spot on a giant's face. Then it became an immense sea of agile pollywogs.

She couldn't fathom being sixty-four. It was such a funny idea. Paul sang so sweetly, as if from an imagined time, some distant future—maybe on the deck of a large ship cruising to a balmy isle. Her laugh led her to lovely, happy Rita. Maybe it was Rita who had run off to meet the man in the motor trade. Now she was happy and free of him, but still in the motor trade, so to speak. Checking her line of meters and then having tea.

Ann was hardly aware of Jimmy until "Good Morning Good Morning" began, with the farmyard sounds. Jimmy and his drawings of Bugs and Porky and the farmer Fudd. Pigs, chickens in the henhouse in Kentucky, gamboling spring calves. Home was far away. That home—undulating, blue and green, the scent of gardenias on the porch. She could hear her mother calling the pigs. *Soo-eeee!*

A pitch-black thought interrupted the holes in Blackburn, Lancashire. A field of land mines, helmeted figures running across, strafing sounds above. Strafing. There had been so much strafing lately. She said that aloud. "Don't worry about strafing," Jimmy said, lying beside her, staring at the ceiling. She had to pee. Didn't she?

By the time the last note of the last song faded, she felt she had been on a phantasmagoric journey in Wonderland with Alice.

They flung darts at Jimmy's dartboard until Chip stopped them. Then they ate peaches and sucked the pits. Later Chip gave them fascinating orange Popsicles. Ann hadn't realized Chip had brought them.

"I bought them," Jimmy explained when she inquired. "What difference does it make? Why do you have to get everything straight? All worked out, in rows. Maybe they brought themselves. Maybe they flew."

"Shut up, Jimmy," said Chip.

Ann didn't like what Jimmy said. She didn't speak for a while. Maybe she *was* too organized. But she hadn't realized that bothered him.

"Here, let's listen to Stockhausen," said Chip. "A change of mood."

Ann and Jimmy sat on the couch and closed their eyes while Stockhausen played—freaky tape loops and eerie graveyard sounds. Ann couldn't tell whether to cough or swallow. Her breathing was off, not quite right. She felt that something was trying to get out.

"Oh, man," said Jimmy.

"Man oh man," said Jimmy.

She heard the whales singing to Stockhausen of the ancient history of fabled sea serpents. If sound waves could wend through outer space they could also descend into the ocean's deeps. All the songs of 1967 were traveling, sonar-motivated melodies bearing secrets. A sinking bathysphere was scouting the ocean floor to collect all those songs. You don't know what's happening, do you?

You are out of your depth, girlie, she heard.

From the observation platform at the top of Hoover Tower, they searched for a distant clock that once had a face but now had only an empty circle. When Ann squinted through Chip's binoculars, she could see a blue clock face. It was ten minutes past two. They should hurry. Below the platform, students were rushing along.

Jimmy said, "The whole fucking universe is out there."

He waved at the people below them on the walkways. Suddenly Ann and Jimmy, at the same moment, looked down at themselves to see if they were dressed. It had been completely irrelevant till that moment.

They laughed at their simultaneous realization and fell onto each other.

Chip was driving. Jimmy was in the front and Ann lay alone in the back seat. The roller-coaster curves that had been so intimidating on a motorcycle now seemed quietly rhythmic, soft and unthreatening. Ann was rocking in a cradle and rolling in a sling hammock. What Jimmy said might be true, she thought. She would have to change. She couldn't be a slave to order. But she wasn't! Not at all. Her books had been in haphazard piles until Jimmy brought the planks and blocks. Her struggle for order was only because she was so naturally disordered. *Entropy* was her middle name.

The redwood trees in the park were too large to see, and there were mossy stumps the size of her kitchen. She and Jimmy were Hansel and Gretel, leaving a trail for Chip. The redwoods were run by the Brothers Grimm. Her eye lit on a spider on the bark of a tree. The spider was green and gold, glistening benignly, glowing like a jewel in a narrow sunbeam. Everything here was friendly. The redwoods reached upward like Jack's beanstalk, aspiring, grasping, groping for sun. She tried to hug a redwood, but it was magnelephant. She had to let it hug her. Where was Jimmy?

He grasped both her hands and said, "This is like the Garden of Eden—after Bob Dylan came through."

"Xanadu," she said.

"Xanadu to you too, Toots."

Everything was beautiful. The spider, the leaves, the moss, the ferns, the decay, bugs. There was too much to see. Trying to look at a large view was dizzying. The trees were too large. If she stared at a small patch of bark, a redwood was implied. That was enough. She sat on a fallen limb with her head aimed between her knees at an intricate universe of bugs and fungus. She thought she was at the movies. The arduous plot went on and on.

A large branch of a fallen redwood was the Golden Gate Bridge. Jimmy was walking on the immense log, balancing himself on it, teeter-tottering his way along. Chip, sprawled on a stump, reading his book, called, "Be careful, Jimmy."

Jimmy was beckoning. "Come on up here!" He made his way back to Ann and pulled her up. He held her hand as they walked along the big log. The log was still strong and hard, not rotted, even though they saw that it had fallen long ago. "Redwoods don't rot," Jimmy had told her. "Your bookshelves will last longer than I will."

They were in the redwoods for hours, days. The light dimmed. Chip, their sergeant, kept them on the path through colonies of ferns. They poked along slowly. Ann's mind was sharp. She saw Keats here, Shelley there. She tried to remember something Jimmy had told her about Coleridge, about his wonderful mind squeezed shut by his buddy Wordsworth's high-handed twaddling.

"Xanadu," she said. "Do Xanadu."

Obligingly, Jimmy began reciting "Kubla Khan."

In Xanadu did Kubla Khan
A stately pleasure-dome decree:
Where Alph, the sacred river, ran
Through caverns measureless to man
Down to a sunless sea.
So twice five miles of fertile ground
With walls and towers were girdled round . . .

"There he goes again," said Chip, tucking his book in his leg pocket. "Rafting down the River Ralph."

Ann had been rereading the poem lately, savoring the mellifluous but dramatic tones, the sensuous melody. She had forgotten she had been looking forward to sex on acid. But then that thought escaped.

If you felt disembodied, what could you do? Desire was like an envelope she had dropped into her purse. Where was her purse?

Jimmy, pointing to her, meant that she was the damsel with the dulcimer—who else? She was wailing for her demon lover!

A savage place! as holy and enchanted . . .

Jimmy was tottering and weaving on the log.

Five miles meandering with a mazy motion . . .
Ancestral voices prophesying war!

Coleridge the poet seemed a seer, envisioning all the wars to come, she thought. He wouldn't be surprised at all by Vietnam. Ugly thoughts scattered.

By the end of the poem, though, she felt the sensuous pleasure of the milk of Paradise. She was in Paradise, with Jimmy. She was "meandering with a mazy motion." It was true—the earth was breathing in "fast thick pants," and even the fallen redwood tree was breathing. She laughed. All she could say was "Wow."

"Let's go," Jimmy said. "I feel the dark coming on."

"'At one stride comes the dark,'" Ann quoted out of nowhere. She was seeing a horror movie: Coleridge's ancient mariner meets the spectre-woman on the skeleton ship.

"I almost know that damned 'Kubla Khan' by heart myself," said Chip, as he hustled them along the trail towards the car.

"Keep your 'fast thick pants' on, Sarge," Jimmy said. "Hark! What's that? A patch of sunlight?"

Ann could see a bright yellow stump just off the trail. "What is that? Let's go see."

The surface of the stump was alive, dozens of slimy blaze-yellow creatures wriggling together. A mass of little snakes. Ann grabbed Jimmy's hand.

"It's banana slugs!" cried Chip. "They're mating."

"How do you know?" Jimmy asked.

"I've studied mating," Chip said. "I've been studying it all day."

"Then it's an orgy," said Jimmy.

Ann touched a slug. It was slippery.

"Don't touch," Chip said. "Salt from your sweat will have a chemical reaction. A pinch of salt would make it melt."

"Are they like snails?" Ann asked. Salted snails would melt in your stomach.

They stared at the slithery creatures, stretching and touching, glomming onto one another. They were over six inches long, in tangles. Jimmy had a smile on his face, his lips curved in the same shape as one of the slugs, the curve of a banana.

"Slugs on drugs," said Jimmy. He slapped his forehead as if he had just divined the key to the universe. "'A flash of golden fire.'"

Bright yellow. Ann saw clouds of bright yellow.

"They're fucking," she said aloud.

At an Indian restaurant later, the familiar smells of Sanjay's cooking blared like horns. Ann thought she was supposed to chew each bite thirty times, sip tea, fold more naan, plop on chutney. The meal was long and funny, and the flavors were deep and sensuous—clever, Ann said. Yellow and cinnamon. Then somewhere there was a movie. *What's New Pussycat?* Each scene was a dreamlike world of its own, like Dante's rings of hell but intensely real. She forgot at times that Jimmy was beside her. He was holding her hand like a potato. The theater lights gleamed on, and she was with Jimmy in a slow-moving throng, cows heading into the barn for milking. Chip had gone ahead to get the car. Or maybe he had gone to church.

Jimmy was quiet. His face sagged. He shooed Ann into the back seat and shoved himself into a heap beside her.

He jerked his head away when she tried to touch his face.

"What's wrong?"

"Just a headache," he said. "Are you O.K.?"

"Yeah, I think so." The movie was still in her head, scenes flashing.

"Chip, can you take me home and then take Ann home? I don't feel so hot."

Jimmy told Chip that Ann would sleep with him. Chip shrugged.

"Sure, that makes sense. Fair play." But they were kidding.

Ann somehow thought that would be all right even though she knew it wasn't, but it was what people were doing—sharing with friends, from the goodness of their hearts. Jimmy hugged her goodbye silently and suddenly she was in the front seat with Chip. Chip, who had been the kind friend all day, was still kind to her as he drove her home. She tried to imagine going to bed with Chip, who was attractive enough, though the jumpsuit really was not flattering and she wouldn't be able to get Porky Pig or Yvor Winters out of her mind. Then she remembered Pixie.

"Don't worry, Ann," Chip said as he opened the car door for her. "Sometimes Jimmy ODs on altruism."

"Is that what it is?"

"Surely you know that about him by now. Jimmy doesn't think he should have anything for himself, so he tries to share everything."

Chip walked her up the stairs to her door. Ann unlocked her door and flipped on the kitchen light. Chip followed her.

He said, "I think Jimmy had early lessons in self-doubt."

"That's not all bad," Ann said, picturing her and Jimmy, bowing to each other in a drawing with the tagline, "No, I don't doubt you."

"Can I go get you anything, Ann? Do you need anything to eat? Donuts? Pretzels?"

"No, thank you."

Chip was a walking palm tree, tall and thin, with a tufty head.

"I'll go back and check on Jimmy."

"Please."

"Let me take a whiz first."

While Chip was in her wine-dark bathroom, she lost track of him. When he reappeared, she was staring into her cupboard, mentally alphabetizing the soup cans and spices.

"Your bathroom is like a cave," he said.

"'Caverns measureless to man.'"

"You poetry freaks."

"Good night, Chip," she said at her door. "Thank you for taking care of us." Chip gave her a warm hug and skipped down the steps, Porky Pig riding the jumpsuit piggyback. She watched as Chip pulled away in Jimmy's Mustang.

"Poetry is not conversation," she whispered to the darkness.

She did not sleep right away, and the next day she was still tripping mildly. The normal chaos of her thoughts became bright colors, fragmented and sent through a kaleidoscope. She saw faces everywhere in the everyday patterns around her—book spines, windowpanes, shadowy maroon tub tiles. The cabbage roses in the carpet grimaced underfoot.

Chip telephoned to check on her. He had stayed overnight at Jimmy's.

"Was he still awake when you got there?" she asked.

"Yeah. He claimed he was O.K. I told him I got you home safely. He's still asleep now."

"What was wrong with him?"

"I don't know. Jimmy's just strange sometimes. He gets a stubborn notion in his head. But remember what I said about his generosity. He would do anything for you."

Ann didn't want Pixie to get the wrong idea in case she had seen Chip leaving the building the night before. But Pixie scoffed at Ann's moral quibbling.

"Sex is just sex," Pixie said. "Jimmy's only testing you."

"Haha."

"You know everybody's sleeping with everybody. It doesn't mean anything. It just means nothing."

"I don't think that's true. And it's not true that everybody is sleeping with everybody. It would take somebody like Chip to solve the math problem of the exponential sum—"

"That's what I mean. Sex with him is science."

Jimmy appeared at the door late in the morning.

"Hey, Snooks," he said.

"Sheepish grin, if ever I saw one," Ann said. She hadn't combed her hair. She glared at him.

He flopped onto the bed with a grunt.

"When did you wake up?" he asked.

"Seven or eight. I don't know. Too early."

"Did you get enough sleep?"

"I don't really know. I'm too mixed up. It seems so odd that it's daytime."

Jimmy reached for her hand and pulled her down beside him. He hooked his arm around her shoulders.

"Was it all right yesterday?"

"It was strange. It still is."

"I'm sorry. I shouldn't have brought you along. Sorry I freaked out on you. You never know how it's going to turn out. But you're O.K.?"

"I'm O.K.," she said.

"Chip did a good job, didn't he?"

"Unh-huh."

"You were all right, weren't you? You didn't get depressed?"

"No, but you seemed a thousand miles away." She tousled his hair. "You split somewhere between the redwoods and the restaurant."

"Do you want to go get some waffles?"

"No. I'm still a little whirly."

"I was feeling crazy last night," he said.

"Are you O.K. now?"

"My head still hurts."

She massaged his neck for a while, and he moaned.

"Is that better?"

"Mmm. I'm sorry I had to send you away. It was getting weird for me. I just had to get by myself, and I knew I could trust Chip to make sure you were all right. He took care of us all day. He did a good job, didn't he?"

"You already asked that. But he shouldn't have left you. He was our guide. I shouldn't have left you either."

"I was O.K. I had some things to think about."

"What things?"

"It was just some bad stuff, and I didn't want you in the center of that. How about you? Do you feel changed like I said you would?"

"I don't know yet. Something happened. I don't know what it is."

"Don't you, Miss Ann?"

She was staring at a child's socks. A simple pair of striped socks. The little girl was waiting for the bus with her mother. The mother eyed Ann suspiciously. The destination sign on the bus was like a label for the coming day. A chartreuse sign on the side of the bus said,

(WHERE ARE YOU GOING?)

At the supermarket, she gazed at beets—large jewels with hairdos. Outside, she noticed a curled leaf on a bush. The leaf was shaped exactly like a great blue heron. As she drew closer, she saw that it resembled a praying mantis. But it was neither, though both assumed prayer-like poses to seek prey. It was only a leaf, but it was also a heron and a mantis.

Ann delayed her summer trip to Kentucky, afraid to go—with her peculiar, revised mind.

Hopewell, Ky.
June 28, 1967

Dear Ann,
   Hope you're coming home soon, but I know you've got your school work. Be careful, you'll study so hard you'll wear out your brain. And the airplane ticket costs so much. It come up a cloud this afternoon that was purely black. When it started sprinkling rain I had to run out and gather in the wash. I just rolled up the clothes and didn't have to sprinkle them down to iron. . . .

Love,
Mama

"What does she mean? Jimmy asked.

"She put a sprinkler head on a ketchup bottle and she sprinkles the clothes with water and rolls each one up into a ball and lets them sit in a basket for a few hours while the moisture distributes through the shirts and makes them ready to iron—a little bit damp but not wet. She calls it 'sprinkling down.'" Ann was manhandling a soup can, grinding it open with a balky can opener. "That was exhausting to explain! And I never even thought about it in my life. I just knew it."

"Do you sprinkle your blouses with a ketchup bottle? That's fascinating!"

"No. I have a steam iron. I don't need a ketchup bottle. Do you want some soup?"

He nodded. "There are just so many things to know."

Ann imagined herself ironing Jimmy's shirts, a domestic chore that would give her pleasure. Someday they would live in a house together and she would iron his shirts. She would cook their dinner. But she had sworn she would never pick up after a man the way her mother did. She could see her father's dirty castoff farm duds making a path across the floor.

She was living in a fairy tale. Jimmy hadn't talked about his empty bucket lately, but since the acid trip something had changed in him. The change was abstract, as if he wasn't always paying attention.

"What's going on in your heart, Jimmy?" she demanded. "What goes on in your mind?"

Ringo's voice ringing in her head, Mama wringing the wash.

"Am I tearing you apart?"

"Yes." *You are breaking my heart.*

It was only later in the day that she realized they had been speaking in song lyrics.

On Tuesday afternoon, a week after the acid trip, they were walking through the Arizona Garden on campus. In the past day or two, she had been losing the lingering hallucinogenic flashes, but the bizarre shapes of the cactus plants spooked her. Many of the cacti were tall and phallic—sentries, gate posts, Greek columns. Others were spheroid and bumpy. A myriad of pincushions. Pink round flowers were pasted onto shiny green surfaces like cake decorations. Some suggested the interior of millefiori paperweights.

"This place is freaky," she said.

"And you've never been here?"

"No." She shivered. "It seems like a good place to be raped and then thrown into a patch of prickly pear."

"There's no good place to be raped," he said.

Jimmy steered her to a bench. "Let's sit here. I'll watch out for roving cacti. I won't let them accost you."

He let go her elbow. She touched his knee, but he did not react.

She said, "When I was little, I cut my arm and needed stitches. At the hospital, while I was under ether, I dreamed about a horde of little cartoon figures jabbering in high voices. They resembled those little cacti over there."

She pointed to a grouping of small, round plants with random offshoots like thumbs.

"Cartoons, huh? That's odd. The Greek word for cactus is *cardoon*. Or maybe it's Latin."

Ann thought that she and Jimmy both snobbishly insisted on using *cacti* as a plural because they had both had Latin in high school.

"Ether," she said. "Weird. I guess I started on drugs early."

She said that to be funny. Or ironic. But Jimmy said, "I have something to say."

This was an alarming place to hear some sobering news. "What?" she blurted.

"I have to go to Chicago," he said.

"Is your family all right?"

"Well, they're never all right. Anyway, I have a few things to tend to there, and it seems a good time to go."

He placed his hand on her knee. "Ann. Snooks. Listen to me. I think it's better anyway if we don't see each other for a while."

She stared at what seemed to be a tragic theatrical mask, the face of a squat cactus.

"What do you mean?"

"I'm just not ready," he said. "For you."

"Why? What's wrong? I don't understand."

"I don't measure up to you." Jimmy lifted his hand and slid a few inches away. "I'm sorry! I'm saying this badly. But we need to take a step back."

Her head was lowered. She couldn't look at him, but he turned toward her.

"I have to think things over. Oh, Ann. Ann. Ann, listen to me." He lifted her chin and placed his other hand on her shoulder. He gazed straight into her eyes.

"I think you agree with me too much," he said. "It makes me feel I don't know you."

"Of course I agree with you!" She grabbed his hand.

"I think you expect too much from me."

Ann stared at pebbles on the path.

"I don't know what I'm doing," Jimmy said. "You know I have to be clear about things. I have to see where I'm going." He turned and stared straight ahead, folding his hands in his lap. "Maybe the long drive cross-country will do me good," he said. "Driving will help me to think."

"I can't speak," Ann said.

"What a shithead am I," he said. "I'm like a mud puddle in your way."

"You're not a mud puddle. What a thing to say."

"Then you admit I'm a shithead."

"No!"

"I don't deserve you," Jimmy said, and he stared off into a community of tall cacti that seemed to be encroaching like space aliens.

Ann thought she would never understand why Jimmy felt unworthy.

The average Stanford student or professor felt superior in some way. But both she and Jimmy felt something lacking in themselves, and together they tried to fit their broken pieces into a whole. She believed that this was the chemistry that brought them together. But now she imagined a multitude of microscopic cactus spines separating them.

"I don't deserve you," he repeated.

"Poppycock," she said. Big, teary blobs ran down her face.

Ann flew to Kentucky for two weeks, taking with her *Humphry Clinker*, *Tristram Shandy*, and the one-volume complete tragedies of Shakespeare. Both she and Jimmy were taking the summer to read for the exam. Jimmy's deferment wouldn't be affected because he was still enrolled. Two weeks on the farm in a post-acid daze made Ann feel warmly attached to her family, as if she need never leave. She saw her parents through Jimmy's eyes as she imagined bringing him there. But when she imagined hoeing tomatoes and canning green beans for the next fifty years, she was glad to return to California.

Hopewell, Ky.
July 17, 1967

Dear Ann,

When you were here, you acted like you didn't know us. I know your studies are a big responsibility and you have to keep your scholarship, but book learning's not everything.

You read your books all day and was up all hours, so I didn't hardly get to see you. I wanted us to go to Paducah to the white sales. You can get some good prices this time of year, and I know you needed some towels.

You didn't hardly mention your boyfriend, just that you weren't going to see him for a while. I know you must be heartbroke, but you'll get over it.

But I have to tell you that you hurt me when you said I couldn't possibly understand what you were doing in school. That book you had your nose in the whole week—all I did was ask a question.

You said it so quick maybe you didn't mean it, but you made me feel dumb. You made me feel like I didn't know you. I was so full I couldn't say anything then. I know I haven't got an education, but we worked hard to make sure you did so your life won't be as hard as ours. I don't know if an educa-

tion can teach everything you need to know. Maybe there are some things that are not in those books. I was hurt, but I'm not mad. I'll get over it.

Love always,

Mama

Chicago
July 18, 1967

Dear Ann,

I don't know how long I'll be in Chicago. My grandmother is sick and I want to see her as much as I can. I was always very fond of her, and I'm worried. And my dad has kept me busy. I'm doing some research for him on the history of medical malpractice, so I go to the library every day, and here at home I get the chance to swim twice a day, so that's a boon.

I'm glad we didn't part on bad terms. I didn't want to make you cry. You were so understanding, and I know I can always trust you. I liked what you wrote about trusting me to figure out what I'm doing. I hope we are both taking the time to reflect on our relationship while we devour that scrumptious reading list. What a crock. I can't fathom what is the good of knowing some of this vapid, jejune, submental folderol from bygone days. "Thanatopsis!" But Chekhov is good. And "Piers Plowman" is unexpectedly hilarious. A vision of a "fair field full of folk" is irresistible. I thought of your father, the *quintessential yeoman farmer, tilling and reaping.*

I'm reading Siddhartha by Herman Hesse. It's not on the list, I know, but what the hey. . . .

Patience and prudence,

Jimmy

She was surprised to learn of his attachment to his grandmother, and she wondered if he was making an excuse for staying away. She realized that although he criticized his parents mercilessly he was tied to them just as she was to her own parents. She had been shocked by her mother's letter, but it was true that in some ways her mother didn't know her. She felt Jimmy had misunderstood her too. She did not really believe he could break up with her. It would be like denying a sunrise. It had already happened; it couldn't be rerouted. Frank the psychologist said she was being melodramatic.

"What can I do to help him with that feeling of worthlessness?" she wailed.

Frank didn't want to hear about Jimmy. "Shouldn't we be looking at you? If he does want to break up, then how are you prepared to deal with it?"

Frank hadn't made her cry like that before. It seemed cruel. She believed Jimmy loved her. If he said he wasn't ready yet, by the end of the summer he surely would be. Or if not, she would be ready to assist him, to take on the burden of his indecisiveness and despair. She had not lost him, after all. It made sense that they spend some time apart. He had told her she should feel free to see others, but she wouldn't. She wondered if he would see other girls, but she couldn't believe he would. She didn't want to think about that.

The war hummed its familiar refrains. *Hey, hey, LBJ.* Jimmy had left his TV with her, but the news of body counts was depressing, so she stopped paying attention. Ann didn't need coffee that summer. She tore into the stacks of books she had accumulated for the exam. Her mind seemed clearer now, her reading more confident. Instead of cramming material to regurgitate, she read attentively, without becoming diverted by longing for Jimmy. It took effort to tear herself away from an absorbing novel. She read slowly, drawn in by the astonishing brutality of an Icelandic saga, or the quiet beauty of a Shakespeare sonnet. Her old habit had been to grasp the gist of a work and go on, hurtling through bundles of material like an Evelyn Wood speed-reading demon. But now every facet of the kaleidoscopic display of Western literature shimmered with psychedelic significance, sensory impact, uniqueness. Bites of catnip, the opposite of Jimmy's "submental folderol." *Folles de rôles*, she thought. The languorous rhythms of Dylan Thomas made her forget to eat. She could halt on a glittering passage and imagine the author dreaming it up— trampolining for joy. Whitman and the lilacs, Woolf and the lighthouse, Poe and the raven.

Chicago
July 24, 1967

Dear Ann,

I had a fight with my dad, who I think is a hypo-
crite and a coward. But never mind. My mother is
the nutcase! The pair of them deserve each other.
I'm starting to see the dark humor in their marriage. I'm in my old room, with all my model trains
and planes. It's a kid's room. They still see me that
way. And they don't see how obvious their lies are
beneath their smooth facade. If the country club
knew the TRUTH, they would have to kill themselves, I guess. I'm exaggerating, but it's like Mom
would flip out if someone thought she hadn't made
the bed that morning or sent a thank-you note for
some crappy present. I embarrass them no end. In
the living room Mom has a framed graduation photograph of me in a suit. She introduced me to a
golfer lady and then showed her the picture. She
said, "This is what my son really looks like—if he'd
cut that hair. Blah blah." I just walked out of the
room. . . .

Chip sent me a Grateful Dead album. Oh man!

Love,

J

Jimmy wasn't a great writer of love letters, she realized. He could have quoted a whole Shakespeare sonnet by heart if he had wanted to. She wished he would declare his feelings more effusively; his reticence made her restrained, not wanting to push herself at him. Girls traditionally were supposed to play hard to get, but this was Jimmy, she reasoned, and with Jimmy it was always real, not games.

When Ann pulled into her parking spot, she saw a police car driving away from the landlady's house. Jingles, standing on the side porch next to her giant pot of elephant ears, was speaking with Sanjay. She clutched a light, frothy shawl around her sunflower sundress.

"Mrs. Sokolov had a robbery," Sanjay said when Ann approached. "She is very upset."

Jingles barely glanced at Ann. "It was my husband's favorite possession. He bought it in Spain, when we worked there. It reminded us of Russia."

"A sculpture," Sanjay said. He indicated the broken window near the back of the house.

"You've seen it," Jingles said to Ann. "You see it every time you pay the rent."

"Have I?"

"The ballet dancer. It was like a Degas, only better. Georgiy always thought it was superior."

There was so much clutter in Jingles's house, Ann could not call the dancer to mind. Apparently the burglar had reached through a lace curtain and grabbed the statue. Jingles surmised that little barbed buttons on the dancer's bodice had clung to the curtain and the robber ran off—curtain rod, curtain, and all.

"He didn't expect the curtain to stick to the dancer," Jingles said.

"The curtain rod was found in the alley," said Sanjay.

"Did you hear a car drive off?" Ann asked.

"I heard the window break and then a thud like a stone when the table fell. I had to make my way from the front room upstairs and down the stairs. I wasn't very fast. And I wasn't scared, until now." She coughed, then adjusted the decorative tortoiseshell comb in her bleached hair.

"Don't be frightened, Mrs. Sokolov," said Sanjay. "It appears that the burglar had seen the dancer and knew where it was. That was his goal."

"Everyone here has seen my little dancer," Jingles said. "I keep the curtain there so no one can see it from outside, so whoever stole it has been in the house."

Jingles seemed to be growing more upset even as Sanjay tried to reassure her. She dusted an elephant ear with two fingers.

"It could be in one of the apartment units right now."

Ann and Sanjay looked at each other. Sanjay turned to Jingles, who was teetering on the top step.

"Mrs. Sokolov, I am going to bring you my special curry this evening. You must lie down and rest, and do not worry about your dinner. I will bring it."

Pixie remembered the ballerina statue.

"It was nothing like a Degas dancer," she told Ann.

"It was made of plaster or something. Ceramic, maybe, and it was bright colors. The skirt was orange and the girl had a pigtail coiled around the top of her head like a bird's nest. Unforgettable."

Ann said, "I never noticed it."

One afternoon, Chip dropped by to check on Ann. He was staying at Jimmy's place and teaching a course called Cybernetics through the Ages at the Free University. He wasn't seeing Pixie now. He was going out with a girl named Amy, an undergrad history major who he said could whistle Brahms concertos and had a tattoo on her butt. "She's into growing orchids," he had said. "I don't know how she does that in a dorm."

Chip sat at the table. Ann wiped up spilled sugar.

"I know you like hot tea, so I'm going to make some for you."

"Sure thing, thanks." He drummed his fingers on the table. "What are you listening to these days?" he asked.

"The Airplane, the Doors. The usual." But *Sgt. Pepper* made her anxious, plunged her into uneasy thoughts about the day of the trip. "Jimmy likes that Grateful Dead album you sent him."

Chip recommended some new Bay Area groups. In her flurry of reading for the exam, Ann had not been listening to the radio.

"What do you think is going on with Jimmy?" she asked after she had poured boiling water onto the tea. The tea was loose leaves of Darjeeling. Pixie had given her the teapot, an apology for saying Jimmy was a jerk for going to Chicago without Ann.

"I've known Jimmy three years, and he's always been restless, full of questions."

"Did he have another girlfriend?"

"Oh, he went out with plenty of girls, but he didn't seem to get serious about one till there was you."

"Really? Why is he in Chicago? I was afraid there was some girl back home."

"No. He never wants to go there." Chip ran his hand through his unruly hair. "I talked to him long-distance the other day."

"He hasn't called me."

"I called him to find out something about the gas stove. I should have just called the landlord."

Ann checked the teapot. It was Japanese with little blue kimonos on it. Ann was Jimmy's only real girl-friend. That thought reassured her.

"He said he had a fight with his dad," she said. "I guess he meant argument. I don't know what about."

"It probably started with his hair and proceeded to how much money it's costing to keep him in school and went on to why he didn't enter a worthwhile field, like medicine or law. I think he makes Jimmy feel like shit."

"Then why is he in Chicago?" Ann decided the tea was ready, and she poured it into the small blue cups that belonged with the kimono teapot.

"Do you have any milk?"

"No. I'm out."

He shrugged and dipped his spoon into the sugar bowl.

"Chip, tell me, what do you think is going to happen? I can't tell. I was afraid he wanted to break up, but in his letters he says he cares about me and he loves me. Why isn't he here?"

"Jimmy's very complex," Chip said. He tested his tea. "He's too sensitive."

"What happened to him on that trip?"

"He got something in his head." Chip bowed his head and shook it slowly. "I always think Jimmy's younger than he is. He's a kid. An idealist."

"He's all balled up inside," she said. "That's what my mother would say. I guess that's a yarn metaphor. She'd say his hair wouldn't fit in a bushel basket."

Chip laughed. "What would she say about me if she met me?"

"She'd say you're a sight for sore eyes. If you just got out of bed, she'd say you looked ragged."

"That's my natural look."

Chip's crooked lower teeth and sweet grin were endearing, Ann thought.

After he finished his tea and they had listened to some Joni Mitchell songs, Chip stood up to go. He said, "You call me if you need to talk, O.K.?"

"Thanks, Chip. That's very nice of you."

"You're welcome."

"Do you want Jimmy's TV? I'm not watching it."

"Nah, I have too much studying to do, and I get the news from the radio."

"It's better not to look at the news."

"Do you do all your studying here?" Chip surveyed her dismal digs. Still no curtains.

"Mostly."

"Don't you ever take your book outside or to the library—some other place?"

"Why?"

"It would be good to have a change of scene," he said.

"All my notes and folders and notebooks and my typewriter? It's too complicated."

"Especially the typewriter," he said, nodding at her blue Smith Corona.

"It weighs twenty-six pounds."

"It's odd that you know that."

Chip's bike was in the shop, so Ann drove him home. Seeing Jimmy's little house again made her anxious. She could imagine moving into it with Jimmy when he returned. The front porch had a blooming vine she hadn't noticed before, a bounty of pink flowers climbing up the column of the portico. A tuxedo cat dashed into the shrubbery when Chip closed the car door.

Pixie was at the door as soon as Ann returned. "Was that Chip?"

"Yes, I drove him home. He walked over here after his class."

"I guess we're really through, then," Pixie said, with a sad-clown frown. "Did he mention me?"

"No, he came to check on me."

Ann cleared the table and offered Pixie some tea. Pixie declined and Ann rinsed out the teapot.

Pixie edged toward the door. "I saw Jingles," she said abruptly. "She's filing an insurance claim. She says that dancer's worth five thousand dollars. I would have said junk-shop rubbish."

"I have no idea what things like that are worth." Ann dried the exterior of the teapot. She knew Pixie had paid $4.99 for the tea set. The sticker was on the bottom.

"I grew up in an apartment full of knickknacks,"

Pixie said. "Jingles said Sanjay brought her some curry. Humph! Curry." Pixie twirled on her toes like a ballerina as she left.

The Vietnam War seemed nearer, like an approaching drumbeat. Everyone against the war was showing it in the way they dressed, the way they talked. Ordinary people didn't know what was happening, did they? The Dylan song resonated with new meaning. With the Doors blasting on her stereo, Ann stayed up late with one or another archaic tome on the reading list. Sometimes she suddenly asked herself why she was reading this or that text. Why? Jimmy was right to question the reading list. All summer she was in limbo, longing for his return. She wondered if his mother was washing his pink underpants, or if they had a maid.

Chicago
July 31, 1967

Dear Ann,

You must stop bewailing your dearth of sophistication. First, it's not true. You are sophisticated in your own way, even if your dad didn't have two cars and you weren't in a sorority and didn't live in town. You know more than I do about a lot of stuff. Furthermore, I sense that you're beginning to stand up to Pixie. Good for you!

I'd like to take you for a ride on the el, the elevated train that goes around the city. I love the city from that angle. I didn't realize how much I'd missed it. I want to show it to you sometime. I finished "Piers Plowman," and it made me remember a time when I was in the hospital. I got very sick one winter. They thought I was going to die, apparently, but they didn't tell me what was wrong with me. I overheard my dad say to Mom, "He won't live to be fifteen if he doesn't get over this." I was about nine, so fifteen seemed positively ancient to me. I still don't know what I had exactly, but I got over it and it never came up again. There was a man in the ward who had gangrene and they had to amputate his leg. Afterwards, he lay there in a stupor, moaning now and then that he could feel his leg and that it was still in pain. What's more, he could still smell the awful rotten odor of gangrene. I could smell it too! I told him so. I was in that room with him for a week. And the smell never went away. I'm still haunted by that man with gangrene. He was a farmer, from the cornfields down in Illinois, and he had caught his leg in some machinery. I will never forget how he lay there, with absolutely nothing to do. He didn't like talking, and he wouldn't read. He was a man who had never thought of reading a book. He was used to working, making things, fixing things, and his world was totally upended. I was there in my bed, a busy boy with my books and comics and games. I couldn't even get him to play a game of chess with me. I was wide-awake and occupied with my childish pastimes, but they said I was sick. I think I had a cough, maybe pneumonia. I have thought about that man often, about what you would do if you couldn't do what you were used to, or what you wanted to do. I blamed him and judged him for years. How could he be so narrow? But more recently—I think because of what you tell me about your dad—I've thought he must have had a lot in his head, a lot of wisdom that enabled him to lie there in bed and take what came, to accept it. He must have felt he had been stripped of his manhood. He must have felt a profound emptiness, his whole purpose gone. But he resisted with all his might. And I've come to admire him. He'd have to be very strong to be so stoic. I thought he should have been open to a game of chess, but now I see that he may very well have been embarrassed because he didn't know chess.

This is the kind of thing you dwell on when you go home for a while! You can't go home again. I know.

Love,
Jimmy

Ann, grateful for his encouragement, wrote Jimmy pages and pages of thoughts about her reading, while trying not to be too forward about her feelings for him. She didn't want to pressure him. After Mama's anguished letter, Ann renewed the biblical vow to honor parents. Jimmy's contempt for his parents was unthinkable to her. She tried to encourage him to see their good points. But in his view, his parents were basically dishonest. The way his father laughed about his patients as though they were gullible guinea pigs, his mother's fake hospitality, the hypocrisy of their suburban mores. They wore false-faces like pagan gods.

Chicago
August 6, 1967

Dear Ann,

I have to look at things straightforwardly, without playing games, and yet I know that I am always withholding, always courting mystery and hiding what I'm thinking. I know that. It is one reason I didn't want to be with you for a while. It is so embarrassing to be this way, to recognize my deficiencies and to make you put up with them or even to deceive you with things I don't say. I struggle with this and wish I could be as honest as I expect everyone else to be. Sound effect: big sigh. How did you ever get involved with me, Sugar Snooks? I'm nuts—you know I am. I look at the world and expect it to have some standards and consistency, and yet I know I fall short myself.

Please bear with me. I will keep working at it. I appreciate what you say about the enormous privileges I've had, and maybe I'm not grateful, but is it really a privilege to be conditioned by these maniacs who worship the almighty dollar and think they're better than other people? I know it's indecent to complain about being well off, but I think money is the root of the problem. My dad is raking

in the dough while gossiping behind his patients'
backs. That's wrong. I know I should be more for-
giving, as you suggest, and I'm giving some thought
to that. . . . Here I am, reading Eldridge Cleaver's
prison diaries in Ramparts and wondering, will
there ever be justice in this world? . . .

Love,
Jimmy

Ann was questioning everything too—questioning authorities, rejecting expectations. She was still angry with Yvor Winters for ever making her feel small, angry with Frank the psychologist for questioning her love for Jimmy, angry with Pixie for being so critical. But she was afraid her rebellious streak was flimsy.

When she went to pay rent to Jingles, who was surly and sullen, Ann thought about how difficult it would be to be a landlady. Jingles not only had been robbed but was being deceived. She didn't know that Ann had repainted the pink walls or that Pixie had dumped pink rocks on the bathroom tile. It seemed that there was a big-top show taking place and that Jingles the erstwhile acrobat was missing it. Ann got a whiff of incense inside Jingles's house. It was the same fragrance that came from Pixie's apartment.

"Is that incense?" Ann asked. "It seems familiar."

"Sandalwood. I bought it in the Haight. I went there with Sanjay, your downstairs neighbor." Jingles regarded her skeptically, as if realizing she had told too much.

"I went there with Pixie last week," Ann said. She had not seen Sanjay's girlfriend, Paula, in many weeks.

The Haight-Ashbury hubbub was appealing, yet daunting. Ann and Pixie had sauntered through head shops and Indian import stores. They bought cheap jewelry, sniffed the grass fumes in the air, surveyed the extravagant costumes. Psychedelic music drifted from doorways.

Jingles, standing with arms akimbo, said, "I don't know why those kids in the Haight want to be so dirty."

"Any word of your ballerina?" Ann asked.

"I'll never see it again."

She folded Ann's check and saw her out the door. The plastic flowers in the hallway seemed dusty and grubby. The rear window had been repaired.

After typing several term papers for sixty cents a page, Ann was able to buy two embroidered tunics from the India store next to the restaurant in Palo Alto where she had eaten with Jimmy and Chip the night of the acid trip. She bought a puzzle ring and an Indian bedspread, which she understood already to be clichés. She taped a poster from the Fillmore to her wall.

She was jotting down ideas for a paper, "From 'Kubla Khan' to *Sgt. Pepper.*" It might lead to her dissertation. But Professor MacLean, her new adviser, told her she would have to take more courses in nineteenth-century British before she could ever presume to travel that road between two disparate time periods. Not disparate at all, she fretted. They overlapped intriguingly. She remembered Jimmy playing with tape loops.

Meredith and John invited her to a patio party, a cookout, but Ann declined, saying she had to write a paper. Instead, she wrote a six-page letter to Jimmy about her new psychedelic interpretation of "Kubla Khan."

Chicago
August 10, 1967

Dear Ann,

I will be in Chicago a while longer. My grandmother is not doing well. Mom is distraught and doesn't see how she is affecting everybody with her delusions. But my grandma is a wise old soul, and I think Mom just couldn't live up to her example. When Grandma was in her twenties, she was a flapper, or at least that's how I've imagined her, straight out of a Fitzgerald novel, but now I realize she was too old to be a flapper. She must have been born way back in the nineteenth century. During the Depression, she worked at Midway Airport, and during World War II, she worked on the Navy Pier, where they were training sailors. I try to get her to talk about those old days, but it exhausts her.

I would like to have her grace and emotional strength. Her skin is sort of yellow, and she shakes. She's really old, over eighty, I think. When I was little, she used to take me to the airport to watch planes take off and land. "One day you will fly a plane yourself," she said. But somehow that never appealed to me. I am so restless in my flight.

Always searching for the meaning of things. Never satisfied!

I'm intrigued by what Hesse says about nature, how each thing always has an opposite and you can't have one without the other. It's chilling to think that a peach is both real and an illusion. I still feel bad that I jumped all over Pixie and the I Ching. I'm not for a minute mystical or religious. I'm more interested in ethics and possibility—what should one do? On what basis? How do we decide what is true, or what is the right thing to believe? Is there a right belief? My head spins around sometimes. Sometimes I feel Heraclitus was the wisest— you can't dip a paw in the same river twice.

Yesterday Grandma told me some extraordinary things, which only underline everything I've been saying about this fucked-up family.

Mom always said her father died when she was an infant and she had no memory of him, but Grandma told me he died when Mom was twenty. So what was going on? I probed Grandma a bit, and she blurted out the whole story. Apparently my mother's older sister, my Aunt Betty, got pregnant in high school. There was so much shame. The young man was a poor immigrant, a Czech. And her father, my grandfather, forced her to leave home. He made her go away and put the kid up for adoption. Grandma thought that was extreme and she tried to get him to relent, but he wouldn't. Aunt Betty went off to some town in Wisconsin for several months. Grandma was heartbroken, and I think she indulges me because she never got to know her other grandson. She doesn't think Aunt Betty ever told the man she eventually married— Uncle Ross, a real-estate lawyer. She settled into a quiet, repressed suburban existence where everything is swept under the rug. Or sucked up with the Electrolux.

Grandma told me this with tears in her eyes. I think she decided it was time to just let it all hang out. She's old, with nothing to lose. I loved her for telling me this. And now I know I have a Czech cousin somewhere!

I'm with Thoreau. You've got to face facts, live deliberately.

I've been working with a neighbor roofing his garage. That's very satisfying to me. I'm reading Aeschylus, ran through the Elizabethan stuff in a hurry, couldn't bear Alex Pope, that old rapist, and am deep into War and Peace. That goes surprisingly fast. I'm glad you're enjoying Ford Madox Ford—don't you love that name? I miss you, Snooks.

I'm lonely without you, and I'm sorry I ever hurt you. Someday I'll make you proud of me. I wish I could do that now. That reminds me. I have a big surprise for you.

Love,
Jimmy

Ann was disappointed that he did not mention her psychedelic "Kubla Khan," but otherwise she regarded his letter as a true love letter. Frank the psychologist agreed that Jimmy wrote a good letter. Later, she thought that Frank was trying to suggest that what she wanted to believe was true was not necessarily the same as what was true.

Ann encountered Sanjay one afternoon as she arrived home from the library with a fresh pile of books. He invited her in for tea and helped settle her books onto the table.

"You have an overload," he said.

"Yes, I barely made it across campus to the car."

Smelling the sandalwood, she wondered just what kind of trip he had made with Jingles to the Haight. He turned on his teakettle and selected a box of tea from several on a shelf.

"What do you think of my Indian outfit?" she asked. She was wearing a purple tunic with silvery trim and her water buffalo sandals.

"I am amused by the rage for India. But it is very nice that you admire our style." He smiled. "The exports are good for India."

"Pixie has a teak elephant the size of a Great Dane."

Ann noticed a small wooden Buddha on Sanjay's desk. His apartment was neat and tasteful, unlike her apartment, which held nothing of interest, nothing artistic. If she typed some more papers, she might buy a Buddha or an Indian-print tablecloth.

"Are you familiar with water buffaloes?" she asked, displaying her sandals.

"Oh, yes. These are popular here now. The protestors like them."

"What do you think of the war in Vietnam, Sanjay?"

"I don't judge the individual," he said. "The soldiers. But the war is not good."

"How do they see us in India?"

"We are always looking at America," he said. He placed two small yellow cups on the table. "America is so powerful, and when we see America become involved in a place where it does not know the people—the customs, the history—then we worry. But I can't speak for everyone. India is a large country, with many points of view."

"Do you want to stay here after you get your degree?"

"Probably." His smile was broad, showing his gums. "There are many opportunities for research. And I always want to find out things."

He lifted the teapot and began to pour. "This is a tea for peace," he said.

One afternoon, following Chip's advice, Ann drove
to Foothills Park. There were few people in the park
except for workmen repairing trails. She found an attractive clearing near the parking area. After brushing
away the rough debris from beneath a eucalyptus tree,
she spread a towel on the ground, which was soft and
springy. She had brought an egg-salad sandwich and
a Coca-Cola. She read about half of Samuel Butler's
Erewhon. The Beatles song "Nowhere Man" played in
her head. Her eyes followed a line of large ants trek-
king to a heap of wood chips. Some kind of wood-
pecker rat-a-tat-tatted. An airplane droned. She kept
remembering the acid trip with Jimmy—playing at
the redwoods park, balancing on the fallen log. Something had changed that day, something that caused
Jimmy to leave. The acid had walloped her, but it left
no dark mysteries.

Erewhon was forgettable, satire on a time gone by.
She skimmed, then tried reading Boethius. She had
plunged into the reading list with no particular plan,
just flitting around among many styles and periods.
She was still glowing from Jimmy's recent letter, his
love letter. Although she was warmed by his report
about his grandmother's confession, his problems with
his family seemed overblown. Shouldn't he be more

understanding of his mother now that he knew about her sister's past trouble? He was free. He didn't have to sleep in a room with his toy trains.

She left Foothills Park late in the afternoon, intending to go down Sand Hill Road to find the Palo Alto Tree, the towering sequoia that Albert had urged her to visit. When she went there in April, she had been too excited about Jimmy—his hair, his warm hands—to consider why the parallel journeys of the explorers Boone and Portola stirred Albert so much. There seemed to be an almost mystical significance for him.

Just after she turned left on Junipero Serra, the car began vibrating and an awful racket from the engine, a hammering and clanging, shook the car. The engine quit. She managed to pull onto the shoulder below an embankment and glide on the grass to a stop. The car was silent. The ignition did nothing. Grabbing her purse, she made her way up the embankment in her floppy sandals, the scrub grass scratching her ankles. She could see some buildings ahead—a gas station and a small market. She was hot from the walk, and her ankles itched. At the market, after using the restroom, she bought a Coke, then asked for a telephone. As she searched the Yellow Pages for mechanics and tow trucks, she pondered whether to call Pixie, or perhaps

Meredith and John. But maybe a wrecker would let her ride in his truck. Ann had taken her car to a mechanic in Palo Alto, but she could not remember his name or the name of his business.

Ann was relieved to see a highway patrol car arrive outside and a tall officer emerge.

"Can you help me, please? My car broke down." She pointed past the street to the embankment and the highway below.

"Old black Chevy?"

"Yes, you saw it?"

"I called in a report," he said. "Why did you leave it?"

"I had to get help."

"You should have stayed with the vehicle."

Ann was embarrassed. How was she to know? She had never had a breakdown, but now she had an inkling of what her parents had worried about when she took off in that old junk heap for California by herself.

The patrolman suggested a certain wrecker and waited while she made the call. The wrecking company seemed to know the place in Palo Alto where she had had her car repaired once. She finished her Coke and left the bottle.

In no more than half a minute, the patrolman sped her to her car to wait for the wrecker. She gathered her belongings from the front seat.

"I'll give you a ride," he said. "I'm not supposed to, but I'm going that way."

He was slim with a hard mouth. She had heard that these patrolmen were called the CHIP guys, for the California Highway Patrol.

As she watched her aged car disappear behind the wrecker, reared up like a horse on its hind legs, she felt as if a string of unaccountable losses was piling up—Jingles's dancer, Sanjay's girlfriend, Jimmy off in Chicago. And the GIs in Vietnam, she thought a moment later. She thought of what Jimmy had said about Heraclitus. Things change.

The patrol car, with the CHIP lettering, was long and sleek, with a busy dashboard. Mesh grid separated the front and back. The tall CHIP guy locked her door. He could have shut her in the back like a prisoner, she thought as he flew into traffic.

"Oh, you drive fast!"

"Routine," he said. He adjusted his visor and rearview mirror.

"Where were you driving from?"

"Foothills Park."

"Weren't you afraid?"

"No. Should I have been?"

"Something to think about. You know, a young,

pretty girl needs to be a little more careful. Things can happen."

"What things?"

"I think you know what things."

He zoomed through a yellow light and screeched to a stop at the next red light.

"Did you hear about the bombing?" he asked.

"No. Where?"

"LBJ bombed Hanoi. It's about time, I say."

"I don't have a car radio. I may not even have a car."

"I've got to hand it to him, supporting our guys like that. We have to remember what we're fighting for."

"What's that?"

"We're fighting against communism, of course! Don't you follow the news?"

"You said we were fighting *for* something. Then you said *against*."

"We're fighting for the American way! What's wrong with you college students? College kids are just afraid of getting drafted! I'd go if they'd let me."

"Well, maybe that would suit you."

The CHIP guy left her at the corner of her street, and she walked through the back alley. Her parking place seemed forlorn. She noticed an oily patch on the pavement where her car had been. The black spot was shining with rainbows.

Ann had to pay fifty dollars to have her car junked. The oil had run dry, and the noise she had heard was thirsty pistons clanging, the death rattle of the car. She could not remember the last time she had checked the oil. She signed her car over to the mechanic, Al Wesson. She should have remembered his name. Her mother used Wesson oil to fry chicken. Was it synchronicity if you hadn't noticed?

"I wish I could fix it for you, dear," Al said. "But the engine's shot. A car can't run without oil, and if it runs out it just bangs itself to death."

He offered her a ride home, but she said she'd walk.

"I'll have to get used to it," she said.

"I can round up a used car for you, dear. I can get you a good deal."

Dear?

"What will you do without a car?" Pixie asked. She was playing the Who and burning incense. Ann still didn't get the incense fad, the point of it.

"I don't know. Stay in my room and study, I guess."

"I'll take you anywhere you have to go. Just let me know. But you'll need wheels sooner or later."

"Will I? I can take the bus to campus, and the grocery is only two blocks."

"What about a bike?"

"Maybe."

Ann felt utterly foolish. She hadn't grabbed the big picture—a working automobile. There was no excuse for being careless about her car, not thinking to check the oil. She had been sitting beneath a eucalyptus, oblivious to its majesty and its history. She had been reading books, retreating into another century.

Hopewell, Ky.
August 10, 1967

Dear Ann,

Your daddy was out cutting down a dead tree in an electric storm. When he started in on it, there wasn't a cloud in the sky. He was having trouble with it, trying to get it to fall the direction he wanted it, and he kept hacking at it, first one side then another. I was watching from the window when it come up a cloud and there was lightning and thunder before he could get it down. I was a wreck, watching from the window. But he got the job done! He come in soaking wet, saying his Sunday-School lessons (ha ha!). . . .

Love,
Mama

Chicago
August 20, 1967

Dear Ann,

Dad took me sailing Saturday. He got a new boat last year, a twenty-one-foot sloop. He's very happy about it because the fittings are the latest. He has to keep up with the Davy Joneses, you know. I told him he should have a mermaid figurehead, or some scrimshaw work on the fiberglass prow, or at least a few whale teeth, but he just glowered at my blasphemy.

Out on Lake Michigan, you understand how Walden can be a mere pond, even though when you're at Walden you'd call it a lake. When you go out a certain distance, Lake Michigan seems like an ocean, and it can be quite dangerous, but I always felt, even when I was a kid, that there was something landlocked about it. I always wanted to know why—why sail in a loop out in Lake Michigan? It was not fulfilling to me. It wasn't like the Irish boarding those ships and escaping the peat bogs. They had a goal.

Although I realize now that I really love sailing— the challenge of dealing with the air and the wind and the water—when I was a kid it became just a matter of humoring Dad and his hobby. By the time I was in high school, summer Sundays on the boat got to be an obligation, and all through college I was contemptuous of it. Mom liked the sailing outfits and the picnic basket. She liked the idea of sailing more than sailing itself. She liked having cocktails at the yacht club, but on board she was likely to sneak down into the cabin and take a nap.

Dad and I must have sailed hundreds of hours together through the years, but I don't remember ever talking about anything. He has the kind of assurance that means you don't need to discuss anything since all the answers are laid out. That always stifled me. I was too full of questions. He'd complain if I tried to read a book when it was calm. Dad loved those books about lone adventurers like Joshua Slocum, who sailed alone around the world, but he wasn't really an adventurer himself. He liked the equipment, outfitting the boat.

I thought about all that when we sailed on Saturday. We didn't talk, just nautical terms like "coming about" and "jibe ho" and "shiver me timbers." I liked the wind on my face and the physical sensations of working the sails. I liked seeing other boats come close, the people waving.

We were out there about three hours and we made small talk, and then we got into an argument about Martin Luther King. I told him how King linked racism and poverty to Vietnam when he spoke at Stanford. King said, "Riots are the language of the unheard." And Dad just shrugged. And he said, "Think of where they'd be now if we hadn't built this great nation with their help." He said he didn't mean anything critical. He was just saying that's how it was, in slave times. He wasn't going to lose any sleep over it. A remark like that just fills me with hopelessness.

When I questioned him, Dad did what he always does when you cross him. He closed his lips really tight and made his steely face. There was both rage and smugness on his face. It was impenetrable. I can't think of any literary character like him. But I kept thinking about Odysseus and Columbus and the Vikings, all those great sea voyagers. I probably think too much in terms of epic journeys.

You said I shouldn't hate my parents. I know I said once that I did.

I don't really, I guess. You're right that I'm tied to them. They are a major part of who I am, but

*that just makes me hate myself. I don't want to turn
into a boring yachtsman in a dapper cap spouting
scuttlebutt from the poop deck.*

Anchors aweigh, my love,

Jimmy

Hopewell, Ky.
August 21, 1967

Dear Ann,
That cat Whistle Britches got killed on the road in front of the barn. Your daddy found him when he got the tractor out. He threw him in the ditch. He was out mowing in the sun and nearly had a heat stroke. It come a scorcher. I cooked lima beans for dinner with scalloped potatoes and the rest of a shoulder I had been whittling at all week. All evening I set in the breeze on the porch and shelled beans. Then for supper I made a blackberry pie. I know how you love that. Wish I could send you some! Ha ha! Your little brother has been up to no good. He's girlfriending already! One of the McKinley girls from school. He saw her at Ed's barbecue joint and I think they're sparking. Your daddy said he had to wait till he could drive before he could go on dates.
You didn't say much about your boyfriend when you were here last. I hope he came back to you and you're still happy with him. If he's the right one, that is. If not, there's plenty of fish in the sea. . . .

Love,
Mama

Jimmy returned several days before the exam. He had driven from Chicago in just under three days, crossing the Sierras at night. It was a long, lonesome trip, he said, and Ann thought about the melancholy stretch of desert she had driven across the previous summer. Jimmy's car had a radio, though.

He had written to expect him sometime that day, and she was waiting, with her hair fresh and combed. It fell nearly to her shoulders now. She wore one of her new Indian tunics. When she spied his dust-streaked car from the window, she refrained from running down the stairs to greet him. But at the door, they flew at each other in a joyful embrace, like lovers at the end of a movie.

"There'll be a quiz after," he murmured, as they rolled onto her little bed.

They dug into each other, grasping and gasping. His hair was a blanket. She wrapped her face in it, a curl tickling her nose. He tasted of cigarettes and mint. He jerked her skirt down her legs and over her feet, her panties following. She unzipped his jeans, and in moments all of their clothes were on the floor.

Being with Jimmy again was like swinging on stars. His pliable, strong body moved like a healthy young cat—fluid, expert. Their hips locked together in a motion that made her visualize wheels. They both said "I love you" to each other. The bed was hard but noiseless. He stayed inside her for a long time, holding her tight, their bellies slapped together. They lay face-to-face, on their sides, holding each other quietly. After a while, when they sat up against the pillows, he told about the drive across the mountains, the songs he listened to, the way he had missed her. The summer with his parents was like an A-bomb test site, he said. He got out before the blast. His grandmother was better. He was glad he'd had the time with her. His parents, he had realized, would never change, and he gladly left them there in Suburb, America.

"My parents don't know anything I'm doing," she said. "I live in two worlds."

"But your parents are authentic. I keep telling you that."

"You haven't met them."

"But I know they're real and true. Your dad has a tractor."

"A neighbor got his foot cut off in a tractor accident. I guess that's real."

"Don't make fun of me."

"I'm sorry."

"It's O.K."

They showered together in the dim light of the burgundy bathroom. It was like being in a dark, cozy cave, bathing in a warm stream. They soaped each other and rubbed against each other. His penis, pink and sudsy, flew up, at attention.

"Not again!" Jimmy said. "Behave yourself!"

Ann greeted the intruder. "Hello, there!"

"He has been very excited about seeing you," Jimmy said, "All across the Great Plains he couldn't sit still."

After the shower, Jimmy fumbled with the top button of his jeans. His striped summer shirt looked like something his mother might have bought him, Ann thought. She had noticed his new white underpants.

"Did your car really die? And you're walking everywhere?"

"It's O.K. Pixie gives me a ride sometimes. Or Sanjay, downstairs."

Jimmy lit a cigarette, his first since his reappearance.

"Let's go see what kind of shape my place is in."

"Do you want to take the TV? I didn't watch it much."

"No, you keep it."

Ann tidied her hair and stocked her bag with what she called *overnighties*.

"I wasn't making fun of you," she said as they went out the door.

"I know."

Chip had gone away for the week so that Jimmy and Ann could have Jimmy's house in private. He had dropped Amy and impulsively asked Pixie to go with him to the hot springs at Big Sur. After dark in the public pools you could get "nekkid," Chip had told Ann, which made Jimmy laugh when she told him. Ann wondered why she and Jimmy had never been to Big Sur.

Jimmy unlocked the door and they went in. It smelled of lemon polish.

"He's cleaned it up for you," Ann said.

Jimmy opened the refrigerator. "Bacon, eggs, butter, juice, bread. Wow. Good old Chip."

"I'm sure Pixie helped."

"So they hit it off after all, huh?"

"I think Pixie was hot to go to Big Sur."

Jimmy had brought only a small duffel bag of clothes and a few books. "I left *War and Peace* and all those big books in Chicago."

"Are you ready for the exam?"

"I didn't get through half the list. No, I'm not ready."

She had heard that line before—about not being ready.

"I'll take it later," he said.

He had said he loved her, but she knew something was different. It was strange that Jimmy was postponing the exam. He seemed to be clinging to her, as if afraid he would lose her. It wasn't jealousy, she thought, for she had given him no reason to doubt her. It was likely his lack of self-confidence, that troubling emptiness inside him. He was reading a Hemingway novel, which was not on the reading list. But enthusiastically he helped her to study for the exam, quizzing her and reviewing her reading and encouraging her to articulate her views on *Erewhon* and *Humphry Clinker* and other abstruse works.

That week they spent all their time—when they weren't lolling in bed—preparing her for the exam. They didn't go out. He brought Chinese food and pizza. She stayed most of the week at his house.

"You are going to blow the mind of one Yvor Winters," Jimmy said. "He is not going to believe how brilliant you are. He will be so ashamed of himself."

"I'm not worried about Yvor Winters. He's retired now anyway."

"But he's still around, casting his spell."

"I'm still mad at him over Emily Dickinson."

"They are going to waive the dissertation and offer you a professorship without blinking," Jimmy said, tweaking her ear.

"That's crazy."

"I mean it. You're good at this, a lot smarter than me."

That wasn't true. She didn't know why Jimmy was being so attentive while withholding things about himself. In his letters he had warned her that he did that, but she was reluctant to probe.

"You can do anything," Jimmy said. "Remember that."

The exam was less difficult than she had expected. Perversely, she had refused to read "Thanatopsis" and there was a lengthy question about it, but the other topics were familiar, even easy. She could have written all day about the New England Renaissance and was glad of the chance to expound on her theory of Louisa May Alcott's significance in it, even though she knew the Stanford literati would scoff. Still, she was quite sure Jimmy could have done better on the exam than she had.

"I skipped the question on 'Thanatopsis.' I didn't read it after you said it was so awful. I read it this morning. It's a horrid poem!"

"I had to memorize it in high school," said Jimmy.

"Oh, please don't recite it! It's just too dreadful."

"I'm sure there are worse."

"Probably."

"You deserve a celebration. I've got tickets at the Fillmore."

"For what?"

"Guess—"

It was Big Brother and the Holding Company with Janis Joplin.

Watching the powerful singer in her cluttered duds, Ann felt exhilarated. Since she arrived at Stanford she had been tumbling along in an inevitable rush toward something she could not define, and now for the first time she felt optimistic about her academic future. Yvor Winters could have his heyday and she could have hers. She would defiantly write about the modern mind of Samuel Taylor Coleridge—*STC Meets the Beatles*—for her dissertation. And she would throw Janis Joplin in too—the lava flow of her harsh voice, raw in its volcanic spewing. It might belong.

In the car driving home from the show, Ann and Jimmy listened to the Doors' "Light My Fire," the long version. Ann felt its turbulence and desire matching the urgency deep inside. She had heard the song so many times that she could anticipate the precise instant in the long organ interval when Jim Morrison would resume the vocal.

The day ended softly, sweetly, as she and Jimmy lay entwined in each other's arms, his hair making a pillow for her. She thought she heard rain, then remembered that it never rained here. It was the kitchen faucet dripping. It seemed attuned to the pleasure of hearing the singer at the Fillmore, like a new force of nature that echoed in Ann's memory.

She woke up in the middle of the night. Jimmy was thrashing and murmuring.

"Can't you sleep?" she asked.

"No." He went to the bathroom and peed. When he returned, she was sitting up, jarred awake.

"Do you feel all right?" she asked.

"I guess so. My mind has the collywobbles." He turned on the pole lamp by the bed.

"What are you worried about?"

He lit a cigarette and blew smoke across the room.

"Are you really awake?" he asked.

"I guess so. I'm sitting up, talking." She pulled the comforter under her chin. The ceiling fan made a cool breeze.

He rose and turned off the fan. He pulled on a T-shirt and sat on the side of the bed. He wore no pants.

"I have to do something," he said, twisting to face her. "It's why I didn't take the exam." He clasped her hand. "Promise you won't hate me."

"Why would I ever hate you?"

Slowly, he exhaled a stream of smoke like a cloud on the conversation.

"Don't hate me." He flicked the cigarette ash into the ashtray on the night table. "I told you I had to do something, and well, I did it. . . ."

"Good. Now maybe we can get a crop out—as Mama would say." She was trying to tease him, but he frowned.

"I want you to understand this, Ann. It's the hardest thing I've ever had to do, the hardest decision I've ever made, and you've got to accept it. I can't deal with it if you don't. Please don't be upset with me. I need you. Come over here. Let's get up."

He lowered her onto his reading chair by his desk and settled the comforter around her. "I'm serious. Look at me."

"What are you talking about?" She reached up and clasped his arms. "Out with it."

"I joined the army."

"What?" She pulled the tail of his T-shirt as if pulling it could silence her scream. "No! No!" She burst into a thunderclap of tears. The comforter fell from her shoulders.

"Yes, I'm afraid so."

"*Why?*"

He held her for a long time, back in the bed, while she cried herself out. She would lose him, he would die, he would be gone. This was the end.

"But you hate the war," she said, still sobbing. "We should be fighting against the war."

"But I do. I am."

"It's two years?"

"Three if you volunteer. I go in the fourteenth."

"*Why?*"

"You know why. Haven't I made that clear?"

"No." Ann knew that Jimmy had felt the draft wasn't fair to the underprivileged, but who would question a draft deferment? Chip, she remembered, had been definite about avoiding the draft.

"I thought you had been talking hypothetically," she said without meeting his eyes. Her shock had turned to a quiet fury.

He lit another cigarette. Her head was in his soft lap. They didn't speak.

"How could you do this to me?" she said finally.

He grew angry then. He had never been angry with her.

"It's a question of what I'd be doing to myself, and ultimately to both of us, if I didn't do this. You don't have to go along. You can just drop me. I may regret this, but I wanted to do it. Now I've done it."

She sat up. "Why didn't you tell me? Why did you stay away? Why did you lie to me?"

"I don't know. I'm a chicken, I guess—the same way

I used the deferment to hide. I just couldn't tell you. I didn't want to worry you and interfere with your reading for the exam."

It wasn't in her nature to scream or even to raise her voice or argue stridently. But she could bawl. She went to the bathroom and stood facing the mirror.

"Why didn't I figure this out?" she asked when her cries died down.

"Don't make me feel worse. I know I wasn't being straight with you. You know I couldn't tell you long-distance."

"But you thought I knew what you were going to do? How can I read your mind? I thought you were reading for the exam. I thought you were in Chicago with your dying grandma."

"That was all true."

"Why didn't you want to be with me?"

"I just couldn't make you worry all summer when you were supposed to be studying." He swabbed her eyes with his fingers. "I tried to break up with you, to spare you all this. But I wasn't that strong."

"I really don't understand."

"I couldn't live with myself if I kept the deferment. I would apologize a thousand times to you, but it would never begin to be enough. And you ask what is fair. Are you being fair to me?"

"What do you mean?"

"I mean what I've really been struggling with."

"What? Tell me."

"I've told you. Why should I have the advantages? I hate that. It makes me feel like some shiny frat boy with—oh, a goddamn blue Mustang. It's just not right."

"I know." She embraced him, giving in to his reasoning, but she felt helpless. Cigarette smoke, ugly and harsh, clouded the bed.

He said, "I didn't decide right away. It wasn't at all clear."

He stubbed out the cigarette in the ashtray, but a faint wisp of smoke escaped from the butt.

They were quiet for a while. Ann couldn't think of what to say. She did not understand how he could shoot somebody. She could not imagine Jimmy ever agreeing to kill.

"Now you see why I couldn't put my mind to the exam," Jimmy said. "It all seemed so irrelevant. I'll take it when I get out."

"You said you weren't ready . . . for me. Is this your way of breaking up? Is this how you wanted to do it?"

"No, no, no. I want you." He caressed her hair and lifted her chin gently. "I had thought maybe it was better to tone down things, so you wouldn't be so wrapped up in me. I didn't want you to miss me."

"But I *will* miss you. You can't change that." She stroked his hair and ran her hand along his cheek, but he didn't respond. He was somewhere else. She said, "You said you weren't ready for me. How can you be ready for war?"

"I'll be back. I'll be ready then."

They ate bowls of cereal, and Jimmy gave her coffee in his Porky Pig cup. They hadn't slept. Ann's eyes were raw from crying, and the cereal was harsh on her throat. As Jimmy tilted his bowl and drank the last of the milk, she imagined him gulping food in a mess hall.

He had signed up in July, in Chicago, and he would return there to report for duty. Since it took weeks to process an enlistment, he had decided to stay in Chicago for the summer. He had implied that staying in Chicago and not telling her was a gift to her, so she could concentrate on her exams. She had trouble focusing, he reminded her.

He hadn't enlisted immediately. There were so many pros and cons. He had walked past the recruitment office in Oak Park several times, and when he went inside to ask questions, they didn't take him seriously. He challenged them by asking why kids who couldn't read a map were being promised the moon.

He had the impression that the army wasn't interested in volunteers who asked too many questions.

Before they would accept him, Jimmy was required to take an aptitude test. "Guess what I qualified for," he asked Ann.

"I don't know. Underwater surveillance. Swimming? Tank driving? I don't know."

"Typing. I'm going to train as a clerk-typist."

"Typing? That's what *I* do."

They laughed, then howled. Jimmy touched her cheek. "You said typing was women's work. See. I'll be safe in an office filling out forms. So you won't have to worry."

She still didn't understand. "I thought you wanted to trade places with some poor boy sent into the jungle with a rifle."

When Jimmy learned that he would not be sent into the infantry, he had reconsidered. He worried that he wouldn't be taking the risk, that he would be typing up the death reports of those who had. It wasn't fair.

"Your friend John was right—they don't want guys like me. Too much education. But then I thought—if we get more educated people in there we can fight it from the inside."

Jimmy ran his fingers through his hair compulsively and tried to pull it back into a ponytail.

"I thought about the campus protests, going to jail, burning draft cards, and all that. And it seemed flimsy to me. We're all just snot-nosed, spoiled kids raised on *Leave It to Beaver* and *Father Knows Best*, and we can't imagine going off to fight. We're afraid we might stub a toe. Or touch poison ivy. And I thought about what you said about wasting the investment in education, and I wondered if I'd be throwing away my life on an immoral war just to spite my dad. I was in a quandary, and I kept reading the philosophers like someone consulting an oracle. Plato on the philosopher kings was a laugh. None of them could paint me a clear picture."

"I'm not surprised."

In the end, Jimmy simply couldn't get over his feeling that it was wrong for people in authority to be sending the disadvantaged to lay their lives on the line.

He laughed. "I know it's far-fetched, maybe absurd. But I thought if they see it's their own kids, or kids like them, going over there, they'd think twice. I can fight the military from the inside, I thought. Report what's really going on—like going undercover. I'm not sure how. Maybe I'm naive."

"That's possible."

"If five million draft dodgers suddenly joined the army, they could gum up the works from the inside. So my gesture is universalizable. Kant's moral imperative—

your actions should be universalizable. If you ask, what if millions did it . . ."

Ann, listening numbly to Jimmy's passionate outpouring, tried to follow the lines of his thinking, but they blurred. She had to admit he made a sensible case—however idealistic. It disappointed her that he hadn't bothered to consult her or Chip while agonizing over his decision. Now joining the army was a *fait accompli.* Fate.

Over the following days, as they continued to talk, Ann began to suspect that if Jimmy's father had been a military man, Jimmy would have burned his draft card or fled to Canada. But his father had avoided service in World War II because of his asthma. He didn't have asthma, Jimmy insisted.

"That's so weak," Jimmy told Ann. "I don't want to be like him."

Yet he did feel weak and unprepared for army life, he said. He knew he had been coddled. But he was physically strong because of the swimming.

Ann pointed out that Jimmy wouldn't have been born if his father had died in the war. "So you can't wish otherwise."

"But I wouldn't know the difference if I never existed," he said.

"That's an odd way to look at it."

"Sometimes I think being born during a war is a metaphor for my whole existence."

"That sounds melodramatic," she said.

Men were a mystery. She knew only that something in male nature had to take off—to be alone, to ruminate, or to go to war. Some things they couldn't do with women. They weren't ready. Odysseus shot off to the Trojan War, then dawdled on his way home to Penelope, who was weaving her tapestry over and over to keep from going mad.

Ann asked Frank the psychologist about this. She hadn't been to see him in a month, and she let it rip. If men had difficulty making commitments to women, how could they commit themselves so easily to war? Was war more important? More appealing?

"I've never seen you angry before." He rubbed his knees as if trying to get warm. "Maybe that's a good thing."

"And another thing, how can Jimmy be so self-sacrificing, so generous? Is that normal? And if he is really so moral, why did he hurt me this way? Is this supposed to be for my own good?"

"You have some very big questions," said the psychologist.

"Will they shave your head?"

"I suppose so."

"I don't want to give up your magnolious hair."

"I can cut it and give it to you before I go."

He made her laugh. "It would be a pillowcase full," she said.

She ran her fingers through his poodle locks. His hair was clean and feathery. She buried her head in it. The hair would have been so alarming to her parents if she had taken him to Kentucky. She dreaded the sight of his bare head, his curlicue curls shorn. Although she did not want to make him feel bad that he had joined the army, she found it hard to hide her disappointment, her hurt. She didn't deserve this. Yet she couldn't remain angry with him, for she saw how troubled he was, how difficult and earnest his decision had been. He seemed to share her own heartbreak, as if his choice finally was not a choice but an inevitability—like being drafted.

"Can't you get out of it somehow?" she asked one evening.

"How? Go AWOL? Shoot my foot?" He grasped her hand a little too hard. "No, I have to do it. I said I would."

"I'm giving you my car," Jimmy said. "And will you keep my books and records for me?"

"Your beautiful car?"

"My ritzy, obscene luxury symbol. I should just give it back to my dad—or shove it off the Navy Pier. But you need a car, and I want you to have it."

He seemed aware of how final these parting gifts might be. Although she insisted she was just keeping them for him, he made a point of signing the car registration over to her, just as she had signed away her oil-dry Chevrolet to Al the mechanic.

Jimmy showed her how to check the oil, and they drove to the beach with Ann behind the wheel. They said little. The day was sunny, a brilliant glare that seemed insulting. Fog would have been more appropriate.

On the return, they checked the tire pressure and picked up a pizza, but neither of them could eat.

She had a suggestion—a card game.

They played hearts, then gin rummy, which evolved into something like strip poker. They laughed all evening. How they loved to laugh, she thought later.

On campus a marching band was practicing earnestly atop Hoo Tow. The season was turning, ever so slightly. When Ann parked the Mustang at her apartment, she saw Jingles gathering litter from the base of her weeping red pepper tree. The tree was loaded with pendulous clusters of rosy berries.

Hopewell, Ky.
October 1, 1967

Dear Ann,
    I reckon you're lonesome now without your boy-
friend. I imagine that was what was bothering you
when you were here. I don't know why he had to
join up, but I know when your Daddy went in he
felt he had to, there was so much meanness in the
world. I went with him on the bus to Louisville and
didn't see him again for six months when he was on
furlow. That was the hardest time of my life, and
you were just a little thing, squalling. Everybody
said you were squalling for your daddy. I wish we
had met Jimmy before he left, but when he comes
back I bet he will be ready to pop the question . . .

Love,
Mama

The next months seemed like the fog over the Bay. Pixie moved in with Chip at Jimmy's house, and they invited Ann to share the place, but Ann wanted to be alone. On the roiling campus, demonstrations and teach-ins were continual. The antiwar crowd scorned the soldiers. Ann had never imagined herself with a soldier boyfriend. Now she had to defend a soldier—a soldier who was the unlikeliest fighter. She wondered if Jimmy's notion of sacrifice and noble service was just a fantasy, like her own ideal of romance and marriage. On alert, she walked around campus as if she were a soldier herself. Ripe pomegranates falling from the trees on campus made a gory red mess on the ground.

Her classes staggered her brain. She had lost focus. Coffee wasn't working. With a sliver of a pep pill, the first she had taken in months, she wrote a paper on T. S. Eliot—that stuffy old banker. She played Jimmy's records. His Brubeck records. Saint-Saëns. Miles.

So many of the songs on the radio that autumn were insipid.

"Incense and Peppermint"
"Daydream Believer"
"The Letter"

Fort Leonardwood, Missouri
October 28, 1967

Dear Ann,
   Greetings from Fort Lost-in-the-Woods. Viet-
nam couldn't be more desolate than these Ozark
hills. We have to learn to navigate out there in the
woods using our wits. It's so easy to get lost. And
the recruiters didn't mention snakes! . . .

Jimmy's handwriting was thorny and irregular, like
newspaper words spliced together for a ransom note.
He wrote about the ordinary—the landscape, the mess
hall, the rain. Ann couldn't picture him in a barracks with a hundred young men training for war—
slogging through mud in a swirling monsoon, with
enemies hiding in the swamp grass. She wrote to him
of pleasant things—books and music. She told him
she listened to "Danse Macabre" over and over and
read "Kubla Khan" and tried to hear his voice. She
wanted him to think of her with warmth and longing.
She wanted to be steady, strong, alluring—an Abys-
sinian girl in a song, a memory to be revived. There
was no guidebook, no etiquette prescribed for writing to a soldier. She wanted to remind him of the red-

woods, the Beatles, the beach, the movies, the car rides, the bookshelves. All of it was sentimental to her. The songs, the places, the arcades along the Quad—all he had left behind. She wondered if he had similar sentiments. Jimmy could be silly, but never trivial.

The Ozarks
November 2, 1967

Dear Ann,

I told you I could shoot, but the first time I shot an M-14 it was like a cherry bomb going off in my face. I don't know what happens to the hearing of soldiers who are out in the field for long periods.

But I will be finished with shooting at the end of eight weeks, and then I start the ultimate challenge—typing! Sorry about my handwriting. Tell me if you need help translating.

Don't worry about what that Twiggy girl says to you. It sounds like she's playing pretend soldier. You can't support the soldiers by donning our garb, nor can you protest in a fatigue jacket without being a fraud, and you can't wear the uniform and know anything about what it means until you've slogged a hundred miles through mud, and until you've had an M-14 cradled in your arms while a DI is yelling at you and calling you names until you truly want to blast him in the puss. Ha, don't I sound like the professional grunt!

Of course Chip's jumpsuit is exempt from all rules.

I liked what you said about some of Faulkner's characters sounding just like your mom and dad.

That makes them seem very real to me. What you said about your Faulkner seminar rings true. I think you're right that such things seem ridiculous now. That is how I felt, but I know that you will become a good teacher, and teaching is a life-giving force. I don't mean to sound shallow, or like I'm putting on a good front. I feel lucky to know you and to be close to you. I know I've caused you misery, but I'm hard-pressed to understand what true commitment is. It's not defined by a ring or vows or some words you're supposed to say. True commitment is not contained in symbols. And yet it is hard to know when it arrives full-blown so that it can thrive without its appurtenances. I'm not making any sense.

Trust? you ask. I trust you to write me wonderful letters, to tell me the truth, to try to understand what I'm talking about, to forgive my mistakes if they're at all forgivable, to laugh when I'm funny but not to laugh at me, and to share your popcorn at the movies. I trust you to drive that meretricious sapphire Mustang as you would ride a wild horse, not because you look good in it (you'd look good even in a dump truck), but because you need a car and can appreciate it when I can't.

Love,
Jimmy

The Mustang sometimes buck-jumped and sprinted, but Ann was learning the nuances of easing out the clutch. She stopped at Jimmy's old house to give Chip a ride to school. Pixie was in the lab all day. Chip shared with Ann a brief letter he had received from Jimmy—light banter about Ludwig Wittgenstein. "Every tautology bites its own ass," Jimmy had scrawled. "That belongs on your jumpsuit."

"That is so goofy," Ann said. She stared at Jimmy's words, then almost broke into tears when she saw his Porky Pig cup on the table.

"Do you think the LSD did something to him?" Ann said now. "Did it send him on a spiral he couldn't get out of?"

"I just don't know." Chip fumbled with his book bag, stuffing in a banana, a lopsided sandwich, and a whole package of pecan sandies. "Something happened to him on that trip."

"What do you think it was?"

"It was a mistake to go to the redwoods," Chip said. "Looming dark trees. Paranoia? Wolves?"

"I barely noticed the trees. I was busy studying bugs."

When Chip didn't speak, Ann asked him about Pixie, if he could imagine joining the army if it would hurt the girl he loved.

"Not if I loved her," he said. "But I don't."

Chip, although intrigued by Pixie, was exasperated by her whims and non sequiturs. Sharing the rent on the house was a good arrangement, he said, and Pixie had a car, but they didn't belong together and didn't know how to split up.

"To tell you the truth, I'm just going to classes like I'm sleepwalking." Chip lowered his head. "Where did Jimmy get such a bird-brained idea? Cuckoo! What kind of scene can that be—prowling around with machine guns in the Ozarks?"

Ann jingled the keys to the Mustang. "Negative capability. That's Jimmy. Maybe he took Keats too seriously."

Fort Lost-in-the-Woods
November 7, 1967

Dear Ann,

*I don't mind telling you now that it's long over,
but that first week of basic training was hell, the
worst week I ever went through. The weather, the
full packs, the merciless drill sergeant, the marches.
It got easier, but the drill sergeant never let up finding creative ways to humiliate us. He humiliated the
draftees every way possible. He mocked those like
me who joined, and he sneered at those in the national guard and reserve. He was harsh with me because I enlisted. The drill instructors are an inch from
your face every morning and you wake up in terror,
but fortunately they're not allowed to touch you.*

*Is the army making a man of me? That old ca-
nard. I never believed it and still don't. True manhood is something more than what you can do with
your body.*

*I expect to get a very brief pass between basic
and advanced training. Do you think you could
come here? You could fly to St. Louis, then take the
bus here. . . .*

Love,
Jimmy

Ann lined up extra typing assignments so that she could buy plane tickets to St. Louis and to Kentucky for Christmas. She typed a philosophy paper on Reinhold Niebuhr, a master's thesis on William Butler Yeats's *A Vision* (claptrap and flapdoodle, Ann thought), and a wobbly treatise on Oswald Mosley. She stowed a hundred and twenty-one dollars in cash in her Freud book. She buried herself in her literary studies, as she had done in her stamp collection over a year ago. The songs she heard on the radio all applied, but not in any specific way that she could analyze. They were not words or meanings. They were just sounds. Some emotions churned in her in response to the songs, but nothing coherent—nothing she could explain—surfaced to guide her.

Chip was there, though. They checked on each other and brought each other food. Pixie was sleeping with an undergraduate history major, but she still lived with Chip. Chip didn't mind what Pixie did. It was of no concern to him. They were just roommates. But he was crazy about her cat, Nicodemus.

Fort Leonardwood
November 20, 1967

Dear Ann,

There's a guy from Kentucky in my unit whose accent sounds a little like yours, but he's not grammatical. He says "ain't" and "I done eat" instead of "I ate." He's really proud—and unconcerned that his words might be incorrect.

Not everything here is what I thought it would be, and I confess I sometimes wish I was in my own room in Chicago, with my mother calling, "Jimmy, get up, you're late for school." My father writes to me now, "Dear Jim," like I'm a grown-up. That is certainly strange. I'm not used to being Jim. Here I'm Egghead or Professor Jimmy or Shitface.

The barracks is really old, from World War II, I think. Everything is wood. Bunks, walls. There's a wood-burning heater in the middle of one long room with bunks.

After basic, we will mostly split up and go into different kinds of advanced training—specialty engineering, electronics, motor mechanics. Typing for me!

One thing has shaken me up—I can't quite grasp this, but the work here is so mind-numbing, so intense, that I'm no longer on a desperate philosophi-

cal quest all the time, trying to figure out everything.
I'm not searching every moment for meanings, or
enlightenment, or alternatives. Suddenly all those
fussy philosophers seem like offstage extras, under-
studies. They're hanging around in the greenroom
waiting for a slim chance to take center stage. But
they have to wait. Every day starts the same, with a
wild jolt that hurls me into a drastic, cruel routine,
and at night the light fades early and the days pass so
quickly that I can't recall if it was today or yesterday
that I got your letter.

I'm freezing and trying to write this with gloves
on. When the heater dies down, the chill pervades
the barracks. Chicago is cold, of course, and I
thought it was cold in Binghamton, but there the
air is so crisp and the sky so blue that you could
walk in seventeen degrees and not notice the cold.
In Chicago the wind is the wind, but in Bingo the
snow is insulation. Here it is the dampness in the
air that is so biting. It feels coldest here.

Love,
Jimmy

Binghamton. If she is in Binghamton, then the out-
come is inevitable. Can't she stop it? She squeezes her

mind to conjure California. In California, the trees do turn in autumn, subtly, and there are occasional blazes of color in unfamiliar trees. In California, it is never truly cold. It never snows in Palo Alto. California is sweet—balmy and zippy.

From the ship's deck, Ann turns to face the setting sun, toward California.

Sanjay always greeted her courteously, occasionally inviting her for a meal. He did not judge Jimmy for enlisting in the army, and he offered a recurring piece of advice: when you are in the river, don't stand still. Ann liked his smile. It was all-encompassing, as if he could accept all viewpoints. He came upstairs to watch TV when there was important news about the war. Sometimes he tried to explain Indian politics to her, and she had the impression that he was quite homesick. He had not seen his parents in two years.

When Ann returned one afternoon from her Faulkner seminar, Sanjay stopped her at the stairs. "Did you hear what happened to Mrs. Sokolov?"

"No, what?" The woman was prone to trouble, Ann thought. Something was always happening to her.

"She found her dancer."

"Where?"

"It was for sale in a classified ad. 'Dancer statuette, like a Chinese ballerina.' She did not tell the police. She has become impatient with the police, as you know. She called the phone number and went to find the dancer herself. She paid fifty dollars for it."

"Jingles would rather pay the money than get mixed up with the police." Ann had learned that Pixie had to pay Jingles three hundred dollars for the damage to the bathroom tiles. Ann did not know how people could throw money around so carelessly. She had saved almost enough money for her plane ticket and the bus ticket from St. Louis to Fort Leonardwood.

That evening Ann saw Jingles taking her trash through the alley. She was dressed in a kimono and a purple cloche. She beckoned to Ann to come indoors.

When Jingles showed Ann the recovered statuette, Ann realized she had seen it before, light-speckled against the lace curtain, like a Dalmatian dog. The dancer wore burdensome flounces, not typical of a Degas ballerina. Jingles had said Diaghilev! Not Degas.

"I'm happy now," Jingles said, fumbling with the belt of her kimono.

Ann went to see Pixie and Chip at Jimmy's house. It wasn't his house anymore, but the Stones poster was still on the wall. The bed was now neatly covered with an Indian bedspread. Beneath Pixie's decorative ceramic roosters and cats, Jimmy was still there.

Chip was in class, and Pixie was writing a paper for her psych history class. Nicodemus was curled on the couch. Ann told Pixie about Jingles and the statue.

"Oh, Diaghilev! That makes sense."

"Sanjay still calls her Mrs. Sokolov."

"Didn't they go out?" Pixie asked. "I'm sure they did."

"Yes, I think so, once or twice," said Ann. "He is very nice. He made me biryani."

"He was meant to be my true love," Pixie wailed. "But he's saddled with that childhood sweetheart. I shouldn't have moved in with Chip." She addressed the cat. "Why did I do that, Nicodemus?" She stroked him for a moment, then asked Ann, "Why didn't you move in here with Jimmy?"

"I don't know."

Ann's eyes hit on a raw crack on the wall. She remembered that jagged line from when Jimmy was displaying his photos of her for the photo dress. She said, "I'm going to see him in Missouri when he finishes his basic training."

"He makes me so angry," Pixie said. "What a dork."

"He had his reasons," Ann said calmly. Then raising her voice, she said, "What do you know about him? What do you care?"

Although Ann thought of herself as storming out, Pixie probably saw her departure as a mild fit of pique. Pixie probably shrugged and resumed the rat mazes of her psych paper.

In mid-December, Chip drove Ann to the airport in the Mustang. She was taking her largest suitcase because she was going to Kentucky for Christmas after she saw Jimmy at Fort Leonardwood, and she had all her presents for the family in the suitcase. A few days later, Chip would go to Chicago to spend Christmas with his family, and Pixie would fly to New York.

At the terminal, Chip walked with Ann to the gate. He said, "Be sure to give Jimmy a piece of my mind, if there's any left." He planted his hands on her shoulders. "Don't worry, Ann. I'm glad you're going to see him. It will do both of you good."

The plane was on time. In a long, affectionate hug, Chip kept saying, "It'll be all right. Don't worry."

As she waited to board, Ann considered what an old hand she was getting to be on airplanes. She counted up the number of trips she had taken by plane. A dozen takeoffs at least. Flying always seemed so urgent. Probably people were making sudden trips of bereavement, but she couldn't discern which passengers were anxious about their destination and which were merely afraid to fly. Airplanes remained frightening, but Ann accepted the risk now. She felt modern, released from the farm fields where she had once been penned. She had tried to explain that image of liberation to Frank the psychologist, and he had said, "You're *Thoroughly Modern Annie*."

For a second, Ann didn't recognize Jimmy. His shorn head made him seem boyish and defenseless, although his hair had already grown out nearly an inch. But the shape of his head surprised her. His head was noble, she thought. His ears were cute.

He read her mind. "I look like a high-school senior," he said.

"You would have been voted Most Clean-Cut."

"Most Likely to Become a Clerk-Typist," he said.

He wore faded jeans and an army T-shirt under a striped shirt and a zip-up winter jacket. As he toted her heavy suitcase down the street, she saw how much stronger he was now. She recalled the white bricks he had lugged awkwardly up the stairs for her bookshelves. The motel was not far, and he had already registered, so she was spared the desk clerk's scrutiny. The room was near the end of the row, and the door was heavy and warped. The door-closing contraption at the top of the door struck her as medieval. Its arm contracted slowly and groaned into place. The dark drapes were pulled shut. Ann switched on a lamp. After bolting the door, Jimmy enclosed her in his arms. With his big new muscles, he squeezed her more tightly than before. They clinched each other, as they had done when they last parted, but now the hug seemed desperate, as if this closeness could harden into stone, or a jewel. The timelessness of that closeness hit her afterwards, many times, as something she could still possess, carry with her like a pebble in a pocket.

They were making love. It was never the same, Ann thought. Each sensation was new. Yet, as always, it was fleeting, elusive. They had learned the right timing for climactic events, which sometimes made them laugh with relief. Jimmy never smoked immediately afterwards, and before long she realized he wasn't smoking at all. He had no cigarettes.

"I gave it up," he said with a shrug.

"Why?"

"Didn't want to do it anymore. Everybody here—everybody—smokes. It's tiresome. And you can't breathe."

"Good. I hate it."

"I didn't know that."

She pinched his cheek. "I'm glad you quit."

She had taken a Dramamine to help her sleep through the excruciating swing and tumble of the bus ride from St. Louis and to quell her anxiety about seeing Jimmy. Now she fought the grogginess. The heavy bedspread was smothering, the dark orange floral design obtrusive. This cover was probably cleaned once a year, she thought. They weren't the first to stain it. She didn't comment on his alarming army-green underwear. It wasn't funny.

"What do you think about when you are alone in your army cot?" she asked.

"I fall asleep before then." He laughed. "Sex. It's all anybody thinks about on base."

He apologized. "No. I think about you. It's more than sex."

She thought he was crying. She was crying.

The next eight weeks he would be at advanced training, sitting at a typewriter, learning how to fill out forms. In basic, there were guys who couldn't read or write. It sickened him that they had been cajoled to join up for the army with high-flown promises of literacy and good jobs after their service. McNamara's morons, Jimmy said they were called. There was a guy named Milton from a little town in Texas who never got past eighth grade. The drill instructor barked in his face and taunted him, making him spell words like *shitface* and *idiot*.

"I bet the kid can't spell *fuck*," Jimmy said.

"Not a word worth knowing," Ann said.

"I don't know about that, Miss Prude."

"Mama calls me Miss Priss sometimes."

He laughed and tickled her under the chin. He said,

"You know, some of these guys who got drafted, these poor guys I was so worried about, some of them seem willing, fatalistic. It's funny. I didn't expect that. And they seem to have more fun."

"I'm not surprised. They would hate Faulkner novels. They'd rather go bowling."

"Fishing," Jimmy said. "They all dig fishing."

Jimmy did not speak of dread or anxiety. He teased and petted her, as if he had no worries other than her own comfort. His usual playful self, though, was subdued. In the night, they could hear army trucks rumbling past. They tried not to sleep at all, but the Dramamine she had taken on the bus still socked her. She was glad to get coffee when the café across the street opened, before dawn. They sat with their coffee while a jukebox played out-of-date songs, lyrics that didn't apply. "Mrs. Brown" by Herman's Hermits. The coffee was evil. The winter sun was bleak and didn't break past the hills until late.

"Ask me a dozen fast questions," she said. "I miss that."

"The mind has to be free," he said, grinning. He twirled his spoon in his coffee. With the spoon poised in midair, he said, "What is the heart of darkness? Where do pencils come from? Is it better to have loved and lost than never to have loved at all? Who said that? Shakespeare?" He scratched his head. "Can't think of any more. I'm worn-out with questions. Where is Da Nang?"

"I wish I could think that fast," she said. "Or quote anything. I couldn't quote two lines from Shakespeare."

"So what? Why berate yourself?"

"I only meant that I admired that you could do it. You don't have to bite my head off."

He inhaled an imaginary cigarette and blew an imaginary smoke ring at her.

She batted the smoke away. "Wasn't it hard to quit? How did you do it?"

"It was a breeze. Nothing to it."

"Are you sorry you joined?" That wasn't the right thing to say, she knew immediately. They had not discussed the future. It was wrong to leap forward.

He sipped the bitter coffee and made a face. "I won't miss those monkey bars. That was the last test, and it was brutal."

She wouldn't probe further. There was no point. A Christmas song played on the jukebox. "Adeste Fidelis." The Mormon Tabernacle Choir, she thought.

"This is our Christmas," she said, her eyes alighting on a flimsy candle-and-wreath arrangement on the café door.

The evening before, they had exchanged small presents. Jimmy gave her a pen-and-pencil set, all he could scrounge locally, he said apologetically. She had brought him a Kurt Vonnegut novel, and Chip had sent a tiny packet of grass. They had decided not to smoke it. Ann didn't want to fuzz up their time together; she wanted to remember it.

"I'm high enough," she said.

"Do you still have acid flashbacks?"

She nodded. "Faces mostly, or sometimes I still have that radical clarity, like looking through a microscope. I can look at a bus or, say, a saltshaker and see it broken down into a reality so intense it makes me feel like I'm flying. My head won't stay on. But it's not very often now."

She wanted to ask him about his bad trip, but she couldn't. They were both reticent, she thought, awkward, as if they were teetering on a curb and trying to keep balanced. After ordering more coffee and going through fastidious motions with the milk and the spoon and the paper napkins, Jimmy finally spoke.

"All right. The army is the pits. I admit it. But I'm determined to be cheerful. I'm having a blast! I didn't want to drag you into it—the absence, the waiting, the uncertainty. How could I do that to you?"

"Never mind that now," she said, reaching across the table for his hand. "In grade school, when we played marbles, or jacks, we played for keeps. Remember that? We're playing for keeps."

"Are you sure that's what you mean? If we play for keeps, then if I win I get to keep all your marbles. It's not sharing. You don't want to lose your marbles."

"Smarty." She slapped his hand. "That's not what I meant. For keeps. It just sounds sweet."

They returned to the motel room, walking arm in arm like Bob Dylan and the girl on the cover of his first album, except for the joy. A cleaning woman was in the doorway of the next room, her junky cart waiting like a scavenger bird, but they didn't have to leave until checkout time, eleven. Ann's bus was due at 11:25. Jimmy double-locked the door and they fell back into bed. The sheets and blanket were lumpy humps, which Jimmy kicked aside.

"I want to see you all over," he murmured. "Memorize you."

"Do you want to draw a picture?"

They laughed.

"I just want you to hold me," he said. "That's all I need."

"I can do that."

"And I want you to remember one thing, Miss Ann. You can do anything. Just believe it. I said so."

In the bathroom, Ann washed her hands with the tiny bar of Dial. She brushed her teeth. The fluorescent light was glaring, and it pulsed lightly. Her new toiletry kit had a see-through plastic compartment for items that might leak, and small plastic bottles for her shampoo and conditioner. She put her makeup on one side and her hair things on the other. There was a pouch for a wet washcloth and another for her shower cap. She packed her things into the kit and wiped the plastic. The kit was a bright floral pattern, with handles, and its two sides lay apart like a book that folded together and snapped. She wondered how many kits like this she would go through in her life. She kept her birth-control pills separate, in her purse, so they wouldn't absorb moisture. She had wondered about stopping them, running the risk. Would that be so bad? She would stop them until she saw Jimmy again, and then she would decide. Then her old question of what toiletries she couldn't do without in the jungle arose. Jimmy would have the army Dopp kit he had now, a mess kit, an overripe-avocado-green blanket, and a lot of regulation stuff that she did not know about. It would be like camping.

Not like camping.

"What a dump," Jimmy said as he opened the heavy, slow door. "But an unforgettable love nest."

They surveyed the room: the fuzzy blanket and thick paisley bedspread with loose stitching, the dark drapes on a picture window. The gaping hole in the ceiling around a plumbing pipe, the frosted window glass in the bathroom, the loud commode. She would next see him in six weeks, during his advanced training.

His blue gaze held her at the door. She blinked first and dropped her head on his shoulder.

His blue eyes.

They sat on a bench outside the bus station, waiting for the bus that would take him back to his barracks. Her bus was due a few minutes after.

He removed his cap. "Here, take a good look at my bald head," he said. She fingered his short hair, only a hint of curl in it.

"You will remember me like this and it won't seem so bad," he joked.

"But I love you without your hair anyway."

"It'll grow back, I promise." Jimmy hugged her

again. "I have another present for you." He rummaged in his rucksack and brought out a grocery bag folded over.

It was his hair.

"'That blows my heart!'" she blurted.

"What?"

"Shakespeare! I'm quoting Shakespeare."

A grievous mistake—imagining him without his hair. If she could make his hair stay on his head, he never could be in the army. The army burrows through her mind, an inevitable course, like a worm through wood.

She stares out the window of the painted ship at the painted ocean. It is nearing twilight. She has been looking at her life through a porthole, like a peep show.

The Christmas lights in Hopewell were still on two weeks later, at the end of her visit with her family. Her father had driven her to the bus station before dawn, after he milked his cows. His hair was graying along his temples. "Don't ruin your eyes a-studying all them books," he said when they parted.

In going out into the world, Ann had rejected the ways of her family, however deeply she loved them. She regretted that her parents didn't get to read Shakespeare. It pained her that she couldn't share Emily Dickinson with them or tell them about Chaucer's bawdy humor or Joyce's verbal flips. The boundaries of the farm—the fences and creek banks—hemmed them in, kept them from the wonder of cities and libraries. And California.

The ride to Louisville was a familiar daylong, meandering journey. During the two-hour wait at the bleak bus station in Evansville, she climbed twice with her cumbersome Samsonite up the steep stairs to the restroom on the balcony. Then, during the jolting jaunt on the hilly Indiana side of the Ohio River, she tried to nap. Her head hurt. A man in the seat behind her snored.

She had not mentioned Fort Leonardwood. She didn't want to argue about the Vietnam War with her father, who was wary of the protest movement. He had earlier applauded Jimmy's enlistment, but Ann saw his fearful glance at Billy, her brother, who had received a hunting rifle for Christmas. Ann had brought him a copy of *Moby-Dick*. Now she wondered if he might want a harpoon next Christmas.

The sack of hair had been mashed, first in Jimmy's rucksack, then in her suitcase. In a letter two days before, Jimmy had kidded her, suggesting she have his hair made into a wig. She recalled her mother's brooch woven from her own mother's hair. Hair craft made Ann cringe.

Albert met her at the bus station in Louisville. He greeted her effusively, embracing her and splatting a wet kiss on her cheek. He wore chinos and a plaid shirt and a fringed buckskin jacket. His brown hair hung in a ponytail. Daniel Boone himself.

Albert brought her a cup of coffee from a lunch counter. It tasted bad. Burned shoelaces. Groggy from the Dramamine she had taken for the bus ride, she needed the coffee.

Rubbing his hands together enthusiastically, Albert demanded that Ann tell him everything. Change was afoot all over the nation—inside and outside, he said, opening his arms wide. "Self-actualization," he said. "'Know thyself' and then jump into the flux."

She laughed and nudged the alarming cup of coffee away from her. She said, "I'm afraid self-actualization is not on my syllabus. It's all I can do to go to my classes and write the papers. And I do typing jobs."

She thought he was disappointed in her. She told him about her studies and they explored *Moby-Dick* for a while. But when she tried to talk about "Kubla Khan," Albert lumped it with what he called the fuddy-duddy theory of education. He loved teaching, claiming it was about people, not books. He still got stoned on occasion. Their talk was pleasant. She avoided telling about Jimmy.

Albert went to the counter to check on her flight. As he turned, a man passing said, "Oh, I thought you were a girl." The man tittered. Albert nodded and seemed about to curtsy, Ann thought. The man walked away, self-satisfied.

"Let people wonder," Albert said, grinning.

The flight was canceled. Ann had a choice. She could fly to Chicago and wait until tomorrow for a connection. Or she could remain in Louisville and take the flight at the same time the next day.

"Stay here," Albert urged her, delight in his voice. "You can crash at our house in Lexington."

"Will Pat mind?"

"No, not a bit." Albert hadn't mentioned Pat, and he rarely wrote of her in his letters. He said, "She's still in Oregon with her family, but she won't mind if you spend the night at our house. Come on, I'll show you Kentucky again!"

They retrieved her bag and started off on the new highway toward Lexington, stopping frequently for tolls. The conversation was rich, filled with laughter and memories. It was a relief, after the heartache of the Ozarks and bus rides and the remorse and stasis of the family visit. Ann remembered with pleasure how Albert had encouraged her, had defended her when her Shakespeare professor told her she didn't have a logical enough mind for graduate school. Her whirlybird way of thinking was her advantage, Albert insisted. When another professor made lewd suggestions to her, Albert warned him away from her and offered to take her side if she wanted to file a complaint.

Albert displayed an air of deliberate abandon, simultaneously with an overly serious adult sobriety. As her freshman teacher, he was electric, and she had been under his sway. Shockingly, he used the word *sex* frequently in class. Sex-crazed Henry Miller was on the syllabus. Later, as her mentor, Albert was sometimes manipulative, charged with purpose, insistent—such as his notion of California—but now as a friend beyond school he seemed vulnerable, Ann thought.

The drive on the new four-lane toll road revealed a different face of Kentucky. It was a broader view, an open landscape, not an intimate scene. Over the years to come, she would observe that Kentucky changed in her eyes every time she returned. And yet it was always its essential self. She recognized a tone of voice—not merely the distinct accent, but an underlying innocence, an outlook. Her own attitude toward it, more than the place itself, kept changing.

"I should always take your advice," she said in the car, a stick-shift VW Bug.

"Why don't you?"

"I don't know."

"You know what you are, Ann? You're perverse."

"You always say that."

"That's another word for *ornery*. If somebody says your mind is fertile, you'll dispute that, and start telling about how dried up and useless your mind is."

"I never said any such thing."

"See? You deny it."

On the drive to Lexington, Ann felt distracted by Albert's forceful optimism and his blatant confidence in her. She had always trusted him, but now he seemed less a professor on a pedestal. His cheerfulness seemed strained. When they reached Lexington, he admitted he was worried about his sister, who was in the hospital. Albert, who was her caretaker, said he needed to stop there.

Ann had never met Iris, Albert's younger sister, and didn't know that she had been intermittently depressed over the last few years, since Kennedy was killed. Albert said she bounced out of it from time to time, with a burst of energy, but in the last year she seemed sunk in a hole. Then on Christmas Eve she had been apprehended out in the middle of New Circle Road, where she appeared to be directing traffic.

Albert and Iris were not close in age—she was twelve years younger. He was overcharged and ebullient, and she was sober and slow, but now she was ricocheting off the walls. In high school Iris had been a cheerleader and a debating champion, and later she worked in state government in Frankfort. This breakdown was out of character, almost like a deliberate rebellion, Albert told Ann.

"Do they know what's wrong?"

He shrugged. "I've tried out every theory I could find in Freud."

"Repression? Hysteria?"

"Freud is a game." Albert slapped the steering wheel and laughed. "The doctor told me about *la folie circulaire*, or circular insanity, a Ferris wheel ride from the lowdown blues to hysteria and loss of inhibition. What am I supposed to make of that?"

"Sounds like going around in circles," Ann said.

Albert said he would never have mentioned this to Ann if her plane hadn't been canceled. "I don't want to worry you with this."

"I hope she'll be all right."

"She's not really crazy." Albert turned into a long, curving driveway. "Here we are. It's the state hospital."

The loony bin.

"You can wait in the car or come in with me if you want to," Albert said.

"I wouldn't miss it," Ann said.

Albert parked near the main building, an aged brick mansion framed by boxwood hedges.

"I'm in the cuckoo's nest," Albert said. "Did you read Kesey's book like I told you to?"

"Not yet." Ann was rummaging in her suitcase, under the Bug's hood, for an envelope of paper flowers, simple pastel daisies, to give to Iris. They were a surprisingly hip Christmas present from a cousin. As they walked to the building, Ann removed the flowers from the envelope and arranged them into a bouquet.

In the hospital lobby, where a warped Christmas tree stood in a corner like a disgraced student, Albert inquired about taking Ann with him to visit his sister. A hefty woman in a gray hospital outfit escorted them through two padded and padlocked doors. Ann could hear loud music, Teresa Brewer singing "Music! Music! Music!" A nickel in the nickelodeon. What Ann heard was Jimmy singing the Russian names in the voice of the pig in the *Pogo* strip. Khrushchev, Pravda, Mikoyan.

A fountain of despair shot up from within her. The army would be like this madhouse.

The smell of frying baloney pervaded the place. Ann had seen the skillets of sizzling baloney when they passed a kitchen door. She was supposed to say *bologna*, but in Kentucky it had always been baloney, just as her aunt Cora was always Aunt Cory. It was a way of talking not learned in graduate school. The sound of their speech flooded back to her whenever she heard her family, and today when she heard Albert.

They entered a large community room with a TV set bolted high on the wall, in a corner. Several patients were engrossed in the TV, and one of them was making faces along with the comedy show on the screen. An aged woman in an orange muumuu was staring at a baseboard. Two women pulled at each other's smocks. Some of the other patients in the room were talking to themselves. An aide handed a pill and a cup of water to a slim old woman in a miniskirt.

"Here comes Iris," Albert said.

Iris, her scarlet lips moving in an exaggerated smile, greeted Ann and Albert. Her face was too thin for her excessive paint job.

"I'm so happy to meet your new wife, Albert. It's about time you got hitched! Lordy, I'm so happy for you. Are these flowers for me?" She snatched them from Ann. "So pretty. They'll let me have a vase of water because I am the champion of the corridor. I have accrued more goody points than anyone in the ward for the last five years. They said so in gold writing."

Ann did not know if Iris was normally so effusive and so heavily made-up, or so flamboyantly dressed in a kimono and beehive hairdo.

Iris said to Ann, "His old wife was a bitch. I'm glad he got rid of her. He always got along better with his students."

"Stop it, Iris!" Albert said good-humoredly. "You're traveling in unknown territory."

Albert tried to shepherd Iris to a corner couch, but more patients were crowding around her. Iris said they flocked to her because she gave people comfort. She pulled one of the flowers from the bunch and gave it to the thin woman in the miniskirt, who began picking the petals off. After dropping each one to the floor, she unwound the paper wrapping from the wire stem and let it float down.

Albert was consulting with the room warden about his sister, asking what Iris needed, wanting to know about the state of her room, her things. The patients milled around Ann and Iris.

"I am the mastermind," said Iris, panting. "I have a dream book and you are dreamers in it. Would you like to have a copy? I have seventy-three of them. I will fetch them."

Iris moved her hands as though wearing elegant gloves, and she brushed imaginary smudges from the shirt she wore beneath the kimono.

"There," Iris said. "Isn't that nice?"

Some yelling erupted in the corridor. An aide went to the door, peered through the glass, and waited for someone to unlock the door. The door opened and the aide went through.

"That floozy just does that to get attention," Iris said. "You can count on it. If she doesn't get attention she will have a fit." She yelled at the door, "Tough tittie!"

"I'm sorry," Albert said quietly to Ann, squeezing her arm.

Ann had been curious, amazed, and now she felt sad for Albert's burden. Iris had been a joyous little sister, he said, much petted by the family.

The flowers had disappeared, taken by a short man with a limp.

"He steals everything I own!" Iris cried. "You can't have anything decent in this goddamn place. When I get back to my penthouse, I will be running things a little differently. There'll be some changes made."

She repeated the line, in song.

Iris sank onto the cracked vinyl sofa. "Oh, there's no rest for the weary," she said with a sigh. Then she broke into a gentle grin. "You have pleased me so much, Miss Meg."

"I'm Ann."

"No. You remind me of a Meg. Meg you will be. Don't fuss. Mama's right. I'd like to give you a dahlia, but I have no measuring tape. You should wear polka-dotted silk and sip raspberry wine with apple pandowdy." She moved her fingers along Ann's arm like inchworms. "All I get to eat here is a forkful of mush."

She grabbed Albert's sleeve. "Albert! When you and Meg go on your next honeymoon, let me give you some advice."

"What's that, Iris?"

"*Key Largo*. The subtropics. Such a great movie! Faces like Mount Rushmore."

Ann and Albert sat for a while in the car without running the engine. Ann's toes tingled with the cold, but she was thankful for her wool-lined leather gloves. Albert didn't seem to notice the chill. He apologized for bringing Ann there.

"But you're giving me a boost," he said, turning to gaze at her. "It's so good that you're here."

"I didn't know you were having to go through this, Albert. It's such a shock."

"She's been through several phases. And she's calming down. But now they want to give her some kind of heavy tranquilizers."

Albert waved to someone walking past the car. "She secretly always wanted to be onstage, and now she is. But they want to keep her in a stupor."

"She looked pretty."

"This has flummoxed me," Albert said. "She freaks out and what do they try to do? Give her drugs to stop her flights of fancy. Either way, they don't want enlightenment, or enlargement. They want mind control. I didn't O.K. the tranquilizers. I always sort of enjoyed her wild antics, her flippy phases."

"My nose is blue," Ann said, glimpsing her reflection in the shadowed window of the car.

Albert buzzed the car ignition. "Sorry. I was lost in thought. I just don't want them to destroy her spirit."

He said, "The other day this administrator at the hospital sat me down and tried to sell me on how modern the hospital is. It's no longer an asylum! That used to be its name, but now it is a benevolent palace for the mentally unfortunate where they get pampered and loved on by a dedicated staff of angels. He told me some of the horror stories from long ago, to make me think we live in enlightened times now."

"Tell me some." The rush of cold air from the heater startled her. "I have a morbid curiosity," she said.

"I know." Albert patted her knee. He said, "This fellow told me that at one time the patients who couldn't manage their bodily functions were put in sawdust beds. These were wooden boxes like coffins, with a layer of sawdust. The inmates—drugged out of their minds—just lay in these boxes of sawdust, and then all their waste was scooped out in the morning. It made me think of cat-litter boxes."

They ate strombolis at Pasquale's and then smoked a joint in Albert's kitchen. The smoke was relaxing. It made her feel Albert's friendship more deeply. He was a person who embraced people without analyzing them. He always said people were doing their best, and she thought he had a way of bringing out the best in people. It was uncommonly interesting, although awkward, to be with her former professor in his ordinary life, in his house, with his pudgy cat, Peaches, and with the ubiquitous presence of his absent wife, whose clunky pottery and framed needlepoint samplers of Zen parables stippled and studded the house. "The Goose is out of the Bottle" seemed to float above the toilet-paper roller in the bathroom.

Two tokes were enough. Albert saved the rest of the joint in a little metal box. Then he set Miles Davis's *Sketches of Spain* on his stereo.

"What was the best and worst thing about your trip?" he asked after they had listened for a while.

"Waiting two hours at the Evansville bus station was the worst."

"I meant your acid trip."

"I wrote you about that."

"What was the main thing about it?"

She thought about Jimmy, how something was lost between them after that trip. She knew her head was down, as if—out of modesty—she couldn't face Albert.

She said, "Loss of context. It was like grass but extreme."

Albert listened attentively as she described the trip. She tried to tell him in detail what she remembered, and he nodded frequently, recognizing the sensations she described.

He said, "I must have dropped acid every weekend when I was in California."

He jumped up to turn over the record.

They moved to the main room. Albert sprawled on a yellow vinyl beanbag, and Ann sat on a ripped Danish modern chair. Peaches flew into her lap with a thud. The record had been popular when Albert was at Stanford.

"My life in California several years ago was a formative time for me, and I wouldn't trade it for anything. It was such an important part of my life. It's where I got centered."

He lowered his head into his hands for a moment—hiding, or thinking. He lifted his head.

"The openness of California was exhilarating. It was where I was introduced to Zen and mythology, encounter groups. All the stuff I was hoping you would get into. And the Free University—that place was exploding with creativity. You have to be judicious about dope, of course. But it's the place where you work on your head."

"I need my head worked on," she said.

She felt a small burst of courage. For the first time, it seemed to her that Albert had been as young and naive as she felt herself to be. He still possessed an untarnished optimism.

Now he seemed to be pacing the rooms, stumbling a bit to sway with the plaintive goat-herder melody Miles Davis was blowing. Albert slid into an enthusiastic monologue about California as the ultimate frontier. "You follow the sun, you breathe in the limitless possibility of the psyche of America."

"But California ends at the beach."

Albert patted her head.

"That's the point. If all the travelers and seekers just stop at the beach and mingle together, then all that energy has got to explode. That's what I saw in California. People with ideas, a belief in openness and expansion—mind and body. It was sheer excitement, partly the ebullience of youth, and partly real changes that were coming about."

"That all sounds good."

"It's not the love beads and the sandals and the stuff that came after. That's just trinkets, symbols, everywhere now. Long hair."

"Except here in Kentucky."

He laughed. "I'm doing my best to start the revolution." He tugged at his ponytail and flipped it over his shoulder.

"Bear in mind that I was there long before the love-ins, the protests, the explosion of music. It's exploding now, and maybe some of it is tacky, but I was there at the *birth* of the new consciousness. I was in on it at the *beginning*."

Abruptly, Albert grabbed her arm. "Something's got you down, Ann. What is it?"

It took a while, and she had to work up to it. If she said the word *army* right away, she would burst into tears. So she told him about Jimmy and how she fell in love and how they fit together. The Mustang. His trip to Chicago.

As she told him about Fort Leonardwood, Albert shook his head in disbelief.

"I can't feature a young English major in this day and age saying he wants to go fight the Viet Cong."

"He doesn't. He just feels guilty."

"I know what that's like."

"I don't know what to think," she said.

Albert changed the record, something softer than the screeching goat herder. He dimmed the pole lamp and sat on a hassock.

At the end of the first song, Albert spoke. "A young man like Jimmy is pulled in all directions. And he feels guilt if he refuses to go and guilt if he does go. It's a powerful tension."

"A friend said Jimmy joined the army because of a bad trip. Is that a possibility? Could it make you do things you wouldn't have done otherwise?"

Albert shook his head. "That sounds like science fiction. You can make anything out of anything." He laughed. "You won't find platoons of hippies in the army. Of course, acid could open up his mind and allow him to entertain many viewpoints. He might have seen something he hadn't seen before."

"That's what it seemed like."

"I admit I'm surprised." Albert frowned. "Most kids in college are desperate to avoid the draft."

"You asked me what the acid trip was like and how it affected me afterwards. It was like this."

She told him that one day after hearing the Rolling Stones on the radio singing "Paint It Black," she immediately painted her radio black. It seemed the logical thing to do. It was like being in a trance, a character in a movie under hypnosis, and yet it wasn't. It was like being liberated from the brainwashing effects of ordinary surroundings. The tyranny of sensible logic.

"I laughed when I realized what I had done. It was spontaneous. I think that's what you wanted me to find. Just the capacity to let loose."

"That's exactly it," Albert said, grinning widely. "I am heartened and thrilled."

They laughed together. Anything could happen and here she would be, quietly and mirthfully observing a panorama of everything in her world. If only it would stay still.

Ann slept with Peaches on a daybed in a junk-shop study, in her half-waking moments reviewing the day. The heavy cat, like a doorstop, barely moved through the night.

Albert had checked on her before she went to sleep. He brought her Kesey's novel, and he sat on the edge of the bed.

"I have to admit that I always wanted to get you in bed," he said with a loud laugh. "So this is it." He squeezed her shoulder and petted the cat. "I'd be willing, Lord knows, but you have your Jimmy."

"Thank you." She laughed. "That's the nicest rejection I ever got."

"Good night, Ann. I will always be your friend."

She thought he might have meant that he would be there if Jimmy didn't come back. People did the best they could. She thought about Iris and her dream book, the glow on her face from her newfound stature at the former loony bin.

The furnace kicked on, and a gust of air tinkled the Chinese wind chimes in the window. Peaches sighed and twitched.

It was still early for her flight, so before going to the airport Albert drove around the Olmsted-designed parks throughout Louisville. Winter made the landscapes stark, revealing contours of the land otherwise invisible. The cardinals were blatant in winter. Ann counted six in a bush.

"Winter always makes me stop and think," Albert said.

"You can see what is there," Ann said. "No camouflage."

She and Albert had each shared a sorrow, she thought, and that changed permanently what they were to each other. Albert was no longer a mentor, with fanciful advice and urgent directions.

After checking her bag, they walked down the long, curved corridor of the airport.

"We've been too droopy today," Albert said when they reached the gate. "I want you to go on back to school and have confidence that we can get through this thing—whatever it is that's happening to this country."

"I will if you will."

"You go play with your poems or whatever you do at that school, and I'm going to every peace demonstration in the country. We're going to end this war. And then your Jimmy will come home." He hugged her tightly.

"Thank you."

"You'll get through this," he said, his characteristic buoyant optimism resurfacing.

"You will too," she said, her head resting on his shoulder for a moment as they said goodbye. Then he gave her a long hug that felt good, but she pulled away— always resisting, like he said.

A snowstorm in the Northeast had caused the delays in Louisville, but now the flight paths were clear. Ann boarded the Eastern Airlines plane to Kennedy Airport, where she would get the Mohawk plane to Binghamton. The cold, lonely north. The snowstorm that had canceled connecting flights in Louisville the day before had left a foot of snow in the Northeast.

Gazing out the window of the stateroom, she remembers Albert saying the word droopy. *Memory doesn't have to be so droopy.*

In Palo Alto, even though winter is the rainy season, there will be many pleasant days. Who knows what may yet happen at Stanford? She closes her eyes to the Caribbean and dreams up California.

1968

Ann last saw Jimmy in Chicago on his leave in late January. Although his body had grown muscular and hard, he had not lost his gentleness. He was tender with her. She did not detect fear and uncertainty in him, and she did not show her own dread. She reported the pompous claims people made in her classes, and she assured him that her confidence level in class was at an all-time high, although that was probably not true. They reviewed all their good times together. They made plans to go to the hot springs at Big Sur. Chip and Pixie had raved about its sensations—the thrill of canoodling, stoned, in the hot water in the pool at the edge of a cliff, and how bizarre it was to share the scene with unclad strangers. She told Jimmy about going with Meredith to a new futuristic shopping mall. Ann was bored and had no money, so she waited on a bench by Macy's and tried to read the Nighttown section of *Ulysses*. She was still typing manuscripts for spending money. By now photo T-shirts were everywhere—cotton, not stiff linen. Jimmy lamented the missed opportunity, but she insisted it was not important. She told him how it pleased her to drive his Mustang, how it made her feel he was there with her, her own wild pony.

There was an air of make-believe to their last days together before he shipped out. It seemed to her that they both held back, neither wanting to give the other a reason for doubt. There was a gap between them, but they were polite about it. He would not wear his uniform while he was with her because he said it would frighten her—or it would make her laugh at him. As long as they were together, nothing harrowing or alarming was happening. There was no past or future, he said. There was only now. That was from one of his philosopher kings, but she wasn't sure which one. Jimmy was reading some Frenchman who got his ideas from Heidegger.

This was now. Here they were, in Chicago—at the Water Tower, at the Art Institute, at the Field Museum. The temperature was two. They rode the el around and around, then scurried to find warm buildings. And they spent long nights in a rundown hotel, reluctant to sleep, not wanting to erase time. Although his parents were away, he would not take her to their house out in the place he called Suburb, America. His grandmother was thriving in Florida, sunbathing and drinking cocktails.

On a warmer day, he showed her Lake Michigan from the Navy Pier. The day was gray, with low visibility, and rough water beating the pier in great slaps had made swirls of ice. Frozen patches, outlandish sculptures, extended out into the lake.

She huddled beneath his extended arm. "You said you'd take me sailing."

"Not on a day like this." He laughed. "Dad was out in a snow squall once and almost capsized. The lake hadn't started to freeze yet, but there was a sudden snow."

"I've never been this cold."

"Let me keep you warm." He squeezed her close. "My ladylove of Lapland," he said, teasing.

"You're my reindeer," she said. "Giddyup."

Jimmy recalled another of his father's mishaps. "He had rigged up a way to sail in the winter by extending the tiller and pulling the sheets down into the cabin. He could operate the boat from below. He went out one frigid day and of course someone reported an unmanned boat out there. The marine police came after him." Jimmy laughed. "He loved to tell about that. He felt like he'd gotten away with something."

Jimmy turned away from her and gazed out over the hostile expanse.

"This lake can be mean," he said. "But on a clear summer day, in a mild breeze, it can be pure joy."

"I want to remember this," Jimmy said, in bed. "Kissing your soft bubbles."

"Don't let the air out," she teased.

"You're a mystery," he said. "I want to carry your mystery with me."

Hail to thee, blithe spirit!
Bird thou never wert. . . .

"There you go again." She laughed.

"There's a quotation for every occasion," he said.

If Ann could have retained in a notebook—or a photo album, or a tape recording—the fine points and essences of those Chicago days, it might have been enough to sustain her during his absence. The sensations, the silly words, the assurances, the hopeful laughter, the breathtaking sex—everything enigmatic and thrilling about Jimmy. But the leave in Chicago slipped away, and she was in class again.

February 14, 1968

Dear Ann,

I'm mailing this from Oakland just before boarding the bus to the air force base, but you won't get
it until after I leave the country. There was one
thing I meant to tell you in Chicago. That is, I'm
not afraid. I don't go around in dread. I think
Siddhartha—and also acid!—taught me a way of
peace amid danger. And in fact most soldiers sur-
vive, so I won't assume this is a fatal journey. As
long as I have a Zen (?) attitude I should be all right,
though I assure you I will stop short of setting
myself alight.

I heard of a dozen guys just in the last few weeks
who went AWOL from Oakland. It's like the next-
to-last stop on the tour.

I am taking with me special memories of our
time in Chicago, as well as your visit to Fort Leonardwood before Christmas. That crummy motel
with the neon light flashing all night. The lasting
image I have of you is when you turned and walked
away as my bus drove off. I watched you from the
window. You waved, but you couldn't see me. You
didn't notice, but a little dog started to follow you

before you went inside the door of the station. I'm
that puppy dog, following you in my heart while
Uncle Scam kidnaps me in a big green machine.
Sgt. Pepper has plans for me.

Love always,
Jimmy, or Jimbo . . . take your pick

His handwriting was like chipmunks running through an inky maze. She decided that the word was *Jimbo*. That sounded hollow, as if he were trying to adopt a folksy attitude—imagining himself to be authentic, like her parents. Maybe he believed that at first, but now that he was really shipping out, she thought he must be whistling fiddlesticks to thrash his fears. Authenticity—what a romantic notion. He had read too much Heidegger.

In her classes, Ann felt alone. Many of the students who knew Jimmy seemed to shrink from her. She was grateful, for she didn't want to have to explain anything or to accept either their judgments or their commiseration.

The Twiggy lookalike, Elise, who boasted a new Yamaha, like a baby motorbike, was in the Milton class.

"Man, did he have any idea what he was doing?" she asked one day. "That's a bad scene. Jimmy was in my Shakespeare class a year ago, and he *seemed* pretty intelligent."

"He *is* intelligent," said Ann.

"Then why would he do such a dumb thing?"

Twiggy Girl blinked her kohl-lined eyes and patted her bleach job. She wore a leather motorcycle jacket and striped pants with pink ruffles just above her biker boots.

"I wonder," Ann said.

"Hi, Chip?"

"Hi, Ann. Word from Jimmy?"

"I heard the draft deferment for grads is ending."

"Yeah, I know. I heard. All that soul-searching Jimmy did—it was going to happen anyway."

"Jimmy might have gotten drafted, sooner or later. He won't be twenty-four until November."

"If I make it to June nineteenth, I'll be home free."

"What will you do if you get called before then?"

"I might have to go to Canada."

"I thought you were going to the Yucatán."

"I can't speak Spanish, and the weather will be better in Canada."

"You're teasing, aren't you?"

"I wish I knew."

Camp Granite
February 18, 1968

Dear Ann,

I made it here! It took twenty-four hours. We stopped in Alaska, Japan, and Bien Hoa. Lost a day on the international date line. But we get it back on return, like a bottle deposit.

The country is beautiful, what I've seen of it. Tropical, a little like southern Florida.

I'm with a good group of guys here. I entertain them by reciting poems.

Already I've had time to think.

I don't regret my decision. Maybe I will. I've come to realize how much it hurt you . . . and I kick myself. I could kick the living daylights out of that dunderhead I was . . . running off to Chicago without you. We could have had the summer. Already I've matured a few years' worth. Just by crossing the international dateline! It is startling to realize what a child I was. . . . Well, like all kids, I have to grow up, and now I have a job to do. And to start off, I want to confess that I made up that puppy dog that followed you, but it wasn't a lie. I was the puppy. The pup was metaphorical. I wanted to follow you.

As I told you before, I don't live in dread and

fear. When we have a job to do, we have to do it, and we can ask philosophical questions later.

On the plane I read Hesse again and Hemingway, the humble aitches. And I thought about Heidegger.

Hang on to your hat! (That's what my dad always said when the boat was coming about.)

Love,
Jimmy

Camp Granite
Feb. 28, 1968

Hey, sugar,

That's the lingo a GI would use for his baby, right?

The locals hang around here, begging for work. There's a mama-san named Phan who does our laundry. She washes the clothes in a stream here on the compound. She pounds it on rocks, like people did two hundred years ago. She shines our shoes and cleans up. She knows a little English from being around GIs for the last year. The other day, she said something that sounded like "the fucking mess hall." She might have picked that up from us, but it's not something we'd say all the time. The fucking this, the fucking that, I guess. But why the mess hall?

We pay Phan and we try to give her things, but she's not allowed to leave the compound with anything except laundry detergent and shoe polish. I don't know why. But she asked for that, and so we gave her laundry detergent and shoe polish. I think she sells it to the black market.

There is so much routine you'd think we were

still at the U.S. base. Already I am a typing fool. Officially, I'm a redeployment clerk.

A band came from the Philippines last night. Oh, they were awful! They tried to do Hendrix. So funny. Mack took a picture of the singer in white go-go boots. They were like your boots.

That made me miss you like crazy.

Hang on to your hat!

Love,
Jimmy

———

Jimmy's letters from Vietnam came through an APO box in the United States. No postage was required. Jimmy wrote an exuberant *Free!* on his letters where the stamp would have gone. Later, after she teased him about the free postage, he sent her some Vietnamese stamps for her collection.

Camp Granite
March 5, 1968

Dear Ann,

The army encourages us to drink. At the enlisted men's club (ha, don't I sound hifalutin!) we can get a beer for a dime. Last night I got a beer and a burger and then shared a joint with a couple of buddies when I got back to the barracks. Buddies! A word I've never used. I had friends, acquaintances. I never thought of having buddies. Little Buddhas?

In Qui Nhon, I bought some beaded curtains like Pixie's, and I've made a little private space for four of us. I'm on a lower bunk. We have a little fridge for our corner and we get sodas from the PX. It is handy because it is so hot here. I must go through half a dozen bottles a day.

As for my hair, since you asked, we try to grow our hair out, but then some lifer will demand that you get a haircut. It can't grow long, maybe an inch or two. I'm going to grow a beard . . . and see how much facial hair I can accumulate before they make me shave it. You can have a mustache but not over the lip.

There's a mountain vista outside the compound.

It is super beautiful, magnolious! We have a big cannon, and about once a week we shoot it off toward the mountain, just to let everybody know that Camp Granite is kicking. We're near the South China Sea, so the soil is sandy and the place is kind of bleak with all the barracks and supply posts and heavy equipment. But the mountains are beautiful and mysterious, as though they could be hiding the heart and soul of history. Beyond them is Cambodia, a whole different kind of place.

Had to do sentry duty last night—two hours on, four hours off, two hours on. The sentry posts are inside piles of sandbags. Not much happening around here. We just have to watch. The place feels well protected and far from any action. This weekend I'm going to hie to the beach. We have two beaches, Red Beach and Shit Beach. They rim the South China Sea.

I can't listen to "Different Drum" anymore. I don't like the idea that you and I travel to different beats. We follow the same beat. It's the drum that's different, unique.

You can get a cheap reel-to-reel at the PX, and in Qui Nhon there's a store with record albums displayed on the wall. They will make a tape for you. I bought a bootleg copy of Freddie and the Dream-

ers! *I got it as a joke for a buddy named Luke, who has a reel-to-reel. He plays his tapes constantly. I like all his Beatles, the Airplane, Hendrix, Otis Redding. But now I have to listen to Freddie and the Dreamers. Joke's on me.*

In the morning, walking to breakfast in the dark, you could light your path with the glow of joints— people getting stoked for the day.

I type all day and smoke dope all night.

That could be a song. By the way, I miss you. I'm afraid to say I love you, though I do, because it tears me up. (Tears: two definitions—rips and drips.)

Hang on to your hat!

Love,
Jimmy

———

Pixie had an apartment in Palo Alto now, and Ann saw less of her. Pixie was busy with a series of comprehensive exams similar to those Ann had taken in the fall. She was sorry Pixie and Chip had split up, but Pixie shrugged that off.

"I just stopped by to say hello," Pixie said.

It was pouring rain. Ann hung Pixie's dripping trench coat in the shower.

"Any news from Jimmy?"

"Nothing much."

"I heard LBJ just asked for fifty thousand more troops."

"I heard that on the radio."

"It must be getting bad over there."

"Jimmy doesn't say, but you know he's at a base and he works in an office."

"I know. I'm sorry, I just couldn't help wondering and thinking about how you're doing. It must be so hard with him over there."

Ann made a cup of tea for Pixie.

"Sanjay would like to see you," Ann said.

"I'll see if he's home when I leave." Pixie shivered. "It seems so cold today."

Pixie told Ann that on spring break she planned to go with her parents to Greece. They often took winter vacations, but this year they scheduled a spring trip so that Pixie could go with them.

"I've never been there, and my dad wants to show me the ancestral village before it's too late."

"That will be nice. What an opportunity!"

"Yeah. My parents came to New York in the thirties. They were just kids, they said." Pixie laughed. "They had nothing." She ran her fingers through her frizzed hair. "Just think. They ran a little grocery store and now they've got three of them. A success story. I realized I should appreciate them more."

Ann thought about her own parents, farmers, who could not have imagined owning three grocery stores.

"I'll feed your cat if you want me to," Ann offered. "How is Nicodemus?"

"Thanks, but Chip wants to take care of him." Pixie laughed. "That cat has imagination. I think I'll do a study on him for behavioral psych next quarter. I bet I could fool the experts. They'll think he's an Einstein."

When the rain let up, Pixie rose to leave. She set her teacup in the sink. Ann handed over the trench coat.

"Call me," Pixie said. "We'll do something."

Ann watched as Pixie knocked on Sanjay's door, and then she turned inside. For a while that day, she felt that life was normal.

Camp Granite
March 15, 1968

Dear Ann,

Out here in the tropics every minute is like being on acid in a way, it is so far removed from my old life. I'm listening to "White Rabbit." I go to sleep with my head on a surrealistic pillow.

This is more than I bargained for—not danger, but boredom. It feels so empty, this routine that seems so meaningless. Here I am—a redeployment clerk. Type, type, type. Just like you and your typing jobs! I wish I were there with you. I'd never leave you again. I swear I wouldn't.

There are zero words . . . Our old mantra, remember? . . .

Hang on to your hat. . . .

Love,
Jimmy

She had stopped listening to the radio news after the Tet offensive. LBJ kept sending thousands more combat troops, but not nearly as many as General Westmoreland wanted. She remembered Jimmy fretting about Westmoreland. She would not have dreamed when she first met Jimmy that he would volunteer to serve. Jimmy had thought he could subvert the system from within, but he didn't mention that in his letters, and she didn't ask.

Six weeks after she last saw Jimmy, Ann went to the gynecologist for a six-month checkup. It was a balmy day, and Ann had not worn her jacket, but the clinic was freezing. The doctor, with his white coat, glasses, and chart, was a walking stereotype with a stethoscope, she thought. He resembled the comic doctor in the movie she saw with Jimmy and Chip the day of the acid trip.

"Why didn't you call me?" the doctor said, glowering at her file. Ann was swathed in a peppermint posy-print gown, her feet gripping the stirrups. "I sent you a letter last August, asking you to call my office."

"I thought you were writing about the bill. I put it in the mail as soon as I got the letter."

356 • BOBBIE ANN MASON

"No. This was about your test. Your Pap smear showed you had a stage I dysplasia."

"What does that mean?"

"Abnormal cells. Stage I is a change, an early sign of cancer. Stages II to III indicate strong changes, and stage IV dysplasia can mean full-blown cancer."

He spoke without seeing her, his eyes still scanning her chart.

"Why didn't you let me know?" Her alarm was like a siren blast.

"Well, I couldn't chase you down. It would be un-ethical."

"Why? What are you talking about?"

He pushed her shoulder down so that she lay flat, told her to scoot her buttocks stirrupward, then inserted the cold metal speculum, an instrument that reminded her of a post-hole digger. Then with a long swab he jabbed a spot and smeared the specimen onto a glass slide. After slipping out the metal device, he rammed his finger up her vagina and rooted around.

"I'm taking you off the Pill," he said, removing his rubber glove with a sharp snap. "I want to see how you do for six months without it. Meanwhile, I can fit you for a diaphragm."

"I won't need it," she said. *And if I do, I won't get it from you.* "What about cancer?"

"The Pap smear will tell us." He waved the glass slide at her. "When did you have your last period?"

"The last day of January. I wrote that on the questionnaire."

"Was your flow full and vigorous, or scanty?"

"Scanty." *What language.*

Why was it called a flow? she wondered. Did anyone ever really flow? The Mississippi River *flowed*.

"There is some anomaly," the doctor said, packaging the glass slide in a little sleeve. "I want to run a fern culture. Stay right here. You may put your clothes on."

She visualized the network of ferns in the redwood forest. She wondered if the dysplasia he spoke of was caused by LSD. And could the fern culture find out?

As she dressed in her bell-bottoms and Indian tunic, she recalled being photographed in the shortie baby-doll pajamas, the squirrelly, rambling man ogling her. Always there was a man of authority—a photographer, a professor, a psychologist, a soldier, and now a doctor—a man who potentially had her future in hand like a basketball that he might toss casually.

Ann imagined writing to Jimmy that she had cancer. No, she couldn't send him such news. She remembered how Pixie had extolled this doctor—his discretion, his willingness to prescribe the Pill so unmarried women could fuck the night away without a care in the world.

Nurses hurried along the corridor past the doorway, while Ann waited, her thoughts awhirl. She tried to read *Mrs. Dalloway* but could not get through a single paragraph. In about fifteen minutes, the doctor returned.

"The fern culture shows you may be pregnant," he said.

Ann gasped. "How can that be?"

"You know better than I do."

"Could I have both cancer and a baby?"

"I don't see any signs of cancer now, and it has been six months. Sometimes the cells are just a little abnormal because of the mestranol and norethynodrel, but we're checking. I doubt if you have cancer. Don't worry about that."

"Then will you write a letter asking me to call, or will you take the time to call me with the results?" *For God's sake.*

"It's best if you call here, in about two weeks. We can do further pregnancy testing then."

"What do I do now?"

"Just be calm. Wait."

She had read something in the *Stanford Daily* about LSD and broken chromosomes. She wanted to ask if broken chromosomes would prevent having a normal baby, but he dismissed her before she could speak. He slipped out the door with his clipboard, and a nurse appeared then, with a bright smile.

"Do I hear we have happy news?"

"I wouldn't say that. Cancer?"

"Oh. He didn't mention that."

The nurse examined the lab test. "This could mean nothing," she said. "Don't worry about that. Now to the other condition. Have you had any signs—a feeling of fullness? Or morning sickness?"

"Not really. Well, right now there's something. The doctor just explored my insides with a post-hole digger." She felt blood flowing to the center of her abdomen.

The nurse raised an eyebrow. Ann had rarely seen the eyebrow of skepticism in such explicit action.

"I'll make an appointment for you. I think you may be only a month or six weeks, the very beginning."

The overcast day had brightened, and the sun flashed off the parking lot pavement onto Jimmy's blue Mustang. She was a fountain of illegal drugs. Birth-control pills were legal only if you were married. Her bottle of Preludin was a friend's prescription. And Ann had learned that LSD was illegal, even though Jimmy and Chip had led her to believe otherwise. Not to mention grass. She had been an imbecile to swallow anything foreign. She hadn't been thinking rationally. Did she ever really think?

She had said goodbye to Jimmy six weeks ago and had stopped the Pill the day they said goodbye. There were moments after Jimmy told her he had joined the army that she wished—hadn't she?—she could be pregnant. She had toyed with skipping the pills, but she didn't think she had skipped any. Could wishing somehow have an effect on those madly swimming sperm, those little athletes? Swimming Jimmies. She had been like a cheerleader on the sidelines, urging them past hurdles. She hadn't admitted to herself that she had hoped to become pregnant, as a way of keeping Jimmy.

As she drove to her apartment, one dominant thought was how to tell her parents that she was going to have a baby out of wedlock. At one time such a shameful admission would have been unthinkable, but she had been through so many liberating phases just in the last year that the old rules and taboos now seemed as odd as roosters in bonnets. Jimmy was gone. And the Doctor of the Absurd, with his fern culture, had plunked her onto a seesaw—cancer on one end and baby on the other. Cancer/baby. Ann had a case of the jimjams.

But what about chromosome damage? And what were chromosomes anyway? Little Xs and Ys in the cells like alphabet soup. Her mind was fuzzy, mazy. She remembered thalidomide, a drug women had once taken innocently for morning sickness, resulting in babies with horrible birth defects. Whatever happened to those deformed babies? Hidden in the attic, probably.

Shouldn't she have felt morning sickness? Or did that come later? What did she know about pregnancy? All she knew was that the threat had loomed over her young life like a prison sentence until she got the Pill. But now having a baby would be the ultimate commitment between her and Jimmy, ready or not. He wouldn't be pleased. She was afraid to tell him. She wouldn't tell him until she was sure, but gradually she could feel something like a thrill, or laughter, rippling through her body.

The car radio played Janis Joplin's bull-bellowing and screeches. Sometimes Ann wanted to cry the way she imagined Janis Joplin would cry. The couple next door would hear her. Everyone in the building would.

She cruised home in a daze. When she pulled into her parking spot, she met Sanjay, who was arriving home from his afternoon chem lab. He was a teaching assistant, leading a group doing research on lipids. She wondered if he would know what a fern culture was, but she was embarrassed to ask.

"The day is beautiful," he said, smiling.

"Is it?"

"You are not seeing. You must not despair that your boyfriend has gone to Vietnam. He will come back. You must not mourn prematurely."

"I'm not. I'm not. I'm desperately not."

Sanjay had a kind face. He was observant and he didn't sway in the winds of opinion. He seemed sure, solid, a man definitely not hiding an empty bucket. Ann felt bad that the girl from Wyoming had left him.

"You must have dinner with me," Sanjay said. "We will have wine, and I will cook. Come down at six."

"I thought you were a teetotaler."

"I have been in the U.S. long enough," he said, smiling again.

She lay on her bed with her hand on her stomach and listened to Jefferson Airplane. She stared at the ceiling, imagining that the surface was moving like one of the Airplane's light shows and that she was lost in its textures and would come out the other side in another dimension—on the roof? She saw herself hurrying across campus, zigzagging like a rabbit. In a new hat, she went mad. These images appeared before Ann's eyes like urgent orders. *Feed your head!* One of the musicians was talking backwards, someone lost her head, the dormouse was frantic, running around tippy-toe.

Cancer meant you die.

When Jimmy came home they would be a family.

Ann had not been around children since her brother was small. Meredith and John's boys seemed to be over-regulated brats. She would lose her figure and look dumpy. The hateful gynecologist had promised nothing, but the fern culture was highly unreliable, he had said. It was like a radio telescope listening for signs of intelligent life in outer space, Ann thought. Sometimes it heard only imaginary noise.

She had become fond of Sanjay's vegetable curry, its intricate spiciness and the depths of flavors. To her surprise, she liked the wine. It was white and sweet, like apples. She felt comfortable with Sanjay. For a while, she could be diverted. Sanjay had read Hemingway and Steinbeck.

"You are so cultured," she said. "I haven't read so much as a paragraph about chemistry since high school."

He laughed. "But you know more than you think. Chemistry is everywhere."

Her eyes wandered around the chartreuse walls of

the room. Sanjay had subdued the brash color by hanging a paisley Indian bedspread on one wall. His bookshelves and his desk were neat.

He pointed out his parents and his wife-in-waiting in a group of photographs arranged on a small table. She appeared demure and delicate.

"We have known each other since we were children," he said.

"Is it true your parents in India chose a wife for you when you were just small?"

"It is the custom because of the importance of the dowry and the bonding of families. But I think many people understand that by coming to America there is a risk of rejecting traditions." Sanjay smiled. He had a firm jaw and shaggy eyebrows. "My family is torn. They wanted me to come here, to study, but they knew there was a possibility that I would return changed, that I would no longer bow to the old ways."

"My parents may be thinking the same," Ann said. "No one in the family ever went so far away. On second thought, my dad was in the navy, but I don't know where he went. I know they're afraid I'll never come back."

Or that I would come back with an Indian like Sanjay, she thought. Or a long-haired freak who wouldn't hold a job. She believed they would like Jimmy, though.

"Let me refresh your glass," said Sanjay, pouring wine. "Please. Have some more curry." He spooned orange vegetables onto her plate.

Before Ann returned to her apartment, Sanjay placed his hand on her arm and said, "I know you are worried, and you don't know what Jimmy is doing, but please allow me to reiterate my offer to help in anything you may need. I will be here to comfort you because you are just so alone now. Do not forget that you have friends."

"Thank you." She refrained from crying on his shoulder.

The doctor did call. Actually it was his nurse.

"Your Pap smear was normal, no sign of cancer."

"No cancer? That's a relief!"

"No sign at all. The test is often a false positive. That is, the Pill may cause some cellular changes, but it doesn't mean cancer at all. It happens to some women."

"And some get pregnant."

"We think the contraceptive is quite reliable."

"Then how could I get pregnant?"

"There may be circumstances. Maybe you forgot to take the Pill one day?"

It had occurred to Ann that when they said the Pill was ninety-nine percent effective, that could simply mean screw a hundred times and—*voilà*.

She had several rambling letters from Jimmy, sent from the anonymous APO address, and she wrote him every two days, trying to be cheerful. She did not tell him her news yet. She still could hardly believe it, but she was worried about the changes ahead. She couldn't see herself waddling to class in a tent top. Maybe she would even lose her scholarship. She recalled a girl in her high-school class who had not been allowed to finish school after getting pregnant.

How much typing would Ann have to do to make up for the fellowship? At sixty-five cents a page, four thousand, six hundred and fifteen pages. Only a dozen pages a day for a year—if she could get the work. Plus extra for spending money—and a baby. She could do the numbers in her head, but not the baby.

Camp Granite
March 28, 1968

Dear Ann,

I'm listening to Dylan's "Masters of War" over and over. Although I'm friendly, I'm still a loner. Sometimes I feel intensely the unreality of being in this strange faraway place, exiled into a situation I was totally unfamiliar with until boot camp. I still wonder why I am here and don't trust that my instincts were noble. I'm sure they came out of innocence as much as anything. But I am certain that life is about testing and being tested. I would not want to come to the end of my life and find that I had not lived, as Thoreau so eloquently insisted. He went to the woods, but I sought the jungle. I am still so full of questions, and I know it's the questions, not the answers, that are most important. Answers are comfortable and safe, the reassuring salve to the raw uncertainties. But questions are always new, and yet eternal.

Thoreau, come to think of it, was a young man throughout his life. He was always full of questions, always vigorous and vibrant. He may have understood more about love than a lot of old married people do. He knew because he asked questions.

What is love? How should I live? How do birds know where they're going?

I'm running out of reading material. Can you send me anything by Shakespeare, just little paperbacks? And some poems—an anthology of immortal poems or something—and a good nineteenth-century novel. And something you'd like me to read.

Muchas gracias.

Hang on to your hat!

Love,
Jimmy

"Did you hear about LBJ?" Chip was on the telephone. It was strangely early in the morning.

"What?"

"He's not going to run again. He's in up to here with this war and after messing it up he's going to skip out and let someone else fix it."

"Then maybe things will get better."

"Better? With everything that's been happening, it couldn't get much worse."

"That's from a song," Ann said.

"If only songs were true," said Chip.

"It's April Fool's Day. Is this something in the *Stanford Daily*?"

"No, it's true."

Lexington, Kentucky
March 29, 1968

Dear Ann,

Since our winter visit I've had the pleasure of replaying our conversations in my mind. I was glad we had those drives together, and I hope I stimulated you to think about returning to Kentucky one day.

I have good news. Iris is living at home now and is thriving on her new medicine. It will keep her on an even keel, although I have my doubts about the virtues of staying on an even keel. You need to veer and bob now and then, don't you think? Or what's the use of getting high? I reserve the right to soar!

I have been reading The Population Bomb by Paul Ehrlich. This book is so important I want you to drop everything and read it. It will be a good break from those high-minded writers you've been pursuing. I have for a long time had a bone to pick with the modernists, who want to tell you that you can't read literature unless you practically have a PhD. I know you place great value on this pursuit, and I was proud to have spurred you along, but do be judicious about what you take seriously. Be skeptical, Ann. Don't let the academics tell you what *you're supposed to think. It's like anything else. They're all trying to make names for themselves. But most of the world doesn't give two hoots. You have to reach a perspective that includes the opposition—whatever it is, you must consider its opposite. That's the yin and yang of it. I can tell you, for instance, that James Joyce is not the be-all and end-all.*

We had a teach-in and an occupation of the administration building. Mostly hawks hereabouts, but they're starting to lose their feathers. I'm glad to know Jimmy is safe behind a desk on a supply base.

Be true,
Albert

The buzzy feeling in her abdomen was stronger, a busy rush of blood. It was similar to the fluttery heartbeat she had had with the pep pills. She couldn't keep her mind on the novels of Virginia Woolf, a snooty woman who had it all.

Ann assembled the various little things Jimmy had given her. His letters, the Fillmore ticket stub, his paper on Shelley's clouds, the Vietnamese stamps, and the LSD stamp. Carefully, she removed her naked pictures from the photo dress and placed them between sheets of paper. For a moment, she surveyed the images of her slim body, trying to imagine its coming heavy swell. She ran her hand over her stomach.

She found a box, one that had held several reams of typing paper, for the souvenirs and the photos. She squeezed in the paper sack of Jimmy's hair. Every day, in a compulsive ritual, she made a point of touching his hair.

It was after midnight. Ann was writing notes about time in Woolf's *Orlando*. She was listening to "A Day in the Life," the final song of the *Sgt. Pepper* album, trying to relive the acid trip with Jimmy, a memory she rehearsed often, wanting it to last the rest of her life. Paul had just begun singing the upbeat section about running a comb through his hair when she felt a sharp cramp, then a dull ache suffusing her insides.

The blood began. On the commode in a long burst of pain she released several clumps of blood. They resembled chicken livers. That was all. There was nothing to tell Jimmy. There was nothing there. It was gone. Zero words.

"A Day in the Life" was still playing. And then it ended, with the long piano chord, the sound receding for nearly a minute, until there was nothing left.

As soon as Pixie returned from Greece, Ann telephoned her. She was still numb and mournful and had not been able to speak with anyone about the loss. She had tried to make light of it. It would not have been such a calamity if Jimmy were there. They would still possess every possibility.

"So much for your advice about getting the Pill," Ann began.

"What's wrong?"

"I got pregnant—now how did that happen?"

"Really? Is that good news?"

"It wasn't supposed to happen."

"Don't look at me. You must have forgotten to take the Pill."

Ann explained briefly. "It wasn't even six weeks. It was nothing, except that it was something. And then it was nothing."

"I don't know what to say," Pixie offered.

"That's O.K. I just wanted to tell."

"Did you go to the doctor?"

"No, why should I?"

"Maybe for a D and C—to prevent infection."

"Is that like a douche?"

"I don't know."

"I'm just fine," said Ann.

Pixie brought Ann a fishnet sweater from Greece and took her to a party where she said it would be O.K. to wear the sweater without a bra. She wore her own fishnet top, a teal color. She said it was the exact color of the Mediterranean. Ann saw how brazen Pixie was, her large breasts visible, sagging and flopping. To please Pixie, Ann wore the new sweater without a bra, but she wore a blouse underneath. The fishnet sweater was a brassy yellow, not her color.

At the party, a medical student lectured Pixie about not wearing a bra. He said, "A breast is an organ, like a liver or kidney. It's not independent like a hand or foot, which can perform actions. A breast cannot flex or point. It needs assistance and support."

"Fuck you," said Pixie.

Ann, about to laugh, crossed the room to get a bottle of Coke. Her breasts were in jail, behind the mesh pattern, but swinging free.

Camp Granite
April 1, 1968

Dear Ann,

A bunch of us went to Shit Beach today. Not as nice as Red Beach. Farther down is another beach that is also a leper colony. I didn't know there were still leper colonies in the world! Sometimes I feel like I live in a mental leper colony.

I'm learning a few words in Vietnamese. The mountain is called Vung Chua.

Shakubuku. Remember when I said that word to you? I said it like I was saying boo. And you said it sounded like something a witch doctor would say? That word has been reverberating in my mind, like a repeating song lyric. I wake up in the morning and my mind squawks shakubuku at me! Like it's trying to scare me. . . .

Hang on to your hat!

Love,
Jimmy

The mail came in slots on Jingles's porch, and Ann sometimes waited there, forcing herself through small talk with Jingles and a cup of her muddy coffee. When the cheerful mailman brought a letter from Jimmy, Ann would jump up and grab it. She would have read the letter by the time she reached her door. She was unaware of flying off Jingles's porch or climbing the metal stairs. Sometimes she left unsipped a full cup of Jingles's expensive Italian coffee made with a cone filter.

Jingles was pruning suckers from the pepper tree. It must be spring.

Hopewell, Ky.
April 20, 1968

Dear Ann,

Every year I say I'm not going to plant onion slips, I'm going to plant onion sets. They come up better and you don't lose as many. But this year I went and did it again—planted slips—and they're coming along good! I made wilted lettuce with spring onions and reddishes today. The slips were so pretty at Miller's, where I get my cabbage slips. They were like green hair, they were so fine. If you could eat them just like that, little sprouts, that would be larruping, wouldn't it?

My mother and grandmother planted by the moon, but I never saw the good of that. You plant when the ground's right.

We saw on the television a lot of commotion about the war. So many boys going off. Do you ever hear from that Jimmy you were so crazy about?

Love,
Mama

UPSTATE NEW YORK

1968–1970

Ann shut off most of her memories of the long period that followed—the dying end of the sixties. They were as elusive as nighttime clouds. Those months were dark and empty, and she glimpsed only fragments, like floaters in the eye. She was numb, absent, vacant. She remembered hiding in her apartment, which was only a glorified dorm room with its own bathroom—of a horror-movie hue.

She did not turn on the TV news.

Sometimes migrainous auras lit up her vision. Dime-sized blurry blobs danced around the pages of her book like afterimages from light shows at the Fillmore. A faint cross-patch design decorated the blobs. "Take an aspirin to prevent a migraine," the ophthalmologist had advised. But she never had headaches, just anticipatory auras.

> Yvor Winters died.
> The Beatles broke up.
> Jimmy . . .

She barely acknowledged her surroundings. School was a mystery. She hardly knew where she was. It wasn't sunny California. She could withstand Binghamton winters, but she knew she might not have survived the academic rigors of Stanford University. California was only a dream, a place in a song. In 1970, after the student massacre at Kent State, Ann moved into a small house in Vestal. The burgundy bathroom had finally defeated her. Sanjay returned to India. Pixie landed a research job in Kansas. Ann heard from Chip often. After finishing his course work, he had moved to Oregon with an oceanography major who was a gourmet cook.

Chip said on the telephone, "Remember what Jimmy said about Wittgenstein?"

"No."

"Something about how you live in the present, you live forever. That's where you're free—in timelessness."

"Was Jimmy a hero or a fool?" she asked Chip.

"Nobody is one or the other entirely."

"Could he have been both?"

"I wish I'd gone instead of him," Chip said, not for the first time.

Ann was finished with male authority figures. She said that to Frank the psychologist, in their final meeting. LBJ, McNamara, Westmoreland, Dean Rusk. Nixon now. Yvor Winters. Not Yvor Winters. He was only a name on a textbook. Her real bête noire was a New Critic Joyce scholar who had cornered her in the Xerox room and told her she was cute. She didn't mind being called cute, but she resented having her critical insights also termed cute.

"Jimmy thought he had a vision," said Chip.

"It was stupid," Ann said. "Childish."

"I can't argue with that."

"The only way I can go on is to forget him. It was so pointless what he did."

"He thought he did it for you—in a way."

"That's so twisted," she said. "I didn't believe that."

Chip said, "I just remembered the other day something Jimmy told me when we were roommates in Chicago. When he was a little kid, his mother got him a blue tricycle. He was happy with his tricycle, as kids are. His mother took him to the park to ride his trike. Jimmy's dad was a doctor and they were well off, but some of the poor kids from the neighborhood on the other side of the park didn't have things like tricycles. And Jimmy felt sorry for them, so he gave his tricycle to some poor kid. His mother was furious. She tracked down this snot-nosed skinny tubercular underweight raggedy kid and drove over to that family's house—I don't know, some poor shack—and she commandeered the tricycle. As Jimmy described it, his mom just marched in and snatched it. She probably claimed they stole it. Anyway, there it is, Jimmy in a nutshell."

"Of course it was blue," Ann said in a small voice.

March 31, 1969

Dear Jimmy,

Remember the first be-in at Golden Gate Park in San Francisco? I think it was in the winter of 1967, a couple of months before I met you. I found an old Newsweek in your house after Pixie split up with Chip. There was a story about the be-in. And there was a photo in the magazine of a guy browsing at a bookstall, a photo from the rear. I thought it was you. It was just like your duffel coat. It was exactly like you. Your coat, your hair. Rumpled and shaggy. Your build. Of course San Francisco would have been cold, but not as cold as Binghamton! Even in the summer I shivered in those thin Indian dresses, the short skirts.

I thought that was you in the Newsweek photo.

Please . . .

She did not know where to send the letter.

She seemed to be in a dream, but one more painful than waking truth. If she cried out in sleep, no one would hear. No one could wake her from the nightmare. She couldn't conjure up memories of those final black months of the sixties, she realized now, so many years later.

She did remember John and Meredith's moon party—
July 20, 1969. They had been unfailingly sympathetic
and helpful, as they had promised. Their boys had shot
up like cornstalks and grown seriously competitive about
a basketball hoop nailed above the garage door. Guests
were laughing and drinking margaritas. The astronauts
had landed and the excitement had died down. John
circulated a tray of brownies. Ann carried an empty
bowl, a heavy blue piece of Pfaltzgraff pottery that had
held potato salad, from the deck to the kitchen, where
Meredith was rinsing plates for the dishwasher.

"The moon is boring," Meredith said.

"How can you say that?"

"Just think of what it cost."

Ann checked the TV in the den to see what was happening. She rarely watched TV, but now she was alert
to Walter Cronkite's words. Apparently his whole life
came down to this, and his excitement was palpable.
The astronauts, resting, hadn't yet emerged from the
LEM. Only a few other guests were in the den with
the TV, and they were talking about a beleaguered col-
league at the Stanford Research Institute. Ann turned
back into the kitchen.

"Imagine, being ordered to sleep before you can
open the door and step on the moon," she said to Meredith.

"They're probably dead tired. I would be." Meredith clanged silverware in the sink.

Ann called her parents, using the telephone in John and Meredith's bedroom. She could hear the TV muttering in the den. She sat on the bed, evidently on John's side. His corduroy pants lay across a wooden valet, and his tennis shoes were parked below. She had never seen a real valet in actual use. As she listened to the rings, she stared at the pants and shoes.

"The moon!" she said when Mama answered. Ann pictured her mother speaking from the kitchen wall phone and her father on the extension in the bedroom.

"There are men on the moon!"

Mama said, "I didn't hear all of it. It commenced to sprinkling rain, and I had to run out and gather in the wash."

Daddy said, "We saw it."

"There are men on the moon!"

"You're as far away as the moon," he said.

"What?"

"You seem that far away."

"I'll be home soon," she said.

Ann knew right then that she would always remember the sixties as the happiest time in her life, even though it had been so for only a few months of the decade.

"Tranquility Base here," Neil Armstrong was saying in replay. "The Eagle has landed."

Now, in a new century, on an ocean liner, the sixties don't seem so far away. If Jimmy could have watched the moon landing with her, they would have shared their wonder at human beings bouncing through moon dust. That was the kind of thing she and Jimmy had been good at together—sharing elevated moments, the way they had imagined "Kubla Khan" and Sgt. Pepper. They were cosmonauts. Armstrong and Aldrin, throughout their lives, must have felt unique as pioneers. Nobody would ever again have the feeling of being the first to walk on the moon. The sixties were like that, she thinks—just as Albert had tried to tell her. Jimmy would say, "You had to be there."

Hopewell, Ky.
March 27, 1970

Dear Ann,
    The garden is coming up good. I always love to see a little green thing shoot up after I plant. It's a miracle to watch something grow. Everything the plant will be is in that seed. It just needs dirt and rain. People are like that too. A baby just needs milk and food, and somebody to change its diaper (ha ha!) . . .

Love,
Mama

THE CARIBBEAN

2017

Ann's doctorate was a pre-high-tech rucksack—a clumsy, superfluous appendage. She was fond of saying the PhD "didn't take." It sloughed off into the Slough of Despond, she told her husband, Richard. Who needs it?

The dissertation had always been like a watch bird perched on her shoulder. She wrote it on Emily Dickinson, as she had first imagined, but she plodded through and forgot to laugh. She refused a teaching position at a small college in upstate New York. Instead, she wrote a book, a survival guide of sorts, that had not been out of print since. A syndicated column followed, and she never had to take a regular job or type papers. She did not marry until she was past thirty. Richard was a historian whose easy manner and positive nature had attracted her. He never challenged her or intimidated her. Their marriage was affectionate, physically gratifying, undemanding. Richard was orderly and precise, dedicated to fulfilling "what you're supposed to do." That meant anything from helping neighbors to filling out forms properly. He was a stickler for propriety, like someone in a Jane Austen novel. Ann raised a garden and two daughters. It was a good enough marriage, but it was now coming to an end.

If she had split for California in the mid-sixties, as Albert had insisted, she wouldn't have had Emily and Janis. Who might have been her children in a California life? Whom might she have married if she had gone to Stanford instead of Harpur College? Would she, right now, be standing on the deck of a cruise ship?

The dance classes had ended, and merry-making teenagers with their afternoon frappucinos were heading to their poolside lounge chairs. Ann had been muddling through *War and Peace*, a tome on her list since school days, but she couldn't keep the characters straight. She closed her iPad and slid it into its velvet crevice in her bag. She repositioned her sunglasses, then made her way up the crowded stairs to the promenade above the pool deck. Standing at the railing, facing west, she contemplated Daniel Boone at the Cumberland Gap, regarding the wilderness before him and imagining Kentucky.

She had tried to conjure up California—Palo Alto palm trees and pomegranates and Spanish architecture, with red-tile roofs. But the setting seemed at odds with the story. It was a painted backdrop to an intimate stage drama.

She always seemed to be alone, seeking a place where she could be even more alone.

She and Richard would meet Janis in Miami, and Emily would join them two days later, when she got leave from her research job at the State Department. Janis was so dutiful, tactful. When Ann e-mailed her from the ship about Richard's increasing fatigue, Janis didn't say they should never have gone on a cruise, given the precariousness of his health. She accepted that her father's dying wish was to go on a Caribbean cruise. He would have preferred the Mediterranean, but he realized that was too ambitious. Even on this cruise, the sightseeing stops were a challenge. Richard slept ten hours straight after the day in Kingston.

He had never really fancied adventure, but Ann had dragged him places, regretting most—especially the Quantocks, where they got lost in a holly copse between

Alford and Nether Stowey. His idea of travel was to sit in the hotel lobby bar with a Scotch and meet people.

The cruise ship, the *Brobdingnag* or some outlandish name, was ridiculous—at least eight stories high and crammed full. It was as if all the residents of the small town in upstate New York where she and Richard lived had been herded into a tall building and set adrift.

Ann could not face his dying. She resisted. During the cruise she was restless, seeking escape.

It was best to dream of California. In defiance, she had wanted to imagine a romance with a grad student at Stanford who would go on to big things in Silicon Valley, or to teach at Harvard. Or he could run an Australian sheep station. A California vineyard. Anywhere but Harpur College. Anyone but Jimmy. But he inevitably crashed into her thoughts, along with the whole cast of characters from the snow belt—Binghamton.

The blazing-hot, becalmed sea was too blue. Water, water everywhere. Seized by those hypnotic rhythms she once knew so well, she could hear Jimmy, as loud and real as the ship steward who had just been in the stateroom. Suddenly Jimmy was there, and on the following days it was Jimmy she thought of—the way he had gazed at her across the seminar table, the way he gave her assurance and confidence as no other person ever had, the way he wore his plain, saggy old duffel coat. She had never seen hair quite like that on anyone else—the texture, the casual cascade of curls falling into his eyes. Poodle ears. A few years ago, on a BBC-TV comedy-drama, she saw an attractive young long-haired actor who reminded her a little of Jimmy. Then this week, staring at the subtropical sea, she felt Jimmy come roaring to life in her mind. She beguiled herself into imagining that their story could have a different ending in California.

She couldn't stop herself from taking that Keats and Shelley seminar at Stanford.

She thought she had filed Jimmy away—under Life Had to Go On—but now she realized that throughout her married life, he had been a phantom, appearing everywhere she went, always inside her somewhere, in her imagination, her garden, her car. She saw him snapping her photograph, as though he had a vision of her that no one had ever seen, or bothered to notice—the same vision she had of herself. He could see her truly, and she could see his thoughts through the camera lens, in reverse, through his blue eyes. That was mystical malarkey, she had told herself. Sentimental keepsakes. But weren't they as important as poems? She still had the photos from the photo dress hidden in a box with his letters and his bushel of hair. Richard never knew.

Chip knew. Dear, sweet Chip. She kept his letters too.

They came from many places, a travelogue. She kept in close touch with him, and they had seen each other often over the years. He was a loyal friend. She visited him in Toronto, Chicago, California. Whenever they met, she made a swift mental readjustment and saw him as he was in 1967–his lopsided grin, his electro-shock hair. He had six kids and a flock of grandchildren.

Cupertino, CA
December 30, 1995

Dear Ann,

When I was in Chicago for the holidays I went to see Mrs. Marlow, as I often do when I'm in town. She moved to a condo on the lakefront. She's doing all right, but she seemed forlorn, lonely, since Mr. Marlow died. She still looks good and had her hair sculptured and her face polished. I'm surprised she didn't move to Florida, but I guess she couldn't leave that lakefront view, no matter how much she hated sailing.

Anyway, she showed me a letter from a guy who was in Jimmy's outfit. This guy, from Kansas, heaped praise on Jimmy—everybody looked up to him, brave, honest, etc. Nothing new there, but he also wrote about what happened the day the chopper got shot down. He said Jimmy had hitched a ride at the last moment on the chopper. He had to deliver some deployment papers to Saigon in a hurry. Normally they traveled in a truck in the daytime, when it was safer. But the chopper was delayed going back and it got dark. They went down in a patch of forest and the pilot hit the trees.

Ann, I hadn't realized it was dark. We didn't

know that, did we? And I didn't know he hitched a ride. Oh man, hitchhiking through the Vietnam War. Imagine. Well, that's Jimmy.

I thought this added a tiny glimpse into the past, for what it's worth.

And one more thing, this guy in the letter said Jimmy was always reading a book, and that he had a girl he really missed. He read her letters over and over. A girl named Ann. I should have asked to copy the letter for you.

Oh. Anyway, I thought the letter was a nice reminder of the Jimmy we remember.

Well, kick me in the caboose next time I see you if you want to, but I did not go to the grave this time. It was fifteen below, the ice on Lake Michigan was like an ice carnival, and I could imagine Jimmy laughing at me for freezing my butt off.

Ann, I always think of the sixties with nostalgia. It was the best time of my life, and of course the saddest.

Love to you and your family, as always. Sally sends a hug to your brand-new college freshman.

Chip

———

The steward removed a wilted freesia-carnation bouquet and left composed towels—a giraffe and a cat—on
the narrow twin beds jammed together. While rummaging in her bag for reserve lip salve, Ann inadver-
tently sobbed.

"Are you all right?" Richard asked.

"Allergies."

"Why would you have allergies out here on the
ocean?"

"There's all sorts of stuff in the air. The ocean ex-
hales poison. Cruise ship crap, for instance."

She hadn't meant to snap at him.

He had called the ocean *glorious,* a word he often
used without real meaning. Not like *magnolious,* a
word of genuine power, she thought.

"What's on that eternal iPad?" he asked.

"'The Rime of the Ancient Mariner.'"

"The guy with the bird around his neck?"

"Yes."

"Hand me *The New Yorker,*" he said.

"I could read the poem aloud to you."

"I would just fall asleep." He smiled then. "Thank
you."

———

There were more and more periods of fatigue. They skipped San Juan and Port-au-Prince. Ann had thought the cruise would be important, the least she could do for him. She knew she hadn't been the most attentive wife, and she was troubled by her remoteness, her habitual withdrawal into reading. She could bore into a book in an instant.

Now Richard lay in the infirmary, too weak to sit up. The ship medics had jumped, ready to isolate him and test him extensively for pathogens. Ann explained that he had a blood disease. No, it was not contagious, she said. He might need a transfusion. She could give blood. She had done it twice before. It made her lightheaded, but she didn't mind.

She did not know how she and Richard presented themselves as a couple. She was self-effacing, receding into the background, declining her social role (confabs, openings, "cultural events") and refusing to wear the proper outfits. Since the sixties she had had strict rules against pretentiousness in dress—preferring faded, worn garments. But Richard was a careful dresser, fastidious though never flashy. When she first knew him, he was a typical informal professor in jeans who called students by their first names and invited them to supper, but after he became department chairman he became fond of turtlenecks.

"I think you're unhappy, Ann," Pixie had said years ago.

"He leaves me alone," Ann said. "He doesn't get in my way."

Pixie's own husband glad-handed his way along, spouting platitudes. But Richard could build a boat and had even shellacked their floors. He was an agreeable man—reliable, always punctual. Ann often told herself how lucky she was.

"He goes off on those exploratory missions, or whatever they are," Pixie said. "And he never takes you."

"School trips," said Ann.

"I've divorced men for less than that."

In his formal portrait that hung on the Arts and Sciences Teacher of the Year Wall, he was turned slightly aslant, like someone being interviewed on TV. His shoulders signified solidity and dimension.

Now, gaunt and unsteady, outfitted in nautical leisure wear, he was a stranger. He had always been a stranger, really. Not that he was so hard to understand. But she was a mystery to him and he didn't even know that.

Richard was good with gifts, always remembering anniversaries and birthdays, even for many years honoring with chocolate the anniversary of their first meeting, at a chocolate shop in Boston. There had never been a good reason to divorce Richard, as Pixie had suggested. Pixie, a neuropsychologist, had divorced three men on what Ann thought were flimsy pretexts. Pixie confessed once that she had lost count at sixty-six bed partners, including one memorable fling through the *Kama Sutra* with a man who said he was from India but who turned out to be from somewhere else, Ann couldn't remember where. Not Sanjay.

When Richard was first diagnosed, Ann began to retreat even more, sensing that he wanted to be alone, private, with his dying. She behaved calmly, doing what was needed (taking him to appointments, mixing the probiotic smoothies, listening to his familiar laments on the decline of Western civilization), but her mind was turning away. How had they come to be? How had they pulled off over forty years together? It was not a marriage made from youthful romance. It was a sigh of relief, a settling, a feeling of order at last, a normal life with a house and children. But its insides, the vital sparks that would have made it dance and glow, were absent from the start.

When she thought of her folders of letters from the sixties, she could imagine them addressed to a naive Kentucky student at Stanford who was flummoxed by the intellectual sport of the seminar room. If she could start over, knowing what she knew now—but what she knew now was how naive and untutored she had been. No one would believe that.

If she had gone to California, perhaps she would have been swallowed up by the parade of tired images that were always hauled out on TV specials about the sixties—hippies at Haight-Ashbury, a daisy in a gun barrel, dead rock stars, flower children dancing in the mud at Woodstock, antiwar marchers chanting— all accompanied by a soundtrack of a limited playlist of now-mainstream songs. But Ann knew that decade wasn't really like that. The real story had settled to the bottom. Nothing was ever its synopsis. And she did not think she would have encountered much at Stanford that Albert hadn't already told her about. Except for the weather, wasn't 1967 much the same in upstate New York? She might have flunked out of Stanford, but she didn't really believe California excess would have ruined her as long as she held on to a kernel that was herself.

Mama was the key. Without her, Ann wouldn't have survived Jimmy. Mama had had a way of laying things bare, naming what was true.

Mama said, "When you finally told us about Jimmy, your feathers just fell."

———————

In the early seventies, Ann rented an old farmhouse in upstate New York. Intending to follow Mama's example, she planted a garden. Albert had sent her a copy of the *Whole Earth Catalog*. He was living in California again and had helped found the *Catalog*, a resource guide for people wanting to live authentically. (In recent years, Albert claimed the *Catalog*, with its complex network of information, was the infant Google as well as a foretaste of Apple.)

Ann began with an idea of a garden. It pained her that March and April in the North were such cold, bleak months—T. S. Eliot months, a wasteland. She waited. Mama wrote about the March flowers blooming. She was planting lettuce and radishes, clearing brush. Memories of the mellow spring breezes in Kentucky filled Ann with longing. The deep spring snow in the North made her tremble with urgency, an awe of nature. It stupefied her that most people did not embrace its intricacies or notice the tracks of mice in snow or the shiny oval of a frozen farm pond. Instead of observing the grandeur before them, they gabbed about God the personal overseer.

Ann, nostalgic for mild southern rains, was critical of northern rain. She sought spring in Kentucky. On a long visit there, she jotted down what she saw before her—the first glimmers of leaves on trees, the pale green pointillist shimmer of spring, the parley of cardinals in a budding rosebush. She watched spindly granddaddy spiders performing procreation. She saw box turtles doing it.

She regretted deeply that she hadn't brought Jimmy to Kentucky before he went away.

Back in upstate New York, Ann emerged slowly from her dark trance. She learned an alertness that she had not possessed in school without the aid of Preludin or coffee. She began filling a notebook with her wildlife observations from her porch. In particular she watched a short-tailed deer she called Tillie. At first she thought Tillie had been injured, but through binoculars she saw that the bobtail was normal, just short. It was a pleasure to recognize the graceful, slender doe by the blaze of white on her rump. Gradually, Tillie grew somewhat trustful and approached the porch with her fawns.

Ann savored the workings of a day, its preciousness. She noted patterns in the grass, the subtle stages of blooming trees. She transcribed her telephone conversations with her father—exchanges about horses and cows and cats and dogs and mules and goats and hay fields; the hollow tree along the creek, the spring rains that overran the creek banks, the thunderous, rushing water that ripped roots bare with its force. He never mentioned God. He told her about the oak trees. "We have water oak, blackjack oak, red oak, and post oak. Post oak is easy to split—for fence posts." He told her how squirrels calculate the time to cut down the nuts to ripen on the ground. She learned from him how important it was to notice the progression of the seasons. You could slow down a day, make it timeless. Each moment is only now, the only now.

Ann seized time in a late-season snowflake. She could be a robin concentrating on a worm, a cat studying entomology.

Pay attention. Jimmy would have said that.

Ann called her notebook her grief journal. Each day she noted the weather and the view from the porch. In his journals, Henry David Thoreau had always recorded the weather because it seemed so important at the time and it set the tone for the day. In the summer, Ann walked miles of woodland trails, her painful memories fading into her notations of the ducks and hawks, the mountain laurel and moss. She gawked at a bank of gaywings blooming flirtatiously. She tramped alongside a lake. The birch trees tempted her to try swinging them. The clarity of a northern forest made the tangled, snaky woods of the South seem irritating. She recorded the red flash of a cardinal, the misleading mew of a catbird, the silent, slow daytime cruise of a low-flying owl. She scribbled drawings and maps and copied passages from her mother's letters.

A pale bluebird, a female, kept attacking her own image on the side-view mirror of the Mustang. She perched on the arm of the mirror and pecked around, then returned to the mirror and flailed at herself, then hopped back to the metal arm. She was seeking a nest site. Ann moved the car several times before the bluebird gave up and sought a new place to dwell. But when Ann drove, she sometimes glimpsed an alarming mental image of the bluebird in the mirror.

To Ann's surprise, a New York editor asked to publish her journal. Ann had typed her notes, rearranged them, fashioned a narrative through a year, and interspersed the pages with letters from her mother.

Ann called her manuscript *Grief Garden*, but the New York editor didn't want the word *grief.* Such an uplifting, intimate text had to exude positivity. The book wasn't classifiable, confusing the marketing department. Ann suggested that it had an Emily Dickinson edge and a Coleridge flourish and a skittish Beatles irony, but this wasn't a university press book. The letters from Mama made the detestable phrase "down home" dance upon the page for the editors. They toyed with titles.

Letters from Down Home

From Down Home to Upstate

An Upstate Journal
Journey North
Deer Diary

It wasn't any of those titles. It was her *Grief Garden*.

New York settled on a title: *You Are the Bluebird*, which Ann thought suggested some cute symbolism for the reader to decipher.

You Are the Bluebird
By
Ann Workman

She could not have been more astonished by the book's popularity. It was the word *bluebird*, she was told.

It was hailed as an intimate journey into the female mind. Ann was called "the Walden Woman," "a feminist Thoreau." *Feminist* was far too limited a term for anything about Thoreau, Ann thought. Her weekly column was gender oblivious. She wrote about the flora and fauna of both Kentucky and upstate New York, with an annual dispatch from Walden Pond.

On this cruise to nowhere with Richard, she made notes about the "dazzled seabirds" she saw—birds confused by the ship's lights had crashed onto the deck in sad heaps.

She heard Richard calling her name. She opened her eyes. An orderly was wheeling him into the stateroom.

"Is Janis here?" he asked, as he settled into the armchair.

"Not till we dock in Miami."

She moved the towel giraffe and sat on the edge of the bed. She arranged the thin blanket around Richard's bony shoulders.

"I dreamed you were a certified public accountant," he said. "You are so good to me."

"What song is in your head today?" she asked.

Richard claimed he always woke up with a song playing in his head, sometimes a song he hadn't heard in decades.

"'Sea Cruise,'" he mumbled.

"You've been on that one ever since we signed up for the cruise."

"Can't get it out."

She realized that "Within You Without You" from *Sgt. Pepper* had been playing in her own head. Her memory faltered on some of the words.

She shrank into the diminutive bathroom, where she flushed the toilet and ran water to conceal her sudden burst of crying—the spasms and gasps that overcame her. As she removed the stretchy bandage and cotton ball from her arm, the scent of eucalyptus shot forth, and she heard Jimmy quoting Shelley. "'I fall upon the thorns of life! I bleed!'"

Somewhere
April 1, 1968

Dear Ann,

I owe you an explanation.

I see now how much I hurt you last August when I finally told you I had joined the army. I can never make up for that. I didn't expect you to understand my reasoning then. I see now how arrogant and hurtful I was. I didn't want to burden you with my shame and self-loathing, and I didn't want to ruin your life with my pathetic needs before I got myself straightened out and did what I knew I had to do. I thought you would see what a pain in the ass I would be in that state of mind. But I wasn't really listening to you.

What a featherhead I am! Damn, I wish I could explain it better. But what I mean to say now is that I love you truly but still don't want to stand in your way. Just bear with me—by going on with your life—while I meet this challenge.

Something happened on that acid trip. It made me turn a corner. That's when I knew what I had to do. It was as clear as if I had been receiving in-structions from a hypnotist. I don't mean it was a spooky voice saying, "Join the army." You know I don't believe occult rubbish. But one thing acid can do is reveal the hollow space within you. It tells you to surrender to the void. Familiar words? But when we saw all those banana slugs on that stump in the woods, I had a revelation. In "a flash of golden fire," I saw myself as one of a thousand creatures, like Coleridge's water snakes. How did I think I could set myself apart? Hide with my holy defer- ment like a hermit in a cave? The conviction grew in the following days. I felt drawn in, one of them, with a destiny—one I could choose. For a while, I felt I was carrying the burden of the murdered al- batross, but then I realized how vainglorious that was. It was hard being with you while carrying this dread and tumult, so I went to Chicago. I could not go to Canada.

When I come back I will be different, as they say, the thousand-yard stare and all that. I have no illusions. It will be tough. I just want you to be on my side. And I beg your forgiveness. I remember something you said about Keats and Shelley dying so young, how maybe the last thing Keats laid eyes on was pigeon shit outside his window, and Shel- ley's last was clouds reflected on water as he sank down. Bird shit and clouds. That made me smile.

I want you for my whole life, but I have to do

this first, and I think you should not be tied down by me. I hope we will live happily ever after, but please understand that I had to do this. I just had to, if I was ever going to live with myself.

Goodbye, Snooks.

Love,
Jimmy

The banana slugs were only fucking! she had screamed to the wall when his letter arrived. *They weren't fighting!*

Richard was sitting in the rattan chaise, the *Chronicle of Higher Education* open in his lap. He had rallied after the blood transfusion, and he was making notes for a lecture at Colgate in the fall. He sipped the mint tea she had made for him in the tiny coffee-and-tea center of the stateroom. For a while, she watched him. He knew he might never give that lecture, but he wouldn't stop for death.

She knew Jimmy's letter by heart, and now as she watched Richard continue to work, she understood that when Jimmy wrote that letter on the eve of his deployment he had been giving her a clue to his heart, a guide to the "empty bucket." She gazed out at the water, a blank blue as far as she could see.

She heard the teacup rattle. Turning, she saw Richard adjust his glasses, then lift his pen.

For so long, she had thought Jimmy was driven simply by his youthful idealism, but now, observing Richard's hell-bent concentration, she sensed the courage Jimmy must have had all along, even into his last moments, however they happened. A stare into cold foreign eyes, a trickle of liquid falling from a jungle leaf, a reflection of a cloud in a stagnant pool. Bird shit and clouds.

She saw his flashing eyes, his floating hair.

The End

Acknowledgments

My awareness of the California counterculture goes back as early as 1960. Gurney Norman, James Baker Hall, Wendell Berry, and Ed McClanahan had been students several years before me of poet and novelist Robert Hazel at the University of Kentucky, and they all went to Stanford University on Wallace Stegner creative-writing fellowships.

Gurney wrote me dazzling letters about hanging out on Perry Lane in Menlo Park with Ken Kesey and the Merry Pranksters. I got firsthand reports from the early sixties scene as it was happening—*One Flew Over the Cuckoo's Nest*, the Kool-Aid acid tests, the Happenings, the psychedelic bus called Furthur, Neal Cassady, the Grateful Dead. All this was before the Human Be-In and the Summer of Love, 1967.

That scene is legendary, and it entered my consciousness long before the counterculture established itself
and the antiwar movement took off. I have often wondered what would have happened to me if I had gone to
the West Coast after college instead of the East Coast.
I did have a choice. From Kentucky, you went to one
coast or the other. Or else you stayed home. The question prompted this novel, but the characters are new,
not real people in my life.

I write in memory of Jim Hall (1935–2010) and in
friendship to that whole group of Stanford guys from
Kentucky. I salute the memory of our writing teacher,
Robert Hazel (1921–1993). Although he imparted a romantic vision of the writing life, that was enough to
start with.

For this novel, I got special help (coffee, reminiscences, encouragement) from Ed McClanahan and
Gurney Norman. And I drew upon the *Whole Earth
Catalog*, the *Stanford* Daily, and the Stanford University Archives for knowledge of the place in the late
sixties.

Sgt. Pepper's Lonely Hearts Club Band, perhaps the
principal unifying musical event of 1967, has been a
constant in my life since then and was necessary to this
story.

I owe deep thanks to Sue McKaig, from Palo Alto (just

a sleepy town back then); Jan Pendleton (who showed me around her hometown); Ken Fields (Stanford English professor who welcomed me with sixties stories); Gordon Williams and Marc Leepson (not for the first time, for details about Vietnam); James Grady and James Robison (for encouragement and reminiscences of the sixties); Lisa Howorth (who lived in Palo Alto, 1969-70, and had a psychedelic VW bus); and David Polk (a classmate in Bob Hazel's workshop who went to the West Coast after the army). And I thank my friend Lila Havens, who gave me at least a couple of good lines. Thanks also to Pamela Painter for her writers retreat—her house on Cape Cod where I began to write this novel.

My sincere gratitude goes to Jennifer Barth, Jonathan Burnham, Sarah Ried, and all those on the team at HarperCollins. Thanks for welcoming me back to my first launchpad. And I have a permanent debt to Binky Urban, loyal agent and friend from the start of my career.

I am grateful for the encouragement and sharp eyes of my early readers: Karen Alpha, Cori Jones, and Roger Rawlings. And I was bolstered and sustained by the friendship and memory of Sharon Kelly Edwards (1950–2017), my first reader. She told me to hang on to my hat.

About the Author

BOBBIE ANN MASON is the author of a number of works of fiction, including *The Girl in the Blue Beret, In Country, An Atomic Romance,* and *Nancy Culpepper.* The groundbreaking *Shiloh and Other Stories* won the PEN/Hemingway Award and was short-listed for the National Book Critics Circle Award, the National Book Award, and the PEN/Faulkner Award. Her memoir, *Clear Springs,* was a finalist for the Pulitzer Prize. She has won two Southern Book Awards and numerous other prizes, including the O. Henry and the Pushcart. She is former writer-in-residence at the University of Kentucky and lives in Kentucky.

HARPER
LARGE PRINT

We hope you enjoyed reading
our new, comfortable print size and found it
an experience you would like to repeat.

Well – you're in luck!

Harper Large Print offers the finest in
fiction and nonfiction books in this same larger
print size and paperback format. Light and easy to read,
Harper Large Print paperbacks are for the book lovers
who want to see what they are reading without strain.

For a full listing of titles and
new releases to come, please visit our website:
www.hc.com

HARPER LARGE PRINT

SEEING IS BELIEVING!